CUT ME OUT IN LITTLE STARS

BOOK 3 OF THE SATORI CHRONICLES

AMY SUNDBERG

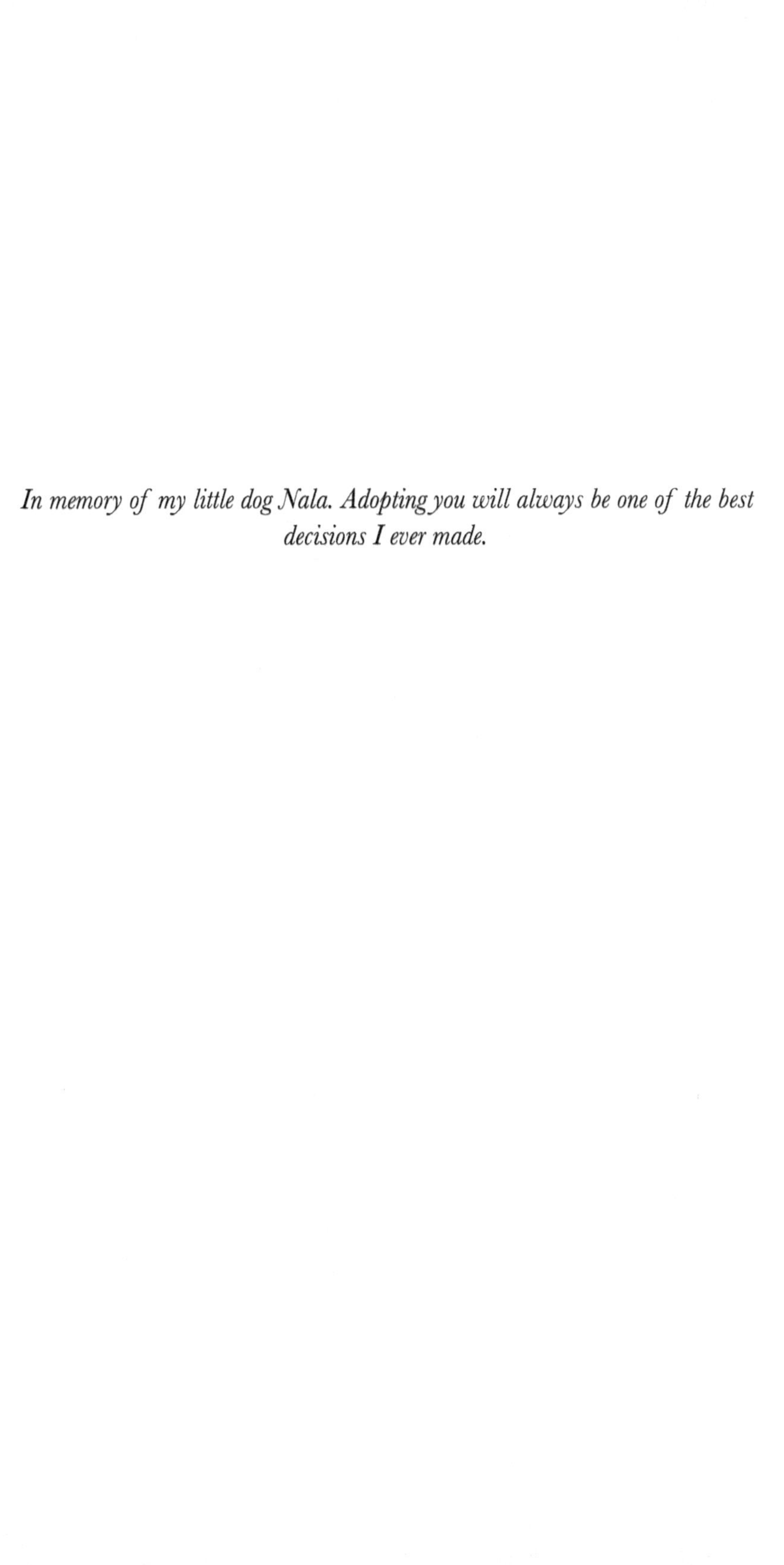

In memory of my little dog Nala. Adopting you will always be one of the best decisions I ever made.

CHAPTER 1

$\mathscr{B}$eing in disgrace doesn't get any easier with practice.

It doesn't escape my notice that the Satori have waited until their starship *Dreamer* has made orbit around Zamavat, our destination planet, before waking me from cryosleep. They want to spend as little time as possible on the ship with me.

At least they woke up Burke and Ereni at the same time. Ereni and I are once more sharing a compartment, and Burke is right next door to us. It's telling that he's not given a roommate in spite of the crowded conditions as the Satori prepare to embark planetside. It's almost as if they think we're contagious and might spread subversive ideas to other members of the mission.

We're not trying to stage a mutiny so I don't know why they're worried. We achieved our goal when we gave my friend Pilvi all the scientific data behind the Second Life transformation process, even if it was without the agreement of our Mission Council. We've been asleep for decades while *Dreamer* traveled to her destination, so not only has Pilvi made the data public in the intervening time, but the entire structure of Arborist society might be different. Arbor has been forced to grapple with the secrets and hidden costs of Second Life, and the Wise Ones, encouraged by my friend Virve, may have shifted into playing a greater role in human affairs instead of keeping mostly to themselves.

I wonder if I'll ever find out what happened after we left. One thing is certain: I've made another leap through both time and space, leaving more people behind me. Pilvi has become middle-aged while I slept, and my twin brother Leo is now very old indeed. I can't bear to think of the possibility that he may no longer be with us.

I don't exactly jump for joy when Burke, Ereni, and I receive our summons from the Mission Council. What could possibly be left to say? We made our decision, and I can't bring myself to feel any real regret. We did what we thought was best, and just because that meant going against the Mission Council doesn't mean it was wrong.

Nevertheless, we shuffle down the corridors to the shabby meeting room at the appointed time. Not all the members of the Mission Council attend our little get-together: only Aimilios, Calixta, and a long-suffering Irisa are present. They sit on one side of the round table, but they don't offer us chairs. I'm surprised they haven't changed their appearances to better match the norms of Zamavat, but all three are still extremely pale and blonde. Aimilios is still wearing unrelieved black, a scowl on his bearded face. Calixta, wearing a standard Satori jumpsuit in aquamarine, thins her lips at our arrival. Irisa doesn't even look at us, keeping her eyes on her qualpad as if she wished she were somewhere else.

At least Irisa and I agree on one thing. I shift my body closer to Burke, who reaches down and takes my hand. On my other side, Ereni plants her feet as though she is about to enter into battle.

Calixta, who has disliked me since we first met, is the one who speaks. "All three of you have been suspended from active duty for your actions on Arbor," she says without preamble. "Ereni and Sienna, you were already suspended at the time you decided to release sensitive information to the Arborist locals in defiance of this Council's agreement with the duly elected government of Arbor. You acted in direct disobedience to the precepts guiding this mission, which emphasize the importance of collaboration over individual decision making. Your decision impacted every member of the mission, including their personal safety. The entire council has met to discuss your cases, and we have decided unanimously to eject you from our mission, effective immediately. This expulsion will be permanent."

Beside me, Ereni doesn't flinch, and I try to model my own deportment on hers. Is it just my imagination or do I detect some satisfaction on Calixta's smug face? She'd argued against my inclusion in the mission before we'd landed on Arbor, and now, as far as she's concerned, she's been proven correct.

Aimilios clears his throat before speaking. "There is, however, the question of Burke." All eyes move to the young man on my right, and my mouth goes dry. "You were doing good work on Arbor," he says. Burke holds himself stiffly, his free hand bunched into a fist. "Your colleagues have nothing but good things to say about you, and the Arborist scientists seemed to find you easy to understand and collaborate with. Furthermore, everyone on the Council still believes that the unfortunate circumstances in which you found yourself on Sanctum were not of your own making and are not something for which you bear any culpability."

I remember Burke's murder trial like it was yesterday. I'd been so afraid he'd be found guilty and killed as punishment for his supposed crimes. Even when I'd testified that my own father was the actual responsible party, I'd been half-convinced he would find some way for Burke to take the blame. That we are both here and safe, standing before the Mission Council, is something to be grateful for, even if the occasion is less than inspiring.

Irisa finally looks up, but she doesn't meet my eyes. She is entirely focused on Burke. "We are unclear how much of a role you played in the decision to share the Second Life scientific data with Chrysalis. Some of us believe you might have been more of a…bystander to stronger personalities who swayed you to turn a blind eye to what they planned to do."

Ereni makes a small sound in her throat. I can't tell if it's a protest or a laugh. Burke hasn't relaxed beside me, and I wonder what he'll say. I'll back him up regardless of his decision. If he wants to deny responsibility for our actions in order to maintain his place on the mission, I can't blame him. It's true he never would have found himself in the position to release sensitive data if he hadn't known me.

"I knew exactly what I was doing," Burke says in a steady, sure voice. "All three of us discussed our options and came to a decision. If any one of us hadn't wanted to release the data, we wouldn't have done it. Besides, I was the one who actually obtained the data. Surely your records show that? I don't see why I shouldn't bear as much responsibility as either Ereni or Sienna simply because my prior job exposed me to fewer difficult choices."

Aimilios's scowl deepens. "I think that settles our debate."

But Irisa shakes her head, distress clear in the furrow between her eyes. "Think carefully about what you're saying, Burke," she says. "You can still have a place with us."

"No," Burke says without hesitation. "I don't think I can."

Irisa bows her head, and Calixta takes over. "We have been in communication with the mission team on Zamavat's surface, and they've suggested you join us planetside to discuss your future." She sniffs. "Very irregular for them to get involved at all, in my opinion." This time her glare is directed at Ereni, who maintains a placid smile.

"When will we be leaving?" Burke asks.

"Tomorrow morning. Diantha has said there is room for you stay in their quarters. Our mission will be housed elsewhere in the city." Calixta sniffs again, clearly not happy that we will be outside her direct supervision. "We have warned her of what to expect," she adds.

Ereni's jaw clenches at that jab. Diantha is her biological mother. While the Satori don't have strong familial ties based on genetic kinship, there is clearly some kind of relationship between Ereni and her mother. Ereni has claimed Diantha is just like another colleague to her, but Burke's reactions have made me suspect there's more to it than that. "I'm sure you have," Ereni replies, and I don't think I'm imagining the sarcasm in her voice.

"What about Kuusta Elo?" I ask. "Where will he be housed?"

I can't believe I'm inquiring about the wellbeing of Kuusta, the Arborist who chose to leave his home world behind due to the shame of his actions. His negligence caused a fire that burned down and killed over two hundred Wise Ones who might otherwise have lived for a thousand years or more, and nobody on Arbor is likely to ever forget what he's done. He'd jumped to leave his planet at the first available opportunity. We aren't exactly friends, but I do feel sorry for him.

Diantha looks like she smells something bad. "I have no idea," she says after a pause. "I'm not even sure he's awake yet."

"Perhaps he should be housed with us," I say. I don't know what impulse drives me to suggest it. Kuusta hadn't exactly been an ally on Arbor. But we'd spent hours practicing on our dirt bikes together, and I'm surprised to find that I feel slightly responsible for him. "I think I'm the one he knows best here."

Calixta shrugs. "We'll see." It's clear she doesn't care what happens to him. She would probably prefer to wash her hands of us all.

"We're done here," Aimilios growls. "Hopefully you've learned something from your misconduct, and you won't cause any trouble on Zamavat." He looks like he doesn't believe we could possibly behave ourselves.

Irisa looks up and gives me one last pained look, and I'm happy to be released. The heaviness of their disappointment lays over the room like a dead thing.

The three of us walk briskly through the painfully gray corridors of the ship, returning directly to our compartments. None of the Satori on this ship will give us a warm welcome. They all know we are the reason we're not still pursuing our mission goals on Arbor.

But when we reach our door, Ereni pauses. "Would you mind if I took a moment alone?" she asks. Her hesitation is the first real clue that the meeting has affected her. She'd been looking forward to such a bright future with this mission, and she'd developed more of a relationship with the members of the Mission Council than either Burke or myself.

"Of course," I say. She nods, her face still completely devoid of emotion, and enters the room by herself.

"I guess you're stuck with me then." Burke waggles his eyebrows playfully. He opens the door to his own compartment and gestures inside. "After you."

Once upon a time, the idea of Burke and I being alone together in such a small space would have scandalized me, but we spent so much time together on Arbor that it no longer feels strange. Measured in my waking hours, it's been less than two years since I left Sanctum, but sometimes it feels like an eternity.

Even though Burke isn't sharing his compartment, it has the same two narrow beds, along with the same depressing gray color scheme. A bag of his belongings sits at the foot of one bed, but otherwise it would be impossible to tell who lives here. Burke folds his tall form to sit on one of the beds, and I sit beside him, burying my head in his shoulder.

"Why does a part of me still wish they liked me?" I moan, finally allowing the stress of the meeting to wash over me.

He puts his arm around me and pulls me closer. "Well, you were trying to gain their approval for a long time."

"I was never going to be good enough for them." The words are both discouraging and liberating. Burke is right; I wanted to please them so badly. But now that I no longer have to try, it feels like a weight has been lifted.

"I can't believe they were considering letting me off the hook." His voice is harsh. "That, as much as anything else, tells me this mission would never have been a good fit for me."

I pull away enough to look up at his face. His mouth stretches in a grim line. "I would have understood," I say. "If you had taken them up on their offer, I mean."

He scowls down at me. "Well, you shouldn't. Injustice is never okay. And for them to think I'd turn my back on the two people that matter to me the most?" He scoffs. "Besides, I was just as involved in the decision as either of you."

"I've been really worried you would regret that decision later," I confess. "Irisa told me you would."

"Irisa shouldn't talk about things she knows nothing about." His voice gentles. "I don't know where people have gotten this idea that you and Ereni are somehow coercing me into doing things the way you want. It's insulting to all three of us. We made that decision together, and I stand by it. I don't want you to think I don't mean what I say."

"I don't." I pause, staring at the beige stripe on the wall as I try to collect my thoughts. "I think it can be difficult for me because I grew up in a place where nobody said what they meant. They'd say what was most useful in the moment. I spent a lot of time saying what I thought my parents would want to hear. Sometimes when you're doing that a lot, it can be easy to become confused about what you actually do want or believe. I guess I worry about making anyone else feel that way. Especially you."

"I understand." He laces his fingers with mine. "But when you do worry, you can remember that I don't come from your world. That isn't how I've been raised." He squeezes my hand. "I'd like for us to be able to trust each other to be honest when it matters."

"I'd like that too." I lean forward and kiss him. I mean for it to be a small peck, but even the small brush of his lips against mine is enough to set my heart beating faster. I give him another kiss and then another, leaning into his touch. He slides his hand to hold the back of my head as we continue to kiss, and I feel like I could sit like this with him forever.

Eventually we pull away from one another. My lips tingle, and I wonder if my cheeks are flushed the way his are. "Tomorrow we go down to the planet," I say. "Are you worried?"

He's looking at me in this special way he has, as if he's thrilled to be sitting beside me. It makes me feel important, and I can't stop the smile from breaking on my face, even though we're talking about something serious.

"There's nothing we can do about it now," he reasons. "We'll just have to wait and see what happens. I'm glad we'll be staying with the other mission group though. Living with a bunch of people who feel personally betrayed by you isn't my favorite thing in the world."

I flinch at his description, however apt. "Do you really think they feel betrayed?"

He nods. "They trusted me, and then I acted against our agreements. Of course they're angry. I would be too."

"I thought you said you think we did the right thing," I protest.

He stands up, running his fingers through his hair. "It's possible for us to have done the right thing and broken people's trust at the same time, isn't it? Life is complicated." He groans and throws himself on the bed across from me. "I can tell you one thing. If I ever join a mission group again, I'm going to be very particular. I'll need to be confident we are actually aligned and that everyone involved feels empowered. Otherwise, the price is too steep. I don't want to make the same mistake twice."

It's hard for me to imagine Burke not being part of a mission group, but I can understand his reluctance. "What about Ereni's mother? Diantha?" I ask. "Tell me about her."

Burke lets out a dry chuckle. "Oh, she's exactly what you'd expect," he says. "You'll see soon enough."

I stand up and put my hands on my hips. "Trying to play the mysterious diplomat again with me, Burke? Because I think you'll find we're past that."

With that, I launch myself on the bed on top of him and begin to tickle his very sensitive sides. We both dissolve into giggles as my attack escalates into a full-throttle tickle war. By the time we call a truce, the sting of that day's meeting has dissipated.

CHAPTER 2

After undergoing the appropriate terraforming process, Zamavat was only recently settled by humans, so it is very different from both Sanctum and Arbor. Humans inhabit only a small portion of one of Zamavat's continents, and there are no real cities. Instead, the colonists have formed small settlements called collectives, each centering around shared spaces for everyone's use: a large kitchen, a gathering space that serves for both meetings and entertainments, a school, a small medical facility, and so on.

That is the only information I have when we land at the rudimentary space port. The other Satori sharing our shuttle look pointedly away from us for the entirety of the flight, but Ereni appears as unbothered as ever. Burke and I both keep our eyes down, and I'm relieved when we file out into a small open-air waiting area.

A warm breeze ruffles my hair, and I feel my body relaxing in the balmy temperature. A sweet floral scent fills the air, and I find myself taking deep breaths, relieved to be back on solid ground. Several rows of green-painted benches fill the space, and a single woman stands to greet us.

She is ageless in the particular way of the Satori, who have extended lifespans: she doesn't look young, but there's no telling how old she is. Her dark brown hair clusters in curls around her head, and her skin is a smooth golden brown a few shades lighter than her hair. She isn't much taller than me, and she has a sturdy build with wide hips and muscled shoulders. She wears a loose caftan, the fabric sky blue with huge white flowers printed on it. She doesn't smile at our approach.

"Diantha." Ereni's voice is just the slightest bit breathless. "It was good of you to come meet us."

The other Satori from our shuttle mill passed us in stony silence. Diantha and Ereni wait for them to pass, not exchanging another word even though they haven't seen each other in…well, I'm not certain how long it's been. Burke and I hang back, not wanting to intrude upon the reunion, but once we're alone, Diantha turns her eyes to us, and a smile finally comes. I blink because it's only now, seeing her smile, that I can tell that Diantha and Ereni are related.

"Burke." She inclines her head. "And you must be Sienna. Irisa has let me have an earful about you."

She looks like she's about to laugh, but I can't help but feel criticized by such a greeting. What exactly has Irisa said? She's made it clear how unhappy she is about my behavior on Arbor.

Diantha turns back to Ereni, who is looking uncharacteristically nonplussed. Looking at the two of them, I realize it's not just their smiles that are similar. They also both carry themselves with a graceful erect posture that would be the envy of any proper Neopolitan young lady.

"So you've come to me for help, have you?" Diantha says. "I suspected this might come to pass."

"There is no way you could have predicted the way events have unfolded," Ereni protests. I exchange a look with Burke. This is not the unflappable Ereni I have grown to know over the past couple of years.

Diantha purses her lips. "I hear you, and yet I find I am not surprised to be meeting you here, even though your mission group has no real business being here, given you had two lengthy missions in your top priority queue, as well as several secondary objectives. Didn't I tell you this mission wasn't the right fit for you? Although from what Irisa has told me, it was even more disastrous than I might have expected, what with forced departures from two different planets."

Ereni frowns. "It hasn't been disastrous." Her voice is haughty as her spine stiffens even further. "We were able to achieve some admirable goals. We established several health clinics on Sanctum, as well as leaving behind the resources for more. And we were able to collect valuable scientific knowledge from Arbor."

Diantha's threatened laughter bursts from her, and her whole body shakes as she gives into peals of merriment. Ereni's face freezes. "Oh Ereni," Diantha finally gasps, "surely you know better than this. Your mission has been one farce after another, along with a healthy dose of bad luck. And you were in the center of the mayhem, just as I would have predicted. You shouldn't let your arrogance blind you to the truth of the events that have transpired."

"I only acted as I thought best." I don't think I've ever seen Ereni looking this offended.

"I told you there'd be a show," Burke whispers in my ear. "Ereni and Diantha have never been easy with one another. They're too much alike, and they both think they know best about everything."

"Yes, but your inexperience was showing itself at every turn," Diantha chides Ereni. "I don't know what Irisa was thinking. Of course, she couldn't have entirely anticipated the actions of her newest mission member." Diantha steps closer to me. "Let me take a look at you, my dear."

I blush under her scrutiny, not at all sure if I like her, even if watching Ereni being so off balance is a tiny bit satisfying. And yet we are depending on her goodwill, all three of us, if we have any hope of leaving our own mission behind. Perhaps we could choose to stay independently on Zamavat, but what we've learned thus far about the planet isn't terribly promising. I don't like the idea of spending the rest of my life on such a minimally developed world, even if the warm climate is a welcome relief.

Diantha's glance moves to Burke, who is standing just behind my shoulder. "And the two of you are romantically entangled, is that right? Irisa told me she was worried about our non-Satori friend exercising undue influence over you, Burke, and I laughed even harder than I did just now. 'Is this the same Burke I knew on Satori?' I asked her when I'd recovered my ability to speak. 'He's as stubborn as they make them, and he has been since he was this high.'" She gestures vaguely below her hip. "'No need to worry about that one being forced into anything.'"

With this pronouncement, I'm beginning to like her a bit better. "Thanks for the endorsement," Burke says wryly. "I'm sure Irisa appreciated your input."

Diantha snorts. "You know very well that she didn't. It was too much like telling her I told her so. And I did tell her about you, Ereni, but she chose not to listen."

This seems to cross some kind of invisible line for Ereni. "I'm very talented," she bursts out. "Irisa was simply giving me opportunities that matched my abilities. I'm not the type of person who can wait patiently on the sidelines."

"No, you certainly aren't." Somehow Diantha doesn't make that sound very flattering. "But a little humility never hurt anyone, my dear, and the lack of it has always been your fatal flaw."

"I learned from the best," Ereni shoots back.

This conversation isn't helping anyone. I step forward. "We were so grateful to hear we'll be staying with your mission while we're here. Thank you so much for welcoming us."

Diantha snorts again. "You might want to keep your thanks when you see what our accommodations are like here. Not that your mission will receive better housing. We've been slowly building more comfortable living places, but those efforts are secondary, and the people who have been here longest get priority."

Surely our accommodations can't be much more rudimentary than our compartments aboard ship? "I'm sure it will be lovely," I say. "Perhaps we can see them now?" Anything to interrupt the bickering between mother and daughter.

"Of course." Like Ereni, Diantha is nothing if not gracious. "I'm afraid I was unable to obtain a conveyance for us, as the rest of your mission will be using those available. We have a bit of a walk ahead."

I look grimly down at my heavy bag of belongings and pick it up with purpose. Ereni might feel free to speak to her mother however she'd like, but I feel like I need to stay on her good side. There's no way I'll complain.

The sun beats strongly from overhead when we leave the shelter of the waiting area. I'd expected to find myself in the middle of a settlement, but there are no other buildings here, just a gravel road that leads away from the spaceport, a beaten dirt path at its edge. One side of the road is lined with rows of saplings, completely different from the trees on Arbor. The other side borders on a field that stretches out as far as I can see, covered with low green plants I don't recognize.

"Rice paddies," Diantha says, anticipating my question. "Rice is one of our major food staples here, so I hope you like it."

Burke looks up into the bright blue sky with a grin on his face. "At least it's not raining." We'd read all about monsoon season on the ship. Just then I catch a bug landing on my bare arm, and I slap at it with a little squeal.

Diantha brings her hand to her mouth and lets out a shrill whistle, making me jump. Even Ereni looks surprised. A moment later, a little girl comes running from the other side of the spaceport building. She's wearing a blue sleeveless top and matching blue patterned skirt, flimsy sandals flapping against the dirt as she makes a beeline for us. Her curly brown hair looks like it needs to be brushed, and a sticky residue circles her mouth. She clutches a rudimentary doll that looks handmade under one arm.

"Time to go home, Theckla," Diantha says. "But first, I'd like you to meet your big sister Ereni and her friends."

Ereni's mouth drops open as the little girl comes to a stop in front of me. "Are you my sister?" Theckla asks me. She can't be more than six or seven years old.

"No," I tell her. "That's Ereni." I gesture.

The little girl looks up at Ereni's tall figure. "You're tall," she announces.

Ereni stares down at the girl for a full minute before shifting her gaze to Diantha. "What do you mean, my sister?"

"I mean that I gave birth to Theckla almost seven years ago," Diantha says evenly.

"You did what?" Ereni looks aghast. "You didn't use an artificial womb?"

"They aren't in common use here on Zamavat."

"And are you…are you raising her yourself?" Ereni sounds even more shocked about this possibility.

"I am." Diantha slides on a pair of sunglasses and holds her hand out to Theckla, who scrambles over to take it. "Like I said, we have a bit of a walk in front of us." Without further discussion, she begins walking down the path that runs parallel to the road.

There is a slight pause before the three of us follow her. When I look over at Ereni, her face has returned to its habitual bland expression, but I can't imagine she's as calm as she appears. Discovering the existence of a surprise sister would be a shock for anyone, but the Satori don't have family groupings the way we do on Sanctum. They raise their children collectively, and while biological parentage isn't a secret, parents don't usually exercise any special privileges or even necessarily interact much with their offspring. I don't know how involved Diantha had been in Ereni's upbringing, but my guess is that Ereni's experience of Diantha as a mother is nothing like the one Theckla is having.

"Are you okay?" I whisper in Ereni's direction. Diantha and Theckla are far enough ahead that I hope they can't hear us.

"I…am…going…to…kill her," Ereni grinds out.

"Happy to know the status quo hasn't changed," Burke says. He's surprisingly chipper given the shocks of the day thus far.

We must walk half an hour before we come to signs of actual civilization, and then I understand more of what Diantha was talking about. Because the settlement is so new, the buildings are practical and simple, with little effort put into their aesthetics. Some of the simple structures are completely open in the front. Tropical plants with large colorful flowers and lush leaves grow in abundant quantities, and a few buildings are crisscrossed with vines that grow distinctive white flowers. I do see a few dirt bikes whizzing down the street, which makes my heart lift, but most people are walking, wearing sunglasses, wide-brimmed hats, and clothing that protects them from the sun. I'll need to obtain some sunglasses for myself as quickly as possible, as I've spent almost the whole walk squinting and shielding my eyes with my hand.

We eventually reach a long low building made from a light gray plaster. "You'll be happy to hear we do have a working sewage system," Diantha announces. "That was one of the colonists' priorities. It's quite a luxury here on the frontier."

I blink at that characterization, but I'm grateful all the same. I don't know what people do when there isn't a sewage system, but I have a vague idea it might be unpleasant.

I'm less grateful when Diantha opens the door to show us a single long room lined with bunkbeds. Ceiling fans spin to keep the air moving in the increasing heat, but the room is still an oven. I wrinkle my nose at the lightly fetid smell. At least there are plenty of windows lining both walls, but most of them are currently obscured by woven coverings, leaving the room dimly lit.

"The communal bathroom is at the very back," Diantha says with a nod. "You may take any free bunk you wish. I'm afraid we've gotten used to being very spartan here." She nods at a big cupboard at the front of the room. "Fresh sheets and towels and basic toiletries are kept there. If you have any medical needs, you should let me know now so we can do our best to obtain what you require."

All three of us are silent, and Diantha nods in apparent satisfaction. "Excellent. Theckla and I live in a little hut just down the way. Let me point it out to you, along with the commissary." Burke and I follow her back outside obediently enough, but Ereni remains in the dormitory.

"Was that really necessary?" Burke asks Diantha in a low voice.

I almost gasp out loud, surprised that he's questioning an elder so openly. But Diantha gives a small chuckle. "You didn't expect me to make the humble pie any easier for her, did you? I thought you knew me better than that."

"You didn't have to take her by surprise about the little girl though," Burke says. We all watch Theckla drawing in the dirt in front of the dormitory with her sandaled foot.

To my surprise, Diantha agrees with him. "You're right." She rubs her forehead, pushing back her heavy hair. "I just didn't know how to go about telling her. I couldn't think of a way that would be kind, so in the end, I decided I could at least be quick. Like pulling off a bandage." She shrugs. "She'll get over it. Ereni has never been particularly sentimental about me."

Burke sighs. "It isn't easy for her to come to you now for help."

"Then she should have listened to me when she was deciding which mission to join, and she wouldn't be in this mess in the first place." She holds up a hand. "I know you care about her, Burke, but she'll survive. You all will." She gives me a curious look. "I take it you're Ereni's protégé?"

Perhaps she simply believes in plain speaking, but I don't appreciate being relegated to secondary status. "I was," I finally say. "But not so much anymore."

"Good for you." She jerks her head. "The hut down there at the corner with the vine with the large pink flowers? That's where I live. And the commissary is right around the corner. It has a messy but colorful mural painted on the front. A nice project for the kids." She smiles. "Group meal times at seven, twelve-thirty, and eighteen hundred. If you miss them, you can scavenge for leftovers and snacks, which are clearly marked. Don't take anything that isn't marked though, or people will get upset. Meal planning is quite a process out here, and everyone is expected to be respectful."

"Will our mission be eating at the same location?" I ask.

Diantha nods. "Yes, but we'll have to do double shifts because there isn't enough space. So they'll be on a different schedule than you." She raises her eyebrows. "How do the rest of your mission members feel about having to leave Arbor?"

I can tell she already knows the answer. "We haven't won ourselves any fans," I say quietly.

She shoves her hands in previously concealed pockets in her caftan. "Well, what's done is done. You're all here now, and we'll figure out what we'll do moving forward."

"It seems like you could use extra help here," I offer timidly.

She lets out a harsh kind of laugh. "We certainly have enough work to go around. These colonists weren't in the best of shape when we arrived, I can tell you that. I know it doesn't look like much, but we've been able to do a lot to stabilize the place." She claps Burke on the shoulder. "Good to see you again, and don't worry. We'll work something out for the three of you."

With that, she strides back the way we'd come. A moment later, the shrill whistle comes again, and Theckla abandons her artwork in the dirt to scramble after her mother.

"This is not what I thought it would be like here," I tell Burke, who stares after Diantha with a thoughtful look on his face. "Do you think Ereni knew?"

Burke grimaces. "She didn't have a clue," he says. "And you know how much she hates that."

She's in a similar position to me for a change. I look up and down the street at the simple, plaster-covered buildings. All the plant life livens up the otherwise bleak picture, a few taller trees giving much needed shade while the brilliant blossoms add a splash of color. It certainly is different.

"I guess you and I will be sharing a bedchamber," I tease, turning to go back inside where Ereni is waiting. "Such scandal."

"I guess now would be a good time to come clean and tell you that I snore," he says with a laugh. "Loudly."

"And here I thought you Satori had solved every problem known to humankind."

He snorts. "About that. Did you know we have an actual sewer system here? So advanced."

It's my turn to laugh, but I quickly turn serious. "I had no idea what a newly colonized world would be like," I say. "It's so… primitive."

He shrugs. "They're building a real city about a hundred kilometers from here. It's on track to be done before the next batch of new colonists arrive, and then momentum should pick up. But the early days are all about basic infrastructure and supplies. Making sure they don't starve to death, that there are no deadly pathogens that need dealing with, that they have shelter and sanitation. New colonies don't have reputations of being easy assignments, that's for sure."

Inside the dormitory, Ereni has already chosen and made up her bed with her usual efficiency, but now she's simply lying on her top bunk staring at the ceiling. "She's raising a *daughter*," she mutters. "Unbelievable."

Burke and I exchange a glance before choosing our own bunks and getting to work settling into our new home.

CHAPTER 3

All three of us are given temporary work assignments. Ereni and Burke are both placed on the building team, but due to my lack of practical skills, the man in charge of logistics has some trouble placing me. He expresses dismay that I don't speak the appropriate language to communicate with the colonists, and I think of my refusal to get an N-CAT with a twinge of guilt. Eventually he throws up his hands and assigns me to be an assistant to a Satori botanist.

"Elias has been asking for an assistant for ages," he says dourly. "And I've been telling him we can't spare anyone. But you might as well make yourself useful. Given your qualifications, this is the best I can do."

Early the next morning, as I blearily eat a thin gruel that I'm sure is as nutritious as it is flavorless, I'm approached by a short, squat man with rough hands and a graying goatee. "I'm Elias," he says shortly. "It's time for us to go."

I leave my gruel without regret and follow him outside to a dirty truck. He gets behind the wheel and I settle next to him, waiting for him to begin to explain my duties. He begins driving, the truck bouncing from the roughness of the road. "I'm looking forward to assisting you," I try, but he only grunts.

After a long pause, I ask, "Where are we going?"

"Need to check on some young fruit trees today," he says. I wait for him to explain more, but he appears very focused on his driving. Eventually I turn my attention to my qualpad, where I dive into a lesson on Kensho, the language the Satori speak on their home planet. I really ought to teach myself the colonists' language, but I can't help hoping I won't be on Zamavat for long.

We drive for a few hours before reaching a grove of baby trees. A rudimentary watering system has been installed, connected to a nearby creek. A small robot scuttles between the trees, and when I ask about it, Elias shrugs. "Easier to have a mobile robot in addition to cameras for monitoring," he says. "I need to know if anything isn't going according to plan."

"What would that look like?"

He squints at me for a moment before answering. "We monitor for signs of disease, unexpected bug activity, problems with the watering system, and the like. We have a successful mango orchard that's further along, so I don't worry so much about the mango trees. But we're testing a new tropical apple variety here as well." He shows me how to differentiate between the two types of trees and then sets me off measuring each individual tree and taking soil samples.

Each day, Elias and I drive to different locations to monitor various kinds of plants. Most of them are related to the food supply in some way; if not our own, then the food that will be necessary to introduce new animal species from the colony's biobank. As taciturn as Elias is, he's willing to answer any of my questions about the plants we're caring for, and his slow, methodical rhythm is soothing after the stress of my work on Arbor.

A week or so after our arrival, I'm resting on my bunk in the dormitory on my day off, a damp cloth draped across my forehead as I wish fervently that climate control had seemed as essential to the Satori as a sewage system. Ereni and Burke are working today, and I can't help worrying that we weren't assigned the same days off as some kind of punishment.

I'm beginning to wonder if both missions will labor together on Zamavat indefinitely. There certainly seems to be enough work for two teams, and without the ambiguities and political maneuverings that my own mission team has struggled with in the past. The colonists are thrilled we're here, relieved to have more labor, and luckily there seems to be an abundance of food at present.

A deep voice interrupts my thoughts. "Trying to pretend you're someplace else?"

I sit up abruptly, the damp cloth falling to the ground, and see Kuusta Elo standing in the space between the two rows of bunkbeds. Along with a long-sleeved beige shirt and beige trousers tucked into boots, he's wearing a large sun hat, and underneath it the skin on his nose is peeling. His cheeks are bright red, and he looks hot. This is the first time I've seen him wearing a light color.

"You made it," I say weakly, as if there was any chance the Satori wouldn't have kept their word.

"This is quite a backwater they've brought us to." He sounds remarkably cheerful. "They've put me to work digging what appears to be an infinitely growing ditch. If my people could see me there, they would no doubt feel that I'm getting my due."

I wrinkle my nose. "How are you getting along not speaking the colonists' language?"

He shrugs. "I work with the Satori mostly, but none of them are interested in talking to me either. They know what I did. They're happy enough to have my help, though. Turns out I'm good for something after all." He rolls his shoulders and winces slightly.

"But you're not digging today?"

"I guess the Satori believe in something called days off." He grins. "I thought you might want to do some exploring. Brand new planet and all that. I ran into Ereni the other day at the build site, and she said she thought our work schedules might be similar."

I perk up at this unexpected act of thoughtfulness from Ereni. "They think I'm soft because of my upbringing," I confess. "And honestly, I can't say they're wrong. After spending a whole day out in this heat, I feel like I'm going to pass out." I'm deeply grateful Elias's truck has an operational cooling system. Riding with him is the only time I'm physically comfortable.

Kuusta looks down at his boots, shifting his weight from one to the other. "I was able to get us two dirt bikes," he says abruptly. "If you feel up to it. I know it's hot."

At this news, I rise to my feet and clasp my hands together. "Dirt bikes? Here?"

He smiles at my excitement. "They have a small fleet of them. Turns out one of the original colonists was a fan, thought they might be good for transportation out here. I don't think they get much use."

"I can't believe you got us dirt bikes." I'm already heading for the door, only stopping to grab my water bottle and sunglasses from the floor at the foot of my bed. "I don't care how hot it is."

Outside the sun beats down relentlessly, but I don the proffered helmet and hop on the bike behind Kuusta. A short drive later, and I'm in temporary possession of my own bike. It's old and battered, with a more robust construction and higher gauge of tire than I'm used to, which means it is probably better for rough terrain. I run my fingers along its seat, wondering if I'll have time to give it a nice wash after our excursion and before the evening meal.

"Want to take it for a spin?" Kuusta asks.

"There's nothing I'd rather do." I hop into the seat, revving the engine and getting a feel for how this beauty runs. We drive off together, Kuusta leading the way as I test how the bike moves and brakes. Once I'm confident I can manage it, we increase our speed and go roaring down the dirt road towards the rudimentary spaceport. I think we might stop when we reach it, but Kuusta doesn't slacken his speed, and I'm happy to follow his lead.

We buzz past huge stretches of rice fields, and I catch sight of the occasional drone monitoring them, assumedly to give the alert when the rice is ready to harvest. Burke has told me they might transfer him from building to robotics soon to help maintain all the robots that make this colony possible. "As if starship technology is anything like utility robots," he jokes, but I know he's just being modest. He's been taking apart and reassembling robots since he was small, he'd told me once.

I try to ignore this new sign we might be stuck on Zamavat for the long term. I don't mind helping Elias with his plants, and I know what we're doing is important. Still, I can't imagine spending the rest of my life here.

But in the moment, my future feels entirely out of my control. Instead, I focus on the bike vibrating between my thighs, the wind pushing against my body, and the sense of freedom that I can finally go as fast and far as I want.

We finally reach the end of these particular rice fields, wild vegetation growing thickly on either side of the road in a sign of botanical success, and we pull over in the shade to have a drink. It's so easy to get dehydrated in a climate like this one, something I've already noticed during my time here. I pull my helmet off, holding my hair away from my hot neck, the sweat making me sticky. The calls of strange insects and birds fill the air, and it's a relief to feel the cool water trickling down my throat.

"So what do you think?" I ask Kuusta, who has settled on a nearby rock to enjoy his own water. "Glad you came along with us?"

He laughs, a bit ruefully, I think. "Maybe I should have taken my chances with one of our trading partners," he says. "It wouldn't have been a long wait if I'd been willing to travel to a closer planet. I just felt like it might not be far enough."

To outrun his legacy, he doesn't say. I wonder what it must be like to worry that news of the most terrible mistake of your life might follow you from planet to planet like a bad smell. "I'm sorry you aren't in our dormitory," I say. "I asked if you could be."

He shrugs. "Your old mission team is polite enough. Not friendly, mind you, but I don't get the sense it's personal. They're just not interested in socializing with anyone outside their group. They aren't especially chummy with the colonists either."

I frown. "The Satori mission that was already here seems a bit more open to new people. Ereni says several of the people she's working with have made friends within the colonist ranks." And Theckla's father had been a colonist, I don't add. Ereni had shared this information with me at the evening meal two days prior, a scowl on her face. She said he'd died in some kind of accident, and I knew better than to ask any more questions.

"It would be easier if I could speak to the colonists." He throws his closed water bottle on the ground. "If I were going to fit in with anybody, it would probably be them."

I settle on the rock beside him, trying to find a comfortable position. "Did the Satori offer you an N-CAT?" I ask.

The look on his face at the mention of an N-CAT is a reflection of my own feelings about the Satori brain implants. "That's not the Arborist way," he says flatly. "I don't need a shortcut. If I end up being stuck here, I'll learn the colonists' language the old-fashioned way."

I cock my head in surprise. "Do you think you might not stay?" I'd thought his agreement with the Satori had only involved transport as far as Zamavat. And in a backwater like this, it's not as if there's regular starship traffic to other planets.

He gives a little shudder. "I sincerely hope I can find another option. I might have been desperate to leave Arbor, but this place is a little…underdeveloped for my taste. Tell me you don't feel the same way."

"I certainly never thought this is where I'd end up," I admit. But like him, if my choice had been between staying on Sanctum and coming here, I think I would have chosen here. Sometimes staying is simply not an option.

"The two mission teams are going to have some kind of formal meeting soon." He picks up his water bottle and takes another long draught. "The woman who has the bunk above me told me. I think she feels sorry for me. She said they have to make an official decision as to how they'll carry on the mission going forward. How they'll divide the duties, whether they'll combine into one mission team or remain separate, and so on."

This is news to me. "They could join together into one mission team?" I ask. If that happens, all Ereni's planning will be for nothing.

Kuusta shrugs. "I imagine they can do anything they want. But chin up. We don't know what will happen."

I sigh. "How can you be so calm?" After all, he's just as helpless as I am in this situation.

He kicks his foot into the dirt. "Same way I stayed calm in politics. All you have to do is figure out what you have control over and what you don't. For all the things you have control over, it's worth making huge efforts. But for all the things you don't?" He stands. "There's no point in worrying about them. Might as well conserve energy until there's something you can do."

He might have a point, but the idea of sitting around "conserving energy" while my future is being decided by other people makes me want to scream. "I can't help worrying."

He grabs his helmet. "Then let's distract you from your worries. You up for some more riding?"

He doesn't need to ask me twice.

CHAPTER 4

I tell Ereni about the upcoming meeting so she can work her usual magic and make sure we're invited. But because we're one of the main topics of the meeting, it turns out the three of us are expected to attend. I'm even put to work setting up the necessary folding chairs in the commissary once the long tables are moved out of the way. It's the only way we can fit all the people who wish to attend from both mission teams in the space at the same time.

The three of us grab seats towards the front since we might be called upon to speak. Ereni gestures at the left side of the front row. "That's the other Mission Council," she whispers. Diantha sits at the far end, Theckla sitting on the chair next to her, messing with a qualpad. The seven members of our Mission Council sit on the right side of the row.

"What do the other Mission Council members think of Theckla?" I ask Ereni.

"My best guess is that our Mission Council is appalled by what they'd see as a lack of discipline, but so far they've probably been polite about it." She cranes her head to get a better look at the people in question. "As for her council, I'd assume they're used to her eccentric ways. They wouldn't have been willing for her to join them if that had been a big concern of theirs."

"So she's always been…unusual?"

"She's definitely not a follower," Burke says. "Ereni takes after her in that regard."

"I am my own person," Ereni insists.

"My point exactly."

Kuusta slides into the chair behind mine. "I'm surprised they let you in," I whisper.

He shrugs. "The Satori are not exactly what I'd call exclusionary. And they know I'm just here to listen."

Irisa stands from her chair and raises her hands, asking for silence. It takes the crowd a moment to acquiesce as people finish their conversations. "Does this feel like another trial or is it just me?" Burke whispers.

"Thank you all so much for coming this evening," Irisa says, "and thanks to the original mission for their warm welcome of us newcomers. While our two Mission Councils have met several times to discuss conditions on the ground and what we'd like to do going forward, we wanted to include all interested mission members in this conversation. We have reached a tentative agreement with one another, and we are interested in receiving your feedback."

Now Diantha stands up and faces the group. "We are happy to have more assistance in our efforts here on Zamavat. As I'm sure everyone is already aware, there is plenty of work to be done while we ready things for the next scheduled colonist arrival, which will be in less than a year's time. Our original group has been here for almost a decade, and we can all be rightfully proud of the work we've accomplished thus far."

A small cheer breaks out from part of the audience. Almost a decade? The thought of staying here that long makes my stomach drop. My heart lifts a small amount at the thought that if I were to stay that long, I'd be able to become a much better botanist's assistant. I could even learn the colonists' language and begin to have a social life. But I can't help suspecting my old mission will always hate me.

"We've decided the best path forward will be to combine our efforts," Irisa continues. "With a greater workforce, we can achieve more than we thought was possible for the new expected colonists, making sure Zamavat is positioned for success as it significantly expands its population. In order to accomplish this, we intend to form one Mission Council between our two groups and draft a new mission statement that will align with the majority of our members."

Excited whispering breaks out in the crowd, and I can't tell if the majority is happy with this turn of events. I know I'm not. There's no way our Mission Council will make things easy for us on Zamavat. Ereni lets out a long breath beside me. I wonder if Diantha had warned her this was coming.

"However," Diantha says after giving people a moment to confer, "we recognize that some people from the original mission may wish for some respite at the end of the expected decade of service. In addition, we don't want anyone who doesn't agree with the new mission statement to be forced to remain in a mission to which they aren't aligned. Given these two factors, we'll be splitting into two groups. We hope more people will want to stay than go, but anyone who wishes to leave will be offered a space in the departing starship."

More murmuring, and then someone behind me raises their hand. "What will be the starship's destination?"

There is a heavy pause. Irisa and Diantha exchange a look, but I can't tell what's passing between them. "It will be returning to Satori," Diantha finally says.

At this news, the murmuring gets exponentially louder, and Ereni grips my hand with a vise-like grip. "Home," she says. "She's going home." Burke is staring up at Diantha with a shocked expression on his face. This isn't what any of us had expected.

"How much time will have passed between when you left Satori and when this ship will return?" I ask.

Burke focuses on me with visible effort. "I don't know," he says faintly. His eyes grow distant while he asks his N-CAT. "Two hundred eighty-three years. Give or take."

I try not to react to the high number. So much could have changed in that amount of time, and yet for Burke, it's only been a couple years. I know the Satori have prolonged lifespans, but they still die in their mid-one hundreds. Which means everyone he used to know will either be dead or away on their own missions when this starship arrives.

"I never thought I'd get to return." He says the words almost as if to himself.

Irisa claps her hands several times until the crowd quietens. "I know there's a lot for all of you to think about," she says. "I know our mission hasn't been away for very long, and I believe we have a lot we can achieve here on Zamavat. The colonists are eager for our help, and that need should only increase when the new colonists arrive. In addition, we are very aligned with these colonists in terms of values, which makes working together that much easier."

"And I know some of our mission has grown quite fond of Zamavat during our time here," Diantha adds. "This will be a decision you'll want to consider carefully, and we want to make sure anyone with concerns has time to express them. Therefore, we have planned for the returning ship to depart in sixty days. We ask for your final decisions on whether you prefer to go or stay in thirty days or less so we can arrange everything properly."

Sixty days feels like both an eternity and the blink of an eye. In sixty days, I'll know whether I'll be traveling onwards to Satori or stuck here on Zamavat for the foreseeable future.

The Mission Councils answer a few general questions, but no one asks what our fate will be. They're too busy wondering about their own decisions. I consider raising my hand, but Ereni catches my eyes and shakes her head slightly. "We can ask Diantha later," she whispers into my ear. "Better to have it be less public."

Accordingly, all three of us are sitting on the bench outside Diantha's small hut by the time she returns home from the meeting, holding Theckla's hand. She doesn't seem surprised to see us. Instead, she gestures at the front door, which is unlocked, and follows us inside.

The room inside is small and almost unfurnished, with only a low wooden table and several pillows scattered across the floor. Several handmade rugs liven up the room, and colorful and inexpert artwork that I assume is made by Theckla is tacked up on most of the available wall space. An off-white dome in the center of the ceiling gives off a mellow light, powered by the solar panels on the roof. A set of blocks is scattered across the floor, along with several simple dolls.

"Theckla needs to go to bed," Diantha tells us. "Be comfortable, and we'll talk once she's settled."

"I don't want to go to bed," Theckla objects, hurling herself onto the nearest cushion.

"You might not want to go now, but if you don't, you'll be cranky all day tomorrow," Diantha says. "I will tell you a story once you're ready and in bed."

"Two stories," Theckla says. She sticks a finger in her mouth, a crafty glint in her eyes.

"Yes, all right, two stories." Diantha's agreement propels the little girl into motion as she rushes through the one door of the house into the adjoining room. Diantha follows her, closing the door behind her. Burke, Ereni, and I stand looking at each other for a long moment. Finally, Ereni shrugs and selects a cushion to sit on. Burke and I choose adjacent cushions, and my knee bumps against his ribs as he stretches out his long form.

We can hear Diantha's low voice through the door, but we sit in companionable silence. What is there for us to discuss? I know both my companions will want to return to Satori if they can. For me, it is clearly the better opportunity, but for them, it's a chance for a homecoming they've been trained not to expect. And since their first mission has gone so differently than I'm sure they imagined, it might be another chance for them.

If the thought of them gradually fading back into their old lives and leaving me behind fills me with a cold dread, the less said about it, the better. I don't want to bring a negative future into being simply by speaking it. And while Ereni has shown she can't be trusted, Burke doesn't deserve my pessimistic anxiety about what a future on Satori would mean.

On the other hand, being able to see Satori for myself is a chance I never thought I'd receive, and I have to admit my curiosity is piqued. While there are many large cities on the planet of Satori, their people live spread out amongst thousands of islands, a fact that informs the overall culture. The city Ereni and Burke come from, Seji, covers an entire island, with parkland in the center and beaches at the edges. It's hard for me to imagine, but maybe I'll be able to see for myself.

Diantha eventually comes back out into the main room, closing the door softly behind her. "I remember when I didn't want to go to sleep," she says with a sigh. "Now I fall gratefully into bed every night. Sleep can be such a respite." She sinks onto her own cushion directly across from us.

Ereni goes straight to the point. "Why is one ship returning to Satori?" she asks. "Surely you have a list of potential missions to either join or initiate."

Diantha shrugs. "Our mission was set up for a commitment of ten years. I'm surprised you don't remember. I seem to recall that before we left, you criticized that component of the mission design. I believe you said it was an insufficient amount of time."

"It's not the way missions are set up," Ereni says, ready to take up the argument right where they left it.

"Missions can be set up as we choose," Diantha replies calmly. "There is no one right way. And by making all missions potentially permanent, we exclude many people with valuable talents to offer. But you know how I feel about this. The point is, our Mission Council made a commitment to everyone who joined us, and we intend to honor that commitment. Now, with the influx of your mission, we can ensure the continuation of the work here, and anyone from our mission who wishes to stay can do so while remaining well supported. In some ways, this is the ideal situation. Perhaps I can thank you three for that."

"I don't suppose it has anything to do with Theckla then?" There is an unusual edge to Ereni's voice.

"This was always the plan," Diantha says. "And I factored that into my own decisions. I've known Theckla would have the chance to see the Satori home planet and be educated there."

"But will you place her in a crèche?" Ereni pushes.

There is a silence. "I will not," Diantha eventually answers.

"Having spent her first seven years the way she has, I don't think it would be responsible. Perhaps when she is older."

"She won't fit in without a crèche," Ereni says. "It will be difficult for her to be on Satori."

"Perhaps. But that's not really the issue here, is it?" Diantha folds her hands in her lap. "This isn't about you, Ereni. The way I choose to raise Theckla in no way impacts my regard for you. The two of you might have very different upbringings, but that doesn't mean they can't both be good."

Ereni opens her mouth, but then closes it and nods. I take the opportunity to change the subject. "I don't see how you recognized each other at the spaceport. Given you've both changed bodies and all."

Ereni and Diantha meet each other's eyes, and it looks like Ereni is suppressing a laugh. I'm glad I've given them something to be united about. "I look just the same as I always did," Diantha tells me. "I know your former mission is big into their alterations, but not all missions are the same. And in this case, there was really no need to change. The colonists wouldn't have cared one way or another, so I decided I'd rather be comfortable."

Burke runs his hand over his altered face. "I think when we go to Satori, I'll change back to how I originally looked. I don't want to be a blond giant forever."

He shoots me a grin, but Diantha raises her eyebrows. "While I support you making any changes you'd like, I'm afraid I can't guarantee the three of you spots on the return starship."

Ereni jerks as if she's just been slapped, and Burke looks almost as surprised. In the silence that follows Diantha's shocking statement, the insect song outside the hut seems to amplify in volume. The cozy room suddenly feels stifling, as if it's closing in on me. An acrid odor fills my nose, and I wonder if I'm smelling my own sweat.

"You know our old mission hates us," Ereni says flatly. "We shouldn't stay here. It's impossible to be professional in these circumstances."

"Perhaps you should have thought of that before you made your choice on Arbor," Diantha returns. Ereni looks like she's about to let loose a torrent of choice words, but Diantha holds up her hand. "Don't get me wrong, I'm sympathetic. If it were up to me, I'd be taking you with me. But we need to wait until we know how many others want to return. I'll do my best for you, but there are"—she clears her throat—"certain individuals who are not feeling very forgiving."

This makes sense to me, but Burke looks aghast. "We've taken accountability for our actions," he argues. "And we've been removed from their mission. Surely they don't wish to punish us? What purpose would that serve?"

"It's barbaric," Ereni says. "You know no one on Satori would agree with such ideas."

"But we're not on Satori right now, are we?" Diantha reaches up to massage the sides of her forehead. "As I said, I'm not unsympathetic, but you came here and dumped this mess in my lap. You can't expect me to work miracles. I imagine I can persuade everyone to agree that the best course of action is for you three to return with me, but I can't make any promises. It will be a process. And in the meantime, you'll need to keep your heads down and stay out of trouble. Is that even possible for the three of you when you're together?"

I shift on my pillow, feeling uncomfortable being part of this conversation at all. "And Kuusta Elo?" I ask. "Will he be given a space on the starship? After all, no one here is angry at him."

Diantha blinks as though I've said something she hadn't expected. "No one has mentioned the Arborist at all," she says. "Your mission seems disinterested in his fate. They fulfilled their end of their bargain with him, did they not?"

"They did." I look down at my lap. "But he isn't happy here. This isn't the kind of place he's used to."

Diantha snorts. "And you think Satori will be?"

"I think he'd like to go." I know nobody else cares about him, but that doesn't mean he should be forgotten.

"And you're willing to give up your space for him?" Diantha never pulls her punches.

"I think we'd prefer if all four of us were onboard that ship when it leaves," Ereni says. "Let's not borrow trouble."

"There may be hope for you yet," Diantha says with a smile. "Now get out of my house. There's nothing you can do. It's best to leave it in my hands. And try to relax." She directs this last at Ereni, and I wonder if she knows how futile her advice is.

Ereni is many things, but relaxed has never been one of them.

CHAPTER 5

I keep reminding myself that Diantha told us to do nothing, but after a few weeks, I feel like I'm losing my mind. Burke and I discuss our future in whispers in our bunkbeds after our long days of work are over, and even Ereni looks unaccustomedly grim.

I throw myself into learning Kensho in my free time now that I know I might need it in the future, but repeating vocabulary words to myself doesn't offer much respite from the uncertainty. In the meantime, I do my best to follow Elias's instructions while we're working together. The longer I work with him, the more impressed I become at the depth of his knowledge and the importance of the work he's doing here on Zamavat.

In spite of the oppressive heat, I enjoy checking on all the plants. Elias seems to take pride in them just as someone from Napoleon would feel about their children. He's an endless fount of knowledge about the ecosystem currently being created on Zamavat.

Occasionally we check on plants closer to the settlement and spend half a day in Elias's lab, which he shares with a zoologist and a geneticist. They keep the space dim, and the zoologist has a penchant for playing intricate instrumental music that creates a calm and intellectual atmosphere. Elias has me doublecheck all his data is appropriately catalogued, and sometimes I generate helpful charts, which he seems to appreciate.

We're in the lab one afternoon, and even though Elias and I are the only people present, he puts on some virtuosic keyboard music in the background. I'm having trouble sitting still, and in quick succession I get a cup of water, do some stretching, and get up to adjust the blinds. "You've been on edge," Elias observes calmly from the terminal next to mine.

An understatement if I've ever heard one. "Will you be returning to Satori?" I ask him. We never speak about anything personal, but I can't help wanting to know, given how all my thoughts center around the starship that will be leaving soon.

"No." He peers closer at his screen, and I see he's examining photographs a drone has taken of some rice paddies. "This, here on Zamavat? It's my life's work."

I feel a stab of something close to envy. I wish I had a meaningful focus like he has. "You're doing wonderful things here," I say instead.

He gives me a wry smile. "But you are hoping to go, yes? Just as I'm getting you properly trained up to assist me."

He doesn't say the words with any venom, and I smile back. "I would like to go and see Satori for myself," I admit. "But I don't know if there will be enough space on the ship."

His smile fades at this. "There should be enough space," he says. "Almost the entire contingent of scientists is staying. And many of the newcomers have stated a desire to remain as well."

I wonder why we have not been given this news. "I hope you're right."

He sits in silence, staring at his monitor, and I think our conversation is over. But just as I've begun scanning rows of data, he speaks. "I suggest you talk to someone from your former Mission Council," he says slowly. "Best to make amends if you can. Healthier for everyone involved."

"I'm pretty sure none of the people on that Mission Council ever want to speak to me again," I confess.

"Nevertheless." His voice stays calm, implacable. "If communication is breaking down about your future plans, it is appropriate to go to the root of the problem."

I think of Diantha telling us not to get involved. Ereni appears to be following her instructions, but she knows Diantha a lot better than I do. Do I really want to leave my future in a stranger's hands?

The thought of speaking to someone from our old Mission Council fills me with dread. I know how they all feel about me. Even Irisa. But Elias has never offered me advice about anything but my duties. And what if I am allowed to leave and I never speak with Irisa again? I remember a time when she had been very important to me.

Our former mission has their evening meal shift after ours, so that night, instead of returning to the dormitory, I lurk around the kitchens, offering to load the enormous dishwasher. I take my time, carefully placing each plate and cup, until the machine is entirely full and the other workers start giving me weird looks that make me suspect I'm in the way. I move to hover in the doorway, looking for Irisa amongst the tables of eating Satori.

I spot her just as she's standing up with her tray and I waylay her at the cleaning station. "Let me take that for you." I give her my brightest smile and take the laden tray from her before she can protest.

"Don't you eat during the first shift?" Irisa asks. Her once-pale skin has tanned darkly in the unrelenting sun, and her hair has lightened to an almost white-blonde. I wonder if the Satori who remain from my old mission will slowly alter their bodies to better adjust to this climate.

I place her tray on the discarded stack and begin to place the items on it in their correct places. "Yes, I was hoping to speak with you. I was wondering"—I glance around the crowded commissary and consider how many of these people hate me—"if you might take a walk with me."

"A walk," she repeats. She eyes me dubiously, then sighs. "Yes, okay. It won't get dark for another two hours."

Irisa leads the way out of the commissary and chooses our direction. We walk in silence for several minutes, and I watch as my sandaled feet slowly accumulate a fine coat of dust. I'm so afraid of saying the wrong thing, I don't know how to start. We walk through the entire settlement without exchanging a word.

"I like this planet," she finally says as we see the beginning of the rice paddies ahead, limned in the gold of the low sun. "I like baking in the heat, and I like the vibrant colors. The air smells so fresh and unspoiled."

I haven't noticed any difference in the air beyond its higher moisture content, but I nod as though I agree. "It's a beautiful place," I say. "I've enjoyed learning the plans for the future development of the ecosystem."

"Someday it will be a veritable paradise." Irisa kneels down and cups her hand around a small, bright pink flower. "And it already has such a variety of plants. And the insects!"

I keep my smile pasted on my face. She reminds me of Elias in her excitement about the insects. I find all the bugs in the settlement to be a constant plague. I have small red itchy spots peppered across my arms and legs due to their regular feasts on me when I forget to use the recommended repellant.

We used to have a few weeks of midges every year in San Marco. They'd gather in great swarms over the canals, drawn by the still water. My mother had detested them, and she trained me to do the same.

"It's a very different kind of climate than Arbor's," I say diplomatically.

"And a very different kind of mission." She rises to her feet. "What did you want to speak about?"

I swallow and try to ignore the queasy feeling in my stomach. "I know I ruined things for you on Arbor, and I'm very sorry for that. I still think it was the right thing to do"—curse my honesty—"but that doesn't mean I don't care about how everyone feels about it."

"Decisions have consequences, Sienna." Irisa starts forward at a more rapid pace. "It gives me no pleasure to say this, but now you have to figure out how to live with those consequences."

I bite my tongue to stop speaking in anger. It is not as if Irisa is blameless for how events unfolded on Arbor, and we both know it.

But I'm not here to offer recriminations. "I don't want to talk about myself," I say instead. "I want to talk about Ereni and Burke."

She raises her eyebrows. "We gave Burke his chance. At my insistence, I'll add. He didn't take it."

"He's a loyal person. That's a positive trait, at least where I come from." After so many pointed comments about how backwards my home planet is, I can't resist the small dig in return. "Ereni and Burke both deserve the chance to return home and start over. They haven't left me to face the consequences alone, but if they had never met me, I don't know that they would have ever thought to share the Second Life data publicly. It was my plan, and I was the one who passed the data along to Pilvi. If you want to keep me on Zamavat forever, go ahead. But they shouldn't lose their futures. They can still both go on to do wonderful things, I know it."

I believe what I'm saying deep in my heart. Both of them are so intelligent, so talented, so ready to work hard to achieve their goals. If they end up stuck here on this planet, excluded from the remaining Satori mission, it will be such a waste. I wouldn't be able to forgive myself.

Irisa finally ceases her quick pace and stares at me for a long moment. "I think you've been misinformed," she says stiffly. "Our mission has no wish to prevent any of you from returning to Satori if that is what you wish. It is simply a matter of space. But as almost everyone from our mission is opting to stay, as well as nearly half of the original mission, I don't anticipate there being any problem in that regard."

The relief hits me so hard, I feel dizzy. Elias had been right after all. I would willingly give my spot to either Ereni or Burke, but being forced to stay here, surrounded by people who actively dislike me, while my friends traveled home, would have been a miserable outcome. Better than all three of us staying, but even so. "Thank you," I breathe.

Irisa looks up at the open sky. "You know we aren't a vengeful society, don't you, Sienna? We aren't like Sanctum in that way." I'm so happy at the news, the condescension in her tone has little effect on me. "And we wouldn't want to mar the harmony of what we're trying to build here."

At one time Irisa had admitted to me that the outcome on Arbor had been partly due to her own actions and lack of care. But her words show me she has rewritten what happened there in her own memory. A small sadness squeezes inside of me at the knowledge. On Sanctum, I had liked Irisa, who had presented as a kind of motherly figure to me during one of my lowest times. But all that has changed, and I realize we'll never return to how things were between us.

Consequences indeed.

"And Kuusta Elo?" I ask. "I know he also wishes to leave." He's spoken of nothing else on our dirt bike expeditions these last few weeks. He's even followed my example and begun to learn Kensho.

"The Arborist?" She waves a dismissive hand. "I'll leave that up to the group that's departing, but I can't imagine they'd care one way or the other."

"Thank you," I say again. "I know that will mean a lot to him."

She looks disinterested. "Is there anything else?"

"No," I say quickly, not wanting to undo my good work. "I won't take any more of your time." She nods, and I make a rapid escape, eager to share the good news with my friends.

Back at the dormitory, sitting next to Burke on his bottom bunk with Ereni sitting on my own bunk across from us, I feel the first wash of happiness settle over my body. Things have been so uncertain for so long, but now we know what we'll be doing next. I can't help grinning as I explain what happened between Irisa and myself.

Ereni shakes her head and starts laughing when I've finished. "What?" I ask her. "Aren't you happy?"

"Of course I'm happy," she retorts. "I'm ecstatic that you called Irisa on her bluff."

"I did no such thing." I hug Burke's arm closer to me. "I don't think it mattered what I said, to be honest. They were clearly always going to allow us to leave."

But Ereni is shaking her head. "I wouldn't be so sure about that," she says slowly. "We like to talk a big game, but we don't always live up to our ideals. You do understand that, don't you, Sienna? All that time we spent studying and preparing you to take the exam, what you were learning is what we strive for. But in practice the Satori often fall short. We're just like any other culture in that regard."

"You really believe they would have kept us here out of sheer pettiness?" I ask. I can't quite believe it. But I remember Elias's insistence that I speak with someone from my old Mission Council, and I wonder.

Ereni shrugs. "I'm genuinely not sure. What I do know is that you having that conversation with Irisa undoubtedly helped our cause. It's one thing to make a vindictive decision in the abstract, but it's another thing altogether to explain that's what you intend to do to someone as bright-eyed as you."

"I don't know that you're being fair," Burke objects. "Irisa has always acted in the best interest of the group."

"But she's changed," Ereni insists. "I could tell on Arbor that she's changed. The specter of two failed missions is hanging over her now. She feels responsible, but also resentful of everything that contributed to the failure. At this point she just wants to save her reputation."

I'm not so sure Ereni is correct, but it hardly matters now. Soon enough the three of us will be fast asleep on a starship en route to Satori. And I'll finally see their fabled world with my own eyes.

A week before our scheduled departure, Diantha pulls me aside one evening at the commissary. She checks to see that Theckla is occupied, coloring with her friends on one of the long tables, before stepping out the door with me. It's been getting hotter, and even though the sun is lower in the sky this late in the day, the heat envelops me like a physical thing. "Is it this hot on Satori?" I wipe my brow unsuccessfully with the back of my hand, trying to remove at least some of the unpleasant moisture.

Diantha wipes the back of her neck with a spare piece of cloth and tucks it back into her pocket. "It depends where you are. The island Ereni and I are from is more temperate, but there is an archipelago of islands near the equator that can be similar to this. Nowhere on the main continent though."

"I'm relieved to hear it." I slouch under the eaves, listening to the early evening chorus of bugs.

"I wanted to let you know that Kuusta Elo is officially coming with us to Satori," Diantha says. "I hear he's started learning our language."

"That's right," I say. "We've been practicing together." I hesitate. "If we could have some awake time during the journey, we would both be able to proceed further in our language studies before we land. I know all the Satori we meet will still be able to understand us because of their N-CATs, but it won't be as good as if we can speak the proper language ourselves."

Diantha nods. "That's what I was going to propose myself," she says. "I will ask Burke or Ereni if either of them will volunteer to be awake for a period of time with the two of you so you can practice with a fluent speaker." She walks back over to the door and checks on Theckla before returning. "There is a small population of people from other planets who live on Satori," she says. "You and Kuusta won't be entirely remarkable. But it is still likely to be a difficult transition."

"I'll have Ereni and Burke." Surely I can rely on them now, after everything we've been through together.

"You will." She paces back and forth in front of me. "It might be a difficult transition for them as well. A long time has passed on Satori since our departures. There will be changes that are impossible to predict. And they may find they miss certain people who are no longer with us more than they expect."

"I think they're aware of that," I say gently.

"It might also be difficult for them to decide what to do next. Both of them have always been driven to join a mission. Ereni has been single-mindedly fixated on that goal for as long as I can remember. But with their experience, they might have trouble finding a mission that would welcome them." She shrugs. "Or perhaps I'm worried about nothing. There's no telling how things have changed in our absence. The majority of Satori might sympathize with your decision on Arbor. It's impossible to tell. But either way, it's not going to be easy. I wanted to tell you that, in case they aren't preparing you for what to expect."

If I'm being honest, I have no concrete idea of what life will be like on Satori. Burke has spent most of his time talking about his studies and his love of sailing, but aside from that, I have a murky picture. "I can adapt." I try to project a confidence I don't feel.

"I have no doubt. But I wanted to let you know, once we've arrived, if you ever need some support, you can come to me." She squints up at the horizon. "I'll be in for some criticism myself once we return, given how I'm choosing to raise Theckla. Those of us who are different should stick together."

I'm touched by the unexpected offer, even as her estimate of how she'll be received by her own people shifts my view of what we might find when we arrive on Satori. One of the Satori tenets, after all, is to refrain from judging other cultures according to their own standards. But what of people from their own culture who choose to do things differently? How tolerant are they then? I'm realizing I'll have a lot to learn after we arrive.

"Thank you," I tell Diantha. "I'm glad you'll be coming back with us." I pause. "Do you expect any trouble? With Theckla?"

"Trouble? Oh no, I wouldn't say that." She brings out the cloth again and mops at the sides of her face. "But the decision I'm making is distinctly unorthodox. I don't expect to be the most popular person. If the Satori when we arrive are anything like those I left behind, they'll accuse me of taking other people's cultures too much to heart."

"Why did you decide to have Theckla?" I ask. I've been so curious, but there has never seemed to be a good time to ask, especially not with Ereni around.

"I was in a romantic relationship with her father," Diantha says. "He was a colonist here, and we became close. But then he died in a terrible accident. Luckily, his genetic material had been catalogued, and we had the means to recreate it." She shakes her head. "I just wasn't ready to let him go." She wipes beneath her eyes, and I can't tell if she's cleaning away sweat or tears. "I don't know if I'll ever be ready."

"Is this a common thing to do on Satori when someone dies?" I ask.

She gives a sad little laugh. "Not at all. No one would ever do this on Satori. But then, I wasn't on Satori when it happened, was I?" She reaches out and clasps my hand with hers for a brief moment. "I need to get back to Theckla. But remember what I've said."

She hurries back inside the commissary, and I think over our conversation. It seems like our homecoming might not be the unalleviated joy for my comrades that I've been anticipating. We'll all need to prepare so we'll be ready for whatever we find.

CHAPTER 6

$\mathcal{B}$urke volunteers to stay awake for the first three months of our journey to help Kuusta and I learn Kensho. "I will happily pass my baton to you," Ereni tells him with a little salute, right before she reports to be put into cryosleep. She'd been woken up an entire year early on our trip to Arbor to help me prepare for the comprehensive exam.

Kuusta, Burke, and I spend most of our waking hours together, speaking in Kensho, writing in Kensho, watching media in Kensho. As always when I'm learning a new language, I feel like my brain is crammed with vocabulary words, and sometimes I mix Kensho with previous languages I've learned. At least I'm finding the accent to be easy, but I can tell from Burke's pained facial expressions that my grammar leaves much to be desired.

It is only at the end of the day after dinner that Kuusta retreats to his compartment, and Burke and I have a few precious hours alone. Even then, we mostly speak in Kensho, but occasionally we lapse into Gallo, my native language. Letting the familiar syllables fall from my tongue feels remarkably soothing after a long day wrestling with my lack of vocabulary.

One night we're snuggling on my narrow cot, him sitting behind me with his arms wrapped around me. I allow myself to lean back on his chest, and one of his hands is intertwined with mine. I never get tired of marveling at how much larger his hands are. "Tell me about Satori," I say to him, leaning back my head. "Tell me why you love it so much. I want to know what to expect."

He strokes my arm with his free hand. "I spent most of my time in Seji. It's a beautiful city, encompassing an entire small island. It's much quieter than San Marco because there are very few private vehicles. There is an extensive rail system throughout the city, as well as electric buses. It's easy to go anywhere you want to go."

I remember the hums of the amphicars in San Marco. "That sounds nice."

"There is greenery everywhere you look," he continues. "Not unlike the cities in Arbor, but the greenery in Seji is different. Lusher. The temperature never gets very cold or very hot. In the center of the city, there's a gigantic park. It covers over a thousand acres, and it's where we'd go to play sports, attend concerts, take a pause in the middle of the day. Everyone loves Akari Park. And everyone loves boating. There are plenty of ferries to take you to nearby islands, and there are fleets of recreational boats. Anyone can reserve a small boat for the afternoon."

"Are those the boats you race?"

I can feel him shaking his head behind me. "No, there are racing clubs, and each club has their own yacht that they care for, clean, repair as needed. Being a member of a racing club is a major point of identity. Many people join a club simply to offer moral support, even if they don't expect to be actively sailing. It's one of the ways the city is organized socially."

"Do the clubs hate each other?" I ask, fascinated. "Our top speeder bike racers had famous rivalries that could span generations."

"I wouldn't say we hate one another," he says slowly. "It is very satisfying to watch a club that has been struggling slowly build itself up and improve. I've cheered on other clubs because I've known they were working hard. Clubs help each other out too, and sometimes members swap to help another team. Racing each other is more about seeing what we're capable of doing together. Occasionally a boat breaks a current record, and the whole of Seji turns out to celebrate."

"That sounds fun." I'm allowing myself to be lulled by his descriptions. "Where will we stay when we arrive?"

"We'll be assigned rooms in hospitality houses. We can stay there as long as we'd like, but most people apply for more permanent accommodation. You can specify any of your preferences, although you won't always get everything you want. But all the living quarters on Seji are pleasant, and even if you end up in a different neighborhood than you're hoping, it's easy enough to get around. Perhaps you and me and Ereni will apply for a place together."

I pause, trying to imagine what he's saying. "Is that…a normal thing to do?" I ask.

"Oh yes." He lets go of my hand so he can squeeze me more tightly. "Young people often live with friends from their crèches. After growing up all together, it would be lonely to live on your own. If I'm being honest, I preferred the dormitory on Zamavat to our beautiful little cottages on Arbor. I never felt at home in my cottage. It was too quiet."

He preferred the dormitory? On Sanctum, the ability to afford a large, private residence was illustrative of how much wealth and power a family had accumulated. No one would ever admit to preferring something smaller and shabbier.

But I have to admit there has been a certain comfort in having Burke and Ereni so close. Even on Arbor, we'd been able to easily walk to one another's cottages. In San Marco, I'd had to take the amphicar to see almost anyone.

"Maybe we should apply," I say. After all, it no longer matters what was normal for me on Sanctum. And I'd rather be near the people who care about me. "Would you prefer to live near the water or near the park?"

"The water," he says immediately. "Not that the park isn't lovely. But I'd prefer to go out on the water every day if I could. Just seeing it makes me feel calmer."

"What else do you love about Satori?"

"I love how warm and friendly everyone is. People smile at each other on the street, and sometimes they'll strike up conversations with strangers. If you sit to eat outdoors at the park, it's common to speak to whoever might have spread a blanket nearby. And people don't hesitate to help each other."

"Doesn't sound like a bad place to be a stranger." Although remembering it's acceptable to ask a random person for help will take some adjustment. "It will be strange not to have any of the Satori from our mission with us." Very few of our party had opted to leave Zamavat. "Especially Irisa. I can't believe she posed as your mother on Sanctum, and I was entirely convinced."

"It feels like such a long time ago."

"Will you miss her?" I ask.

Burke tenses behind me. "She's barely spoken to me since we shared the Second Life data on Arbor. I might miss the relationship we used to have, but I won't miss what it's become."

Consequences indeed. None of us have emerged from our experiences unscathed.

"Tell me something else about Satori." I'll never get tired of hearing about our destination.

"I love how much our people love knowledge," Burke says. "There's such a focus on learning, and continuing to learn your whole life. We would never withhold an education from anyone, not for any reason."

"Could I study there?" The thought of getting the formal education I've been denied for so long piques my interest.

"I don't see why not. It might be a little difficult without an N-CAT, but I'm sure that could be worked out." He starts rubbing my arms. "Do you think you'll ever change your mind about that?"

"Getting an N-CAT?" I feel like we've suddenly arrived at a dangerous conversational topic.

"Yeah. You know they're tiny, right? They're smaller than a human tooth."

I can't help but laugh at his chosen comparison. "I don't choose to have extra teeth installed in my brain either, thank you very much." He keeps stroking my arms, and I force myself to release the breath I'm holding. "I don't know how I'll feel in the future, but I know I'm not ready to do anything drastic right now. I'm still trying to figure out what my future is going to look like. The last thing I need is to mess with my brain at the same time."

"Fair enough. Your grasp of Kensho is getting better every day. I think you'll be able to manage well once we arrive."

I turn to look at him. "Kuusta is having more trouble."

Burke nods. "He'll get it though, as long as he keeps practicing. If he decides to stay on Satori, he'll have plenty of time to learn. He's already told me in no uncertain terms that he will never get an N-CAT."

"He's brought it up at least five separate times." I'm being generous in my assessment. Kuusta has made some kind of remark about N-CATs practically every day. "I think he's self-conscious that he isn't learning as quickly as I am."

"Well, not everyone can be as brilliant as you."

Burke kisses me on the nose, which turns to kisses on my mouth, which turns to kisses in other places, and our conversation ends.

AFTER SEVERAL MONTHS spent studying Kensho, all three of us enter into cryosleep. We're woken up from our long slumber only a day before our shuttle departs for the surface of Satori. Burke and Ereni have both transformed once again during the voyage, this time into bodies similar to those they originally had before they left on their mission. I brace myself for the jarring impact of seeing them for the first time, but for some reason it isn't nearly as disorienting as it had been before our arrival to Arbor.

Burke's eyes have returned to the brown color I remember from Sanctum, and there is no longer such a large height differential between us. His dark hair falls in loose curls around his face, and his skin is a light brown color, with a few darker freckles scattered across his cheekbones. I recognize his smile, and this time instead of giving me a vaguely creepy feeling, it simply reminds me of home.

Perhaps I'm becoming more Satori after all.

Ereni is as gorgeous as ever, with long wavy black hair framing a heart-shaped face. Her smile is also recognizable, and I see she's opted to return to the devastating green eyes she'd had on Sanctum. She's regained some of her curves and stands only a head taller than myself. She wears wide-legged trousers that end at the middle of her calves, along with a matching jacket in turquoise blue. Her shoes are open-toed, decorated with large matching turquoise stones.

"You always manage to look good," I tell her.

"Even fresh from the sleeping pod," she says with a wince. I can relate: my own mouth is still uncomfortably dry, and I keep having an itching sensation that roves over my body.

There is no spaceport on Seji, so the shuttles will land on a nearby island outside of the city of Jundo instead. As members from Diantha's mission gather in the lounge with us, waiting for their turn to take a shuttle down, I can't help marveling at how few material goods any of us have. Whenever Mother wanted to travel to our country house, she'd send a separate amphicar just for our luggage.

We share a shuttle with Diantha and Theckla, as well as Kuusta and a few strangers. When we move to exit the craft, I hang back with Kuusta, not wanting to interfere with Burke and Ereni's first moments back home. But when I descend the gangway, I realize we have to traverse a significant distance of flat concrete in order to enter the actual port building.

The air is pleasantly warm but not stifling as it could sometimes be on Zamavat. The sun is almost directly overhead, and I squint towards the building in front of us, wishing we could increase our pace. But Ereni and Burke are strolling in front of us, for all the world as if they don't feel any sense of urgency now that they're home.

Diantha and Theckla drop back to walk with me. "There will be some minor administrative details to address, given that neither you nor Kuusta were born on Satori," she says in a low voice. "I'll stay with you to make sure the process goes smoothly, but I don't anticipate there being any problems."

That's when I realize she deliberately chose to share our shuttle in order to help me and Kuusta. She must have really meant her offer of support back on Zamavat.

As we enter the spaceport, a strange smell reaches my nose: earthy, pungent, and slightly sour. Ereni laughs at the look on my face as I sniff the air inquisitively. "Many of our buildings are grown from fungi," she says. "They aren't strictly alive in the way of the tree buildings on Arbor, but the growing process does leave a residual odor for several years. And this building is a fairly new addition to the spaceport."

"It certainly wasn't here when we left." Burke is gazing off into the distance, a sure sign that he's consulting his N-CAT. "This space-port has almost doubled in size."

He and Ereni share uneasy looks. I can't imagine what it must be like for them to return to their home after such a long absence, unsure of what changes they'll confront.

The space we've entered feels a bit cramped, with pleasant low lighting. A man with a qualpad steps up to greet us. The Satori in our party are quickly cleared. Burke and Ereni go to a nearby bench. Both hunker down without speaking, and I wonder if they're using their N-CATs to receive summaries of all the changes that have taken place in the last three hundred years. Diantha stays with Theckla, Kuusta, and myself.

The man is perfectly pleasant but almost robotic, asking each of us the same series of questions. He doesn't smile a single time during our interaction. Diantha answers for Theckla, and I find myself imitating my interrogator's grave demeanor. At the end of the conversation, each of us is assigned a unique identification number, a room in Seji, and an appointment with a counselor to help in our transition process. Then we are allowed to proceed.

Kuusta leans close to my ear. "They are very efficient." He sounds impressed.

We pass through a decontamination room, which spills into a huge lobby open to the public. The high ceiling curves above us in multiple off-white swirls, a few glowing skylights allowing natural light into the space. I stop to get my bearings next to a blue marking on the shiny floor, and a bench suddenly unfolds from the designated space. I almost feel like I'm inside an enormous high-tech mushroom.

Two people, looking like they're waiting for us, stand from similar benches that disappear back into the floor. One woman rushes up to Diantha and starts speaking at a furious pace my language skills can't follow. Diantha takes Theckla's hand, gives us a little wave, and follows the woman through the massive space and out a sliding door on the far side.

"What was that about?" I ask Ereni. But her attention has been arrested by another woman approaching us. She moves with grace, standing at almost the same height as Burke, her medium brown skin absolutely flawless. A stylish streak of white runs down her flowing black hair, and she has light wrinkles at the corners of her eyes that speak of someone who has a good sense of humor. Her smile, though, seems uncertain, her eyes darting back and forth between Ereni and Burke.

"My darlings," she says in Kensho, holding her arms out wide. "I never thought I'd see either of you again. I cannot describe the joy I felt when I heard the news of your imminent arrival."

"Lyra?" Burke looks like he's seen a ghost, and he doesn't step forward to meet the woman.

"In the flesh." She beams, looking back and forth between him and Ereni like an inquisitive bird. "Surprise!"

Ereni recovers first, stepping forward to hug the woman and give her a kiss on the cheek. Burke follows suit, but I notice he's holding himself rigidly as he does so.

"Tell us everything," Ereni says when the greetings are done. "How is this possible? Did you change your mind and join a mission yourself?"

Lyra's laugh tinkles pleasantly through the space. I don't know why it makes me feel even tenser. "Hardly. You know how adamant I was about staying on Satori. One of the only things we ever fought about, wasn't it?" She gives Burke a fond smile.

"We certainly wanted different things." He stares at her, a slightly wondering look in his eyes. "You're going to have to let us in on your secret."

"Oh, it was nothing I did. Our scientists made another large leap in their longevity research, and so we're all living a great deal longer than we used to. As you will, now that you've come home."

Given the Satori already live so much longer than anyone on Sanctum, this is monumental news. Even Ereni looks temporarily stunned.

I step into the conversational breech. "Does that mean you're over three hundred years old?" I hope I've chosen the proper Kensho words.

"That's right. A common age now." Lyra turns her attention to me for the first time. "And who might you be?"

"Sienna's from Sanctum," Burke says, stepping closer to me. "She's been with us ever since."

"How delightful." Lyra's words don't sound sincere to me, but it's hard to tell given the language barrier. "I look forward to speaking with you later and hearing all about your home world."

"That is very kind of you," I murmur, reminding myself to be diplomatic.

She steps forward and touches Burke lightly on the arm. "And I am, of course, particularly looking forward to catching up with you. You look exactly the same."

"Well, for me, it's only been a few years since I left." Burke seems to be bracing himself.

"It's true. And you must have thought I would be long dead." Lyra says the words with a surprising lightness, as if she has failed to understand the grief of the space voyager who leaves loved ones behind. I think of my twin brother Leo, now almost certainly dead, and something inside my chest contracts painfully.

"I did." No hint of his emotions shows on Burke's impassive face.

"What a wonderful little reunion," Ereni interrupts. "And I know we're all looking forward to continuing it later. But for now, we've been on a starship for a long time, so I'm sure you'll understand how eager I am to get back to Seji, find our rooms, and get some rest."

"Of course." Lyra displays her implacable smile. "I still live in Seji myself so it will be easy for me to assist you. After all, things have changed since you've last been here." With that she takes Burke's free arm and leads him away, chatting in a low enough voice that I can't hear.

Kuusta looks baffled. "I'm afraid I didn't catch all of that," he says in Truncish. "Who is that woman?"

Ereni sighs. "That's Lyra. She grew up in our crèche with us," she says. "And she was also Burke's first love."

My stomach makes an alarming drop at her words.

CHAPTER 7

However much I'm dying to ask Ereni more questions about Lyra and her history with Burke, I rein myself in. Lyra talks nonstop to Burke for the entire journey to Seji, which involves a train and a ferry. Ereni sits quietly beside me, reviewing updates on Satori with her N-CAT. And Kuusta is glued to the window, curious about the new world in which we find ourselves.

I try to push away my anxiety about what Lyra's presence might mean in order to appreciate the architecture on display. The rail station, which is connected to the spaceport, has been built in a similar style that mirrors patterns found in the natural world. Underneath the curving lines of the high ceiling, I felt like I'd entered an opalescent snail's shell. While the aesthetics inside the starship had left much to be desired, everything we've seen of Satori so far shows much greater care taken to render beauty in public spaces.

The train carries us quickly and efficiently to the ferry, and I wonder that no one has asked us for a ticket or any financial recompense. "I think the public transportation here is free," I whisper to Kuusta.

He nods while not taking his eyes from the window. "We often debated that exact point in the eduskunta," he says. "Our transit service was highly subsidized, of course, and affordable to everyone. But we could never quite bring ourselves to abandon the payment system altogether. But here, I can see how it works in practice." He looks elated at the prospect, and I realize that Kuusta cares more about these practical details of governance than I ever gave him credit for. He had been Pilvi's father's main opponent, and as such, in spite of our strange friendship, we'd never discussed policy at any length.

Once we board the ferry, I go by myself to the upper deck and watch as the boat pulls away from the shore. The wind whips my hair, finally grown out to shoulder length, and I gaze at the azure blue water with something like awe. Wispy clouds float slowly in the sky overhead, and the air smells of salt and seaweed.

It is truly beautiful. I wonder how Burke and Ereni were able to leave it behind.

Lyra finally takes her leave from us at the dock in Seji, and we board an underground train. We are all quiet, taking in our surroundings, but Burke sits right next to me and leans his shoulder against mine. All four of us have been given rooms in the same hospitality house. It will give me comfort to know my friends are right down the hall.

We walk a few blocks to our temporary home, turning onto a pedestrian street. When we pass a cross street, I can see the water is only a few blocks from our location. I point it out to Burke, who smiles. Now that Lyra is gone, he's acting more like himself, and he and Ereni are staring around us with the same wonder that Kuusta and I are showing. "So much has changed," Ereni murmurs. "Without my N-CAT, I wouldn't even be sure where I am."

The buildings we pass are mostly of modest height, six to ten stories tall, and they have a strange architectural style that makes them look like they're almost melting. Some of them are bright red or yellow, while others are more muted shades of orange and brown. We occasionally pass by park-like squares, some with groves of trees, others with cultivated gardens, and some with play structures for children. Shadows fall across the building faces from the late afternoon sun, and a group of children run in the street in front of a large building Burke identifies as a crèche, kicking a medium-sized pink ball back and forth.

We finally stop in front of our assigned building, one of the taller ones we've seen, its walls a deep pomegranate red. A woman behind a counter gives us our assigned room numbers. Ereni and Burke both have rooms on the sixth floor, and Kuusta and I are on the third. She doesn't give us keys, and I realize none of the doors lock. We are simply supposed to trust everyone else to honor our privacy, an idea that makes a knot form in my stomach.

When I wave goodbye to Kuusta and open the door to my room, I am pleasantly surprised. I've been expecting something similar to my compartment aboard the starship, but this room is both more spacious and more carefully decorated. Sun pours through the glass door on the far side of the room, and various paintings of seascapes and sailing yachts decorate the light blue walls. The earthy odor that permeated the elevator and hallways is barely detectable inside the room, masked by a sweet citrus smell.

A large bed with a fluffy white comforter is tucked away in one corner, and a good-sized table stands in the center of the room, surrounded by four chairs. The floor is made of some kind of simulated smooth substance, a light reddish-brown, and a soft blue rug lays at the foot of the bed. While the bathroom facilities are down the hall, the room does have a small sink, cupboard, and electric kettle. I peek in the cupboard to see a few mugs, plates, various tea bags, and several snack bars in different flavors, along with basic toiletries. A cheerful red towel hangs from the side of the sink.

A comfortable chair sits just in front of the window, and after dropping my few things on the bed, I sink into it. My room is at the back of the building, and a glass door opens out onto a small balcony. I have a view of a sheltered green space, a few trees reaching their branches towards me. A path winds between various bushes and shrubbery, several benches tucked along its route. Another building rises up beyond the trees, a mirror of my own except in a mustard yellow color.

I take a breath and then let it out. So this is Satori. It is both completely different and strangely familiar at the same time. The lemon scent soothes me, and the chair molds itself to my back, completely supporting me. The tree branches wave in a slight breeze. I wonder if I'll finally have a chance to catch my breath here after everything that has happened.

But then I remember Lyra and the confusion on Ereni and Burke's faces, and that fleeting sense of peace disappears as quickly as it arrived.

WE SPEND a few days getting our bearings. Ereni and Burke inhale Satori history from the last three hundred years, get up to speed on current affairs, and look up lists of old crèchemates to discover who is still alive and on the planet. Kuusta wanders the city streets while listening to language exercises through his earbuds. And I try to rest and not worry about what the future will bring.

I learn that by giving out my individual number, I'm allowed to get three meals a day in a large dining area downstairs. I'm also able to use the clothing printer on the premises to supply myself with a choice of Satori-style outfits. I pay a visit to the medical clinic a few streets over, where a doctor takes my blood and performs scans with a handheld device. She gives me a few shots, including my annual birth control shot, and declares me healthy and entirely fit for my age. To my relief, she doesn't bring up my lack of N-CAT.

It doesn't take long before I begin to feel restless. I'm not really sure what I'm meant to be doing, and there's only so much Satori media I can consume before I need to take a break. I find myself compulsively studying lists of new Kensho vocabulary words.

Burke and Ereni invite me to have dinner with their old crèche-mate Evander, and I'm excited to meet one of their friends who might be easier to spend time with than Lyra. We meet at his building, which bears the melted look and streaks in coloration common to buildings in Seji.

Evander comes out front to meet us. He proves to be a voluble and friendly man of indeterminate age who gestures a lot when he speaks.

Slightly stout, he's only slightly taller than me, and he wears his hair in a distinctive purple stripe down the middle of his head, the sides shaven clean. His remaining hair is long, and he pulls it back into a tail.

He greets us all with effusive hugs and kisses, even me. "Who would have thought the three of us would be together again," he says. "The universe is full of miracles!" Then he hugs us all again.

After he hugs me for a second time, he pulls back and nods several times. "It's a real pleasure to meet you, Sienna. Any friend of Ereni and Burke is a friend of mine."

He leads us inside and up several floors by elevator. We arrive at a large dining area with at least twenty tables, where he presents the food he prepared himself using one of the building's communal kitchens. "I made that noodle dish you used to love, Ereni." He takes a lid off a serving dish, allowing the savory aroma to speak for his culinary skill. "And don't worry, Burke, I made sure we'd have something sweet for dessert."

Ereni laughs. "I don't remember you being much of a cook, Evander. It looks like you've been busy." She leans over the steaming dish, takes in a deep breath, and sighs happily.

Evander looks pleased. "Cooking is one of my favorite hobbies. I only took it up ten or so years ago, and now I don't know how I managed before." He serves generous heaps of noodles to each of our plates, and we sit down to eat.

"What else has changed besides your cooking skills?" Burke asks with a grin.

"Too much to tell you during one meal, I'm sure." Evander hasn't begun eating himself, but is instead watching our first reactions to his cooking with a large smile. "Right now, I have a leadership position with the Seji Association, making sure our city is well planned and well run. It really is very gratifying, and I get to talk with a lot of people, which I enjoy. But enough about me! Tell me all about your much-vaunted mission. I want to hear everything."

Ereni and Burke regale him with tales of their experiences on Sanctum, Arbor, and even one about Zamavat. He listens with a pleasant expression that makes me think he must be good at his job.

Finally, during a lull in the conversation, he turns to me. "And what do you think of our fine city, Sienna?"

"I haven't explored as much as I'd like," I reply. I turn to Burke. "I was actually wondering if you might want to show me around tomorrow."

Burke turns a little red. "I'd love to," he says, "but I'm going to be spending the day with Lyra. She's promised to help me review everything that's happened since I left."

I don't like the empty feeling this news leaves in my stomach, which doesn't settle when Evander laughs. "Of course you are. I remember when the two of you were as thick as thieves, and she hasn't changed so very much. She still dearly loves to exercise her influence, and helping an old crèchemate just returned from the field is an enterprise with her name all over it. Just don't let her bowl you over, that's my advice."

Burke snorts. "Lyra can be forceful, but she's never been able to run my life. After all, I left for the mission, didn't I?"

"That you did, that you did." Evander sits back with a sigh. "But she's had three hundred years to learn how to get her way."

Burke leans back himself, looking unconcerned. "Three hundred years or not, I still know my own mind." He gives me a wink, and I relax a little.

"You should come with me tomorrow, Sienna" Ereni says. "I'm going to visit Akari Park, and you haven't been yet, have you?" When I shake my head, she smiles. "It's one of my favorite places. Remember when you took me to your Mask Makers Festival? Now I'll finally be able to return the favor."

I know she's trying to distract me from Burke's plans, but I do want to see the large park around which this entire city is built. And there's no one better than Ereni at plotting future plans. She will probably have a whole host of ideas of what I should consider doing next.

"Oh yes, you absolutely must go see Akari Park," Evander says with enthusiasm. "I only wish I could join you myself. Ereni is lucky to get to see it through new eyes."

The next morning, Burke waves me a cheerful goodbye, and

Ereni and I venture forth to the park, dressed in our new Satori clothes that seem adept at keeping me both warm and cool. My sandals are printed to mold to the bottom of my feet, and I sink into their soft cushioning with every step. I don't look so different from the other Satori going about their business around us, and I allow myself to be comforted by my relative anonymity.

Ereni confidently takes the stairs down to the underground train, and we ride several stops to reach our destination. Our train car is slightly chilly, and most of the Satori around me have blank looks on their faces, obviously occupied with their N-CATs. I realize nobody in our car looks particularly old. There are no children either, which makes sense given that most of them would currently be in classes, but the uniform sameness of outward age is a bit peculiar.

What would it be like to live hundreds of years while not aging? I have trouble imagining it, but then, I can't even picture what I'll be doing in five years, let alone a hundred. I wonder if the technological breakthrough Lyra told us about requires the installation of an N-CAT. Will I someday take for granted a lifespan that would never have crossed my family's minds?

We get off the train and ascend, the exit of the station leading directly into Akari Park. A large red gate-like structure looms before us, at least fifty meters high and surrounded on either side by dense hedges. I can't discern its purpose. "Why doesn't it have any doors?" I ask.

Ereni stopped beside me, staring up at the elegant, curving lines creating the top of the structure. "It's symbolic. It's meant to remind us of our values of open doors, open borders, prosperity for all." Her voice sounds a little strange, and when I look over, I catch her wiping away a tear.

"I've never known you to be particularly sentimental," I tease her.

But her expression stays solemn. "I've loved this place since I was a little girl. The first time I learned about what happened to old Earth, I was presented with a simplified version, one that was age appropriate, but even so, I was horrified. Afterwards, I came here and stared up at our People's Arch, and I promised myself I would do everything I could to make sure nothing like that ever happened again. Not on Satori, certainly, and also not anywhere else, if I could help it." She smiles at me, her eyes still glistening. "I suppose I was an ambitious child. And very idealistic."

I smile back at her. "Some things never change."

We walk underneath the archway and into a beautiful garden. It's organized around a large blue-green pond partially covered with blooming lily pads. Small trees wave their white and pink blossomed branches, and several pagodas, red to match the entrance arch, sit at vantage points around the pond. As we begin to stroll around the circumference, we come upon a higher outcropping of rocks, water tumbling down them in a small waterfall that flows into the bigger body of water. The sound of the water is almost musical, and the blossoms smell like candy.

"Did you come here often as a child?" I ask Ereni.

She walks at a slower pace than her usual, giving herself time to take in the beauty all around us. "Not so much when I was young," she says. "Then I preferred the play areas and the group sports. But once I reached my teenage years, I came here more often. I found the atmosphere helped me to think more clearly."

"Has it changed since then?"

"Hardly at all. It might be the only thing that hasn't." She gives a wistful little laugh. "It's all so much to take in. I'm afraid you'll have to be patient with Burke and I while we adjust."

We approach a pagoda directly overlooking the pond and sit on its padded seats, turning our bodies so we can look out onto the water. "What has surprised you the most?" I ask.

"Perhaps one of the most consequential changes is the increase in lifespan," Ereni says after a pause. "When you have an entire population that moves from living for an average of one hundred fifty years to a population that lives for an as-yet-unknown average that is hundreds of years longer, that's going to have cascading ramifications. There are significantly fewer babies being born every year now, for example, which leads to fewer children, fewer crèches, fewer positions in child education, a higher education system that is much more geared towards older people, and so on. I'm also not quite sure if I'm imagining it, but it seems like there is a much more aggressive push towards people serving on missions than I remember. It's always been a deeply respected calling, but now it seems like almost an embarrassment if you're below a certain age and have never been off-planet."

"Do you think that's a bad thing?" I ask.

She taps on a low-hanging branch that extends in front of us, sending a few of its blossoms down into the water. "I'm not sure," she finally says. "Before, I would have said it was an unalleviated good. But now, seeing how missions can go in practice...I don't know. We are certainly collecting more data and cataloging more human knowledge than ever before. But it's hard to guess what the side effects of our increased presence in the universe might be." She shrugs. "I guess we'll find out over time. I might even be around to see it."

I think of the mission on Sanctum, about the health clinics the Satori began and whether they're still in operation now, decades after the Satori departure. Whether my people have made progress in allowing women to receive more education, in having more control over their own bodies, or even in being able to become doctors just like Satori women. How do you calculate the difference having access to medical care might make in a life, or even a society? The Sanctum mission became a mess, there's no disputing that, but there's no way for me to measure the good it might have accomplished.

"But to answer your question," Ereni continues, "I think maybe one of the things that has surprised me the most is all the controversy around these new wormholes."

I'd read about the wormholes just the evening before. One of the Satori missions had brought back the scientific knowledge and technology to create new wormholes in space where they didn't already exist. They had returned with the information some decades earlier, but Satori society remains divided on the question of what exactly to do with such transformative, and potentially destructive, technology.

"Why are you surprised?" We'd seen firsthand how much strife could be caused by transformative technologies during our time on Arbor.

"I feel like I don't know my own people," Ereni confesses. "We've never shied away from adopting new technologies, not like this.

There are always some people who want to be more cautious, of course, and we spend time planning whatever safeguards seem necessary. But just look at the life extension technology. The Satori started experimenting with it on this planet about twenty years after I left, and in another ten years, it had been almost universally adopted. Extending the human lifespan an unknown amount of time has all kinds of ramifications and consequences. But the Satori were confident they could harness the technology and figure out how to best use it, and so they moved forward with it. I've checked, and the decision wasn't particularly contentious, even though in some ways, it has had just as big an impact as creating a wormhole in our sector would do."

"I don't know much of anything about wormholes," I say, "but couldn't you accidentally destroy a planet with one? Possibly even destabilize an entire system?"

Ereni waves her hand as if those suggestions are no big deal. "I'm not saying we shouldn't take every safety precaution. But this seems to indicate a broader cultural shift."

I'm curious in spite of myself. "Well, what are the main points of contention?"

"The side in favor of using the technology to create a wormhole in our system argue that doing so will open the rest of the universe to us. They imagine a planned network of wormholes, deployed by ourselves and others, to link all the human-settled worlds together. They think bringing humanity closer will lead to a new renaissance of knowledge, trade, and the arts, and bring better conditions to more remote sectors."

"And the Satori are the ones who bring everyone together?" I can't entirely hide the skepticism in my voice.

"Why not?" Ereni demands. "If we're the only ones willing to do the hard work, then so be it. If others want to join us, we can work together."

I raise my eyebrows at her. We both know it isn't actually that simple. If the Satori play a large role in planning and implementing a wormhole network that facilitates fast travel between sectors, they will maintain their advantage over other human societies, especially those like Sanctum that are technologically primitive in comparison.

But I'm not ready to argue just yet. "Fine. What are the objections?"

She shakes her head. "They are worried having a wormhole will destabilize our missions, our political system, our very way of life. It would lead to a human economy that spans the universe, a veritable explosion in interplanetary trade. But more than that, it would cause a level of human interaction we haven't seen since we first left Earth. There would almost certainly be ideological differences, tensions, and conflicts, some of which could be disastrous."

"It does sound like this technology would be more disruptive than your lifespan extensions," I tell her. "After all, lifespans are only extended for people who are either here on Satori or were born here, right?"

She grips the edge of the seat. "But that's another issue. If travel was much cheaper and faster, a lot more people would come here. Some would come to visit, some to engage in business, and some to potentially settle here themselves. And as humanity begins to become more interconnected, would we really be able to keep the lifespan extension technology just for ourselves? Who would get to decide? And even if we could, would withholding it be the correct thing to do?"

No wonder the Satori are debating what to do with this new capability. "It would change the way missions operate, wouldn't it?" I say. "People could leave on a mission and then come back to visit before they are finished. They could return more easily afterwards, and the people they had known before would not only still be alive, but much closer to them in age."

Ereni nods. "We haven't even reckoned with how the life extension technology has already altered how missions function. Many missions left before the technology existed, but the members of every mission that has left since its development will be more likely to want to return if their close connections might still be alive. And at the same time, with so few people dying, our population is growing steadily, even with the lower birth rate. If we can't convince people to leave permanently, we'll begin to struggle to sustain everyone on this single planet. Now imagine that same struggle spread over every human-settled world near a wormhole."

I understand just enough to realize this is a decision of monumental importance. "It sounds like you think the Satori should use this technology," I say. "But given all the arguments against it, how are you so sure doing so is the right course of action?"

Ereni sighs. "No one can know what will happen. But the reality is, we didn't create this technology ourselves. We were offered it by others. It's already out there. We don't know how many other societies already have access to it. We don't know what consequences will result from its use. And we certainly don't know how to handle our stockpile of human knowledge when all of humanity is suddenly right next door."

She stares down at her reflection in the pond, small ripples in the water distorting the image of her face. "But what we do know is that if we don't play an active role in deploying it, somebody else will. It might be sooner, it might be later, but this change is definitely coming, whether we like it or not. So I'd prefer the Satori be involved and prepare as much as possible."

I spend a moment reflecting on what she's said. "Have you always been this pragmatic?" I finally ask.

She taps the branch again, and another wave of blossoms fall into the water. "I'm certainly doing my best. I've made some mistakes the last few years, and I'd like to learn from them."

"The Satori who are against using the wormhole technology do seem to have some valid points," I venture.

"I agree. And if we could feel confident about suppressing this technology altogether, I might have a different opinion. But given that I believe it will proliferate one way or another, I think that substantially changes the calculus of our choice. Either way, there's a rocky time in front of us."

I turn away from the water and look at the profile of her face. In time I know it will become as familiar to me as my own, but even now I recognize its determined expression. "The universe is so much more complicated that I thought it would be," I say.

"Isn't that the truth." She looks over at me. "I'm glad you're here,

Sienna. I know I messed up on Arbor, but I wouldn't want to be facing everything here without you."

I open my mouth to reply, but then my qualpad buzzes. I check to find a message from "the Superior Mission Council of Satori" summoning me to an official-sounding meeting in three days' time. I show the message to Ereni. "Do you know who they are?"

Her eyes widen. "Yes." She draws out the word.

I can tell this isn't good news. "What is it? Who are they?"

"They are the governing body for all Satori Mission Councils. Each mission is independent, but the ruling body gets involved in any conflicts between or within missions that can't be resolved by the parties in question. They have a local branch here in Seji." She frowns. "I'm not sure what this could be about."

"Did you get a summons as well?" She gives a minuscule shake of her head. "Well, I suppose I'll have to go."

She puts a hand on my shoulder. "If you like, I'll go with you. After all, I'm the reason you got involved with our former Mission Council in the first place."

I swallow. "Are you sure? I know how busy you are now that you've come back home."

"I've missed hundreds of years of current events on Satori. A few hours won't make any difference at all." She squeezes my shoulder. "I'll come. That's what friends are for. And I bet I can talk circles around the delegates from the Superior Mission Council, just see if I can't."

"That I definitely believe."

We sit for a while longer inside the pagoda, taking in the peace of the scene in front of us. I hope the meeting to come will be similarly calm, but either way, I'm glad I'll have Ereni at my side.

CHAPTER 8

I don't ask Burke about his time with Lyra, and he volunteers very little. I tell myself this is all very high-minded of me, that he would tell me if there is anything I need to know, but I'm also afraid of competing with the bond he once shared with Lyra.

Ereni said Lyra was his first love. I didn't have the freedom in Napoleon to pursue the kind of romantic relationship that seems commonplace between young people here, and I had thought most of my brother Leo's friends had been hardheaded *stronzos* in any case. Even so, the implication of the connection between Burke and Lyra being special is not lost on me.

I suppose Burke is *my* first love. I can't imagine being apart from him for hundreds of years, only for him to return only a few years later in his lived time. Would such a large gap be alienating or would it provide greater perspective? Maybe being around Burke will make Lyra feel young again.

Is it even possible to feel young when you're three hundred years old?

I don't know why I've been summoned by the Superior Mission Council of Satori, but I feel surprisingly cheerful when Ereni and I set out at the designated time. This is most likely just a technicality, and I welcome the chance to think of something besides my uncertainty about my future.

We approach a huge circular building in the familiar red and orange, large arched windows evenly spaced around its circumference. It must be at least fifteen stories high, and there's a separate covered stairway that wraps around itself leading all the way to the top. "We can go up to see the view once we're finished," Ereni says. "You can look all across Seji."

We enter a lobby area via big double doors. A small band is playing off to one side, and several couples are dancing to the music. Small shops line the space, and I wish we had time to stop and explore. But Ereni leads me to straight to the bank of elevators, and we quickly ascend to the eighth floor, which is much less exciting, consisting of several office suites. We enter the proper one and wait in moldable orange chairs that remind me of the ones aboard the starship.

The meeting room falls silent upon our entrance. I'm surprised to see eighteen people present. I know it's eighteen because I count each one with rising anxiety. They all sit behind a long table, and it becomes clear Ereni and I are to stand in supplication before them, as there are no chairs set up for our use. It is very different from our shipboard meetings with our former Mission Council, which while occasionally unnerving, had always been relatively casual.

A man with a prominent nose has us state our names for the record. Several of our interlocutors shuffle in their seats as I introduce myself. "Sienna Tascioni, you have been summoned before us today to answer to a complaint filed in absentia by Mission Council 25390," the man intones. "This is the mission that recently operated in Sanctum, Arbor, and Zamavat. Is it correct that you were accepted as a member of this mission?"

"Y-yes," I stammer. I feel like I'm on trial.

"She received conditional approval, entry level one," Ereni says crisply. "The Mission Council expressed their intent to supervise her closely during her first assignment and then reassess."

The group's attention swings to Ereni, providing me with a

blessed break from their scrutiny, and two women whisper to one another before one of them speaks. "You were her supervisor, were you not?"

"Initially, I was," Ereni confirms. "But later I was removed from that assignment."

Another pause, more whispering. "What was your assessment of Sienna Tascioni while you were still supervising her?" another woman asks.

Ereni stands erect beside me, and I take comfort in her confidence. Surely this is all just a formality? It's hard to believe that our Mission Council took the time from their new mission to make this complaint in the first place.

"She was young and inexperienced, of course, and she hadn't received a formal education as she would have done on Satori," Ereni begins. "However, Sienna has always been a hard worker, and she's very dedicated. She is thoughtful and cares about the quality of her work. I spent a year on board *Dreamer* overseeing her training, and I can attest that she has a thorough knowledge and understanding of the Foundational Principles and the Satori Code of Conduct. Furthermore, she illustrated that she was willing to wrestle with deep ethical questions and remain committed to her principles even at high personal cost."

The first man shakes his head. "Her assignments sound highly irregular. First, she received a direct assignment working within a high-level Arborist governmental office, albeit in a junior capacity. This must have hampered your ability to supervise her, did it not?"

Ereni doesn't flinch. "Yes, it did, and I wasn't enthusiastic about the idea. However, our Mission Council was eager to make the Arborist government happy, and Sienna's assignment was due to their specific request. We did meet regularly during this time period, and consistent supervision was assisted by the proximity of our living quarters."

"And then she was assigned to field research with what is known as a Wise One, in spite of having received no relevant training for such a task," the man continued. "As the only field researcher with access to such a Wise One, this would normally have been an assignment for a senior scientist."

"That was another unusual circumstance," Ereni says. "As you might be aware, Sienna doesn't have an N-CAT. She was the only member of the mission who didn't have one. The Arborists were concerned about possible impacts the N-CATs might have on communication with the Wise Ones. At first they were adamant there would be no communication at all between the mission and the Wise Ones, but when they learned of Sienna's unique circumstances, they were willing to compromise."

The man turns his attention back to me. "What happened once Ereni relinquished her supervisory duties?" he asks. "Who was your supervisor at that time?"

I take a deep breath. "Irisa decided she would take on that additional duty because everyone was so busy. But we didn't have regular meetings to discuss my progress or anything like that. In fact, I don't remember that we had a single formal meeting."

More whispering. "It sounds as if you didn't have much supervision at that point," one of the women says. "Would you say that sounds accurate?"

"I certainly felt like I was all alone." The anger at the injustice of it rises within me. Here I am, trying to start over and instead having to answer this complaint from people who hadn't cared enough about me to help me in my new position. "At that point, the only real support I was receiving was from my Arborist co-worker Pilvi. And perhaps from Kuusta Elo, an Arborist politician who has traveled here to Satori with us." He certainly had been dedicated to training me to race, which is more than I can say about how any of the Satori felt about helping me.

"This Pilvi is the one to whom you released unauthorized data about the Second Life process, is that correct?" the man asks.

"Yes. I consulted with Ereni and Burke, and we decided on a course of action together."

"That's right." I startle at Ereni's interjection. "Since Sienna wasn't being supervised properly, a fact to which I think we can all agree, she ultimately discussed this matter with me, and I agreed with the course of action we followed. Which is why, I have to say I'm surprised that Mission Council 25390 submitted a formal complaint about Sienna and yet neglected to do the same for Burke and myself. One might be forgiven for thinking there is something more at play here. One might wonder why the council would decide to complain only about the person who is not only the most junior, but also isn't from Satori and thus is less equipped to answer such a complaint."

There is a long silence. "That is a serious accusation," the man finally says.

"It is not an accusation," Ereni says. "Merely an observation."

"We will take it under advisement," the man says. "But do you deny that you released sensitive information to locals of Arbor without the approval, or indeed, the knowledge, of your Mission Council?"

"I do not deny it." I hold my head high. I stand by my decision. "I gave the data to Pilvi, and her plan was to disseminate it publicly after the mission's departure."

"Why did you make the decision you did?" one of the whispering women asks.

"I knew the people of Arbor were being lied to by their government, and those lies had become the basis for an ongoing injustice in their society. I felt obligated to act."

The woman purses her lips. "So you see yourself as a whistleblower?"

I turn to Ereni. "I don't know what that is."

Ereni steps closer to me, as if she can protect me through sheer proximity. "Yes. We discussed our options at length, and all three of us decided to act in the capacity of what the Satori would call a whistleblower. As such, while the circumstances with our mission were less than optimal, we still enjoy certain protections."

The woman nods. "We are aware."

The man frowns. "We will continue to deliberate on this case, but are there any further questions for Sienna Tascioni at this time?" He pauses, but no one volunteers. "Very well. In that case, you are excused. We will update you when we have reached a determination."

I don't like how vague he is being, but Ereni links her arm with mine and practically marches out of the room, forcing me to follow her. She moves without stopping until we reach the elevator, at which point she jabs the button for the top floor several more times than necessary, her lips compressed. It is only because I have come to know her fairly well that I realize how furious she is.

She doesn't speak a word, and then we reach our destination. She strides out onto the wide-open plaza, wind blowing her long hair. She doesn't stop until she's gripping the railing at the edge, looking out over the city beneath us. The island is bigger than I thought it would be, but from this vantage point, we can see the coastline limned in white, the azure sea beyond.

"They are petty," Ereni says in a tight voice. "They knew Burke and I would be able to defend ourselves against any complaint they made, and so they decided to try to punish you instead. I guess they hoped we'd abandon you once we made it home." She pushes a strand of hair from her face, and I see she has tears in her eyes. "We're supposed to be better than this. We *are* better than this. I am so sorry, Sienna. I am ashamed of what our Mission Council is trying to do."

I don't understand what just happened. "What would happen if their complaint is upheld?"

Ereni shakes her head. "The Satori believe in rehabilitation, not punishment. But you would have to complete a long course of study and present before a panel of experts who would assess your progress. If they didn't deem it sufficient, the complaint would remain on your permanent record. In practice, that means it would be difficult for you to find another mission that would allow you to join."

A well of embarrassment sweeps over me, but I try to ignore it. "I don't know that I want to join another mission in any case," I say. "If they decide against me, I suppose that will answer one question about my future."

"They won't decide against you. I won't let them." Ereni wipes her tears away with furious gestures. "You are just as entitled as anyone to the whistleblower protections, and if they somehow fail to understand that, we will appeal."

"I've only just gotten here," I say tentatively. "I don't want to cause any—"

"We will appeal," Ereni repeats. "But I doubt it will come to that. Disappointment has turned that Mission Council cruel. I'm glad they're far away, and I'll never see them again."

"The wormholes could change all that," I remind her.

"I almost hope they don't." She hunches over the railing. "I've been wondering if Satori society has fundamentally changed since I left. But this nonsense with the Mission Council makes me wonder. Maybe it hasn't changed. Maybe it's always had deep problems, and I just didn't see them." She blinks, and another tear trickles down her cheek. "Maybe I'm the one who has changed."

Ever since I first met her, Ereni has always been so certain. Regardless of what difficulty we've faced, she has urged us onward, confident we'll be able to manage any consequences that come our way. Even after she placed our friendship in jeopardy, she seemed so sure that anything broken must be fixable.

"We'll figure it out together," I say, and she gives me a pained smile. For maybe the first time, I feel like we are equals. She may be Satori, and I might be Napoleon, but that doesn't make either one of us inherently better than the other.

I feel something tight inside my chest suddenly loosen at this thought. Maybe instead of constantly trying to live up to some kind of Satori ideal that might not even exist, I can simply continue as I am. Even here on Satori itself.

Sometimes I forget the Satori are as human as I am.

CHAPTER 9

hen I share the news about what happened at the Superior Mission Council meeting, Burke stays silent for a long time. We're sitting across from one another at my table, sipping from mugs of Satori tea, which requires a significant amount of sweetener to become palatable to me. The last of the day's sun shines through the blue curtains.

"I should have done more for you on Arbor," Burke finally says. "I know you felt pressure, that you could never be as good as the Satori, but I thought it was just nerves and the stress of such a big change. But our Mission Council filing a complaint against you and not Ereni and myself? It shows their discrimination in action. And now you have to deal with the repercussions here, in an entirely new place. It's maddening."

I feel unbothered, and I'm not sure if it's because the news has made me numb or if I genuinely don't care. "Even if the worst happens, it just means I can't join a new mission. And given my experience with my first mission, I'm not sure I'd want to do that again anyway." There is still the looming question of what I would like to do instead, but I hope I can figure that out regardless of the interference of the Superior Mission Council.

"You and me both." Burke stares down at his tea. "I thought when we got home, things would become clear. And I hoped they would be easier for you as well."

There is a certain freedom in my current position that appeals to me. It's different for Burke; he expected more of his Mission Council, and he expects more of his people. Prior to leaving on the mission, his life had been characterized by stability and a certainty about his life path.

But my position in life has never been secure. On Sanctum, I'd known I had to marry in order to ensure my future, but my options were abysmal at best. Marrying a bully like Enoch Royse would have led to a life guided by fear and wretchedness. And I remember being held as a prisoner by my own father; how could I ever forget?

It would be nice if the Satori could live up to their own ideals, but I certainly haven't been raised to expect any real justice for myself. What had mattered, even in the rich, pampered life of the daughter of a prominent senator, was survival. That justice is even a fight I can consider is something I don't think I'll ever be able to take for granted.

"Do you think most Satori think like that?" I ask.

Burke shakes his head. "I don't think so. If you had asked me back on Sanctum, I would have said absolutely not. But I think we've allowed the amount of knowledge we've collected and our superior technological skills to go to our heads. It's simple enough to say we shouldn't judge other cultures, but when it comes right down to it? It's easy to judge people who seem different, even when we have the best of intentions." He reaches across the table and takes my hand. "I want you to know that as long as you choose to stay on Satori, I'll fight for you. I hope you won't need it very often, but whenever you do, and even if it's every day, I'll be there."

I appreciate his support, but the whole situation is so frustrating. "I don't want you to feel like I need protecting."

"Oh, I know you don't need protecting." Burke raises his eyebrows at me. "Don't think I've forgotten who saved who back on Sanctum." I flush at the reminder. "But nobody should have to stand alone." He pauses. "And also, you aren't nobody. I love you, Sienna."

My heart beats faster at those words, the first time he's said them to me. I don't think I understand exactly what they mean, but I know they're important. I think they might be a kind of promise. They aren't a typical expression on Sanctum, and certainly never before marriage. "We don't know what's going to happen," I say.

"All the more important to remember what matters the most," he says promptly. "And I want you to know how I feel. I should have told you ages ago. In all the chaos, it's never seemed like the right time. But I'm beginning to think there isn't one right time. There's the opportunity of this moment, and I'm taking it."

He looks into my eyes, and I feel like I should say something in return. I want to share how I feel, but he's right. I've always been so focused on the next challenge, I haven't stopped to analyze my feelings. I know the butterflies in my heart when we first met. I know how hurt I felt when we didn't understand one another on Arbor, and when he left. And I know that since he returned, I've been holding myself back the slightest bit, waiting to see if he'll leave again.

But none of that is how I feel right now. I believe him when he says he'll fight for me, just as I believe Ereni. Somehow in the intervening months, when they've been a constant presence in my life, I've managed to forgive both of them without even realizing I'd done it.

Burke still makes my heart squeeze in a unique way when I look at him, even when he's inhabiting a body I'm not yet used to. I want to tell him when something important happens, and I want to work together with him to make our lives better. Is that what love is?

"I think I love you too," I finally say. He beams at my words, his smile stunning to behold in his unfamiliar face.

"There's no requirement for you to say that," he says. "I just wanted you to know how I feel."

"I want the same thing." We hold each other's eyes for a long, heart-pounding minute before I lean across the table to kiss him. I mean for it to just be a peck, but before I know it, we've both gotten up and Burke is holding me in his arms, kissing me thoroughly.

I can't get enough of him, my hands roaming across his broad back, one of his hands gripping my hair. The rest of the world has become silent, receding into the distance as we focus only on one another. My whole body feels shaky, and I don't want to come up for air.

I tug at Burke's shirt, not wanting fabric to separate the two of us, and he finally draws back long enough to pull it over his head in one quick gesture. We stare at each other, a moment suspended in time, as we both try to catch our breath. He has a question in his eyes, and I take him by the hand and lead him to my bed.

If this is love, it's been worth the wait.

THE NEXT DAY I meet Kuusta at an unassuming garage near the beach where we can borrow two speeder bikes. I'd suggested the outing the evening before, having learned that speeder bikes are easily available on the island and that the Satori regularly ride them *above the water*. How can I resist the new challenge?

Since Kuusta and I are both at loose ends while we try to accustom ourselves to this new planet, I feel like we could use a bit of fun.

As experienced as he is with dirt bikes, Kuusta has never tried a speeder bike of the type I'm used to from Sanctum. I walk him through its operation inside the garage, and then he gives it a try, making a loud yelling sound when his bike lifts off the ground for the first time. We ride very slowly up and down the practice road outside the garage designated for just this purpose, allowing him time to grow accustomed to the controls.

I buzz with excitement as we head to the water. A woman at the garage had talked us through the emergency protocols in case anything should go wrong. We both wear life preservers over our clothes, which is particularly important for me since proper young ladies on Sanctum aren't taught to swim. We've been instructed to be careful about boats and other craft, but this short section of the beach isn't open for swimming, making navigation easier.

I look over my shoulder at Kuusta, who is trailing behind me. "Ready?" I shout over the sound of the surf.

He flashes me a smile and gives me a thumbs up, and then we're off. I set a moderate pace to begin, riding my bike at its maximum altitude to make sure I avoid dipping into the waves. I taste salt in my mouth as I frown in concentration, watching the upcoming crests to make sure there isn't an unexpectedly large one. The wind whips against my cheeks, the air cool and refreshing with a distinctive but unfamiliar smell.

I let out a large whoop and increase my speed, checking to make sure Kuusta is keeping up. Knowing I could fall into the water if anything goes wrong only adds to the thrill. This is almost as good as competing in a race back home. I revel in the freedom of leaving everything behind; in this moment, it's only me, the sea, and the reassuring presence of the vibrating bike beneath me.

We stop at an island that's been turned into a public park. It's so small I might be able to see end to end if it weren't for a stand of trees in the center. Kuusta and I put our bikes at a safe distance from the surf before sitting down on the warm sand. I remove my shoes and socks, enjoying the feeling of the coarse sand between my toes. "What do you think about Satori so far?" I ask.

Kuusta lays all the way back on the sand, shielding his eyes with his hand. "It beats Zamavat," he says with a rueful laugh. "I have no idea what I'll do here, but at least I might have a fighting chance of finding something interesting. Although first I'll have to improve my Kensho. I've started taking conversational tutoring with a local do-gooder. I thought I'd take a class, but the only available classes are for children."

I snort. "The N-CAT strikes again. Satori isn't set up well for immigrants, is it?"

"They keep saying they'll give me an N-CAT for free. I don't think they understand why I'm refusing. I'm beginning not to understand myself. After all, it's not as if I'll ever return to Arbor. I can see the Satori thinking I should try harder to adapt to their ways but being too polite to say it." He laughs again. "When all is said and done, it's not so bad. I'd much rather be a pariah for being an uncooperative outsider than for being a mass murderer."

I've become too used to his dark humor to react negatively to his joke. I lay back, mirroring his position, and close my eyes, feeling the sun beating down on my face. I take a long, slow breath, trying to allow the reality of this planet to sink in.

I used to lie outside on my family's country estate, back before my father became a senator. Leo and I would lie side by side, far out of earshot of any adults. I'd take off my nice dress and shoes so I wouldn't get them dirty, and we'd run around digging holes and climbing trees and building entire imaginary worlds until finally we'd get tired and collapse on the ground. Being outdoors had always been such a welcome escape from the rigidity of family life.

My qualpad pings in my pocket, but I'm happy to ignore it. I just want to stay here a little while longer, far from the problems and decisions that crowd me back in Seji. The sand heats my back, and I take another deep breath.

My qualpad pings again, but I stretch out luxuriously. It's not as if I have any pressing responsibilities. Whoever it is can wait. "What do you think of the speeder bike compared to the dirt bike?" I ask Kuusta.

"Not bad. Not the same as competing at a scramble, of course. But I could get used to it."

My qualpad pings for a third time. With a sigh, I sit up and pull it out. I have three messages from Burke: "Sienna, where are you?" he's written. Then, a minute later, "Let me know as soon as you get this."

Then the third message: "There's an unknown alien starship orbiting Satori."

CHAPTER 10

$\mathcal{S}$peculation about the alien starship dominates the news. Burke vacillates between fascination at how different the ship appears from the Satori starships and frustration that he can't learn more about it. He spends long hours poring over photographs of the ship that have been released to the public.

Ereni remains quiet, and when I ask her what she thinks, she swishes her long hair. "I'm sure qualified people are making contact with the operators of that ship and engaging in productive communication. They'll let us know as soon as there's something worth telling." But then her cool façade slips a tiny bit. "We've spent so much time looking for any signs of existence of another intelligent life form. It's hard to believe we may have finally succeeded."

Kuusta remains skeptical. "It's just as likely there are only humans on board that ship," he says. "Never underestimate the ingenuity of humankind. They might be trying to reestablish contact with the greater part of human civilization after generations apart."

It isn't until the next morning, when I am dutifully practicing vocabulary words at my table, that I learn more. An insistent knocking interrupts me, and I roll my eyes at what seems like a fake urgency. I just saw my three friends at breakfast. "Come in!" I turn back to my qualpad.

"I'm glad you're here," Diantha says, and I look up with a jerk. "There's been a request from the Diplomatic Corps. They want to see you in person, and very urgently. I told them I'd come fetch you myself." I notice then that Diantha is breathing more heavily than usual. She has a substantial bag slung over one shoulder.

"What's this about?" I look down at my half-finished cup of tea with regret.

Diantha shrugs. "I don't know. They wanted to send someone who already knew you."

I look between her and my qualpad. "They could have just contacted me directly," I suggest.

Diantha sighs. "Are you coming? We need to travel to Jundo, and the next train leaves soon. You should bring an overnight bag."

As disconcerted as I am by Diantha's sudden appearance, I'm not going to refuse the Satori Diplomatic Corps. I haven't been back to Jundo since we first landed at the spaceport there, so this will give me an opportunity to do a little exploring.

I look around for my bag, which I find stuffed in the bottom bureau drawer. I pack a few changes of clothes and run down the hall to get my toiletries. Upon my return, it takes me several minutes to find my coat, which I finally discover on the balcony.

I try to straighten my clothing and fix my hair before following Diantha into the hallway. "Can we stop at Burke's?" I ask her. "Or Ereni's? I want to tell them where I'm going."

But Diantha shakes her head. "Send them a message. My contact impressed upon me the high level of urgency, and it will take us long enough to get there as it is."

Diantha sets a rapid pace, and I stare mournfully at the kitchen as we pass. "I don't suppose there's time to get snacks?"

She gives a little chuckle. "We can get snacks on the train. If we hurry, we can still catch it."

Only after we were comfortably settled in seats across from each other on the train to Jundo do I ask after Theckla. "How is she liking Seji?" I ask. "And will she miss you while you're away?"

Diantha rubs the bridge of her nose. "She's staying at the local crèche while I'm gone. She's been taking classes with the children there since we arrived. She doesn't like the other children, and she particularly hates her swimming lessons. She has to take them with the very young children, you see, and it's quite embarrassing. But as I tell her, she can't live on Satori and not know how to swim. It isn't safe."

"I don't know how to swim," I admit.

"You should look into addressing that." Diantha gives me a sharp look that reminds me for a startling instant of my own mother. "I'm sure Burke would be happy to teach you. It can be quite enjoyable once you get the hang of it."

I remember Burke suggesting just such a thing a few days ago. I've been so focused on practicing my language skills, and learning to swim…it seems like a real commitment. Like something I'd learn if I were sure I was staying on Satori for the long term.

But maybe, as Diantha is suggesting, I could simply learn for the joy of it.

"Has the crèche given you any problems about Theckla not living there with the other children?"

Diantha's face takes a grim cast. "They say I'm holding her back." Venom is laced through her words. "They say she'll adjust more quickly if she can be just like the other children. And I tell them she can never be just like the other children. She's herself, with her own set of unique experiences, which happen to involve a more intimate bond with her mother figure, and that's okay. A society is only as good as the differences it allows. Learning to accept Theckla as she is will be a good lesson for everyone."

"Hard for Theckla, though," I observe.

She's quiet for a moment. "I hope coming back here wasn't a mistake," she finally says. "I wanted Theckla to know where I come from. I know the Satori believe in tolerance, at least in theory. But sometimes there can be a big gap between theory and practice."

"I hope it works out for you here." As someone who can never go back home, I'd never wish that lack of belonging on anyone else.

"Me too."

∼

WHEN WE ARRIVE at the Diplomatic Corps headquarters in Jundo, we are quickly whisked to a nondescript suite on the twenty-first floor. A long conference table dominates the room, familiar oceanscapes on the walls. A small sitting area has been arranged in front of the tall windows at the end of the room, featuring several comfortable blue chairs with a view out over the city.

I put my bag in the corner before settling into one of the chairs and enjoying the view of skyscrapers, all of which have a beautiful rainbow sheen. The city has a very different character from Seji, but in spite of its huge population, the public transit system seems to run reliably and I'm surprised by the lack of noise in the streets. On our way here, we'd walked by the first open-air skyscraper park I'd ever seen, stretching at least fifty stories into the air, greenery hanging between levels. Diantha told me they use an innovative mirror system to make sure all the plants receive the proper amount of light, regardless of their level.

Diantha settles in the chair beside me. "They weren't sure exactly when we'd arrive, so it might be a bit of a wait," she warns.

I wish they'd tell me why I'm here. Why are the Satori always so high-handed? But I know better to object; I sit back in my chair and wonder if swimming is as terrifying in practice as it appears.

It must be almost an hour before my ruminations are interrupted by a group entering the room. There must be almost a dozen people, but I only have eyes for one of them. I stand up, my heart contracting painfully in my chest. "Gianna?" My voice sounds strange in my own ears. "Is it really you?"

The group halts, suddenly silent, and the young lady whom I've addressed blinks at me. She looks just as I remember: innocent blue eyes, honey-colored hair arranged carefully with matching blue ribbons, flawless olive skin, and a green dress that, while in a different fashion than I'm used to—much simpler, with a shocking lack of frills and bows and embroidery—is recognizably from Sanctum.

She's standing beside another young lady in similar attire, but I only have eyes for Gianna. We hadn't exactly parted on the best of terms. I'd been forced to leave Sanctum for good after I orchestrated a daring street race in order to save her from marriage to Enoch Royse, a particularly wretched young man. But I'd never been entirely sure she'd recognized how terrible he was, or if she'd resented what I'd done, even though it had been for her sake. Due to the vagaries of time dilation during space travel, I'd assumed she'd be long dead by now. But instead, here she is on Satori, standing right in front of me.

"Gianna," I say again. I rush forward and practically throw myself in her arms. Someone from home! And not just someone, but someone with whom I'd been very close, once upon a time. A mixture of relief and grief washes over me as I squeeze her in a most unladylike embrace.

She doesn't respond at first, no doubt taken aback by my impulsive action, but then she returns my hug enthusiastically. We hold each other for a long moment before she pulls back. "You must be Sienna," she says, exchanging a look with the young lady beside her. Her voice is not quite what I expect. "Goodness me, you do look exactly like you did in the pictures. It's as if you haven't aged a day. Mother would be furious if she could see you now."

My stomach clenches. "Mother?"

She gives me a charming smile. "Yes. I do look a great deal like her, don't I? That's what everyone says. I am Gianna Giordano's daughter, Allegra. You knew her as Gianna Costa before she was married."

I take a step backward, suddenly deeply embarrassed. "I see." I try to regain my composure. "You look almost exactly as I remember your…mother."

The young lady beside her giggles. "We had a bet about how you'd react to our presence, and I'm pleased to say I've won this particular wager."

Allegra pulls a frustrated moue at her friend's pronouncement, but that does nothing to stop her. "Oh! I shouldn't have confessed to that, should I?" The young lady puts a hand over her mouth. "Please don't think any less of us, Aunt Sienna. We know betting isn't at all proper, but we were woken up from cryosleep quite early, and we did need to find ways to pass the time before our arrival."

Aunt Sienna? I look at the young lady next to Allegra more closely. She is almost as short as I am, and she has similar brown hair, although hers is arranged in ringlets. Her eyes are an unfamiliar hazel, her nose slightly tilted at the end, and she's wearing the typical gloves and dainty boots of a Napoleon lady. "I did want to make a good impression on you." She looks down at herself ruefully. "We went to so much trouble to get dressed properly."

"And you are?" I finally get out.

"Oh, I'm Novelle. Novelle Tascioni. Your oldest niece. Your brother Leo is my father. He would have been sure to send his love if he'd had any notion you would be here on Satori. What are you doing here, anyway? The Satori wouldn't tell us a thing, but Father always said you'd joined a mission to a planet called Arbor, so we were completely shocked when they told us you were here."

My niece. My *oldest* niece, implying there are others. Tears prick my eyes at this unexpected revelation. "Leo," I manage to get out. "How is he? Is he happy?" I realize the absurdity of my words even as I say them. Leo has surely been dead for a long time now. But the chance for some news about his life overshadows that fact.

Novelle wrinkles her nose. "As happy as anyone, I think." She sounds uncertain. "Although he was always so concerned about all of us kids."

"How many brothers and sisters do you have?" I feel a little breathless at the thought.

"Five," she says promptly. "Three sisters and two brothers. We're quite a brood."

I sit down heavily at one of the chairs at the conference table. Six nieces and nephews. Leo had gotten married, and he had raised a large family, just like the kind we'd always pretended to be part of when it was just the two of us.

One of the Satori officials clears their throat, bringing me back to the moment. "It is truly wonderful to meet both of you," I say. "And very unexpected." I turn to the Satori official beside them, a large man with a bushy mustache. "I assume they're welcome here on Satori?"

The official blinks and looks over at his colleagues. "Of course. Their welcome is not in question." He frowns at me. "But there is the issue of how they arrived."

I turn back to the ladies. "How did you arrive?"

Allegra gives an elegant shrug, looking more like her mother than ever, and Novelle giggles again. "Well, you know Sanctum doesn't have our own operational starships."

The official interjects. "They traveled here on the alien spacecraft."

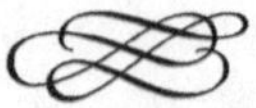

CHAPTER 11

"We can explain," Allegra says quickly. "It wasn't just us, of course."

"We came with an entire delegation," Novelle adds. "We're the only two from Sanctum, but two other planets from our sector wanted to send representatives."

I look back and forth between the two ladies. "You're telling me that the planet of Sanctum elected to send the two of you to represent their interests with the Satori?"

Was it possible my planet had changed so much in so short a time? These two girls couldn't be much older than myself, and ladies weren't allowed to be so directly involved in diplomacy. In my day it wouldn't have been considered at all suitable.

Allegra looks down at her dainty boots, and Novelle lets out a small huffing sound. I know guilt when I see it. "Well?" I feel absurd acting like an authority figure when we are practically the same age.

"The rest of Sanctum might not know we're here," Novelle says in a tiny voice. "I mean, Father and Mother know, of course. And the rest of the family. And a few friends. But it wasn't exactly an official decision to send us."

"Sanctum can't be left out of such an important matter," Allegra interjects. "It is vital that our interests be represented, even if some people want us to stay out of it."

"People in power," Novelle murmurs.

"We've talked about this," Allegra says in a low voice. "We're in agreement, remember?"

"I know," Novelle whispers back. She turns to the man with the mustache. "Can we tell her?"

He sighs. "The entire planet will know soon enough. Just be discrete until the news release goes out, please?"

I nod, uncertain what I'm agreeing to. Novelle claps her hands. "Oh, this is so exciting."

Allegra gives her a quelling look before sitting down across the table from me. She has perfect posture, and she crosses her ankles just as a proper lady would. She is exactly what I would expect from Gianna's daughter. Novelle slides into the chair beside her, flushed with excitement. The rest of their retinue take chairs further down the table, except for a man and a woman who take the opportunity to exit.

"Where shall we begin?" Novelle asks.

Allegra has no such hesitation. "It all began with a strange space anomaly," she says. "Our monitoring systems are rudimentary, I understand, so at first we thought it was the Satori returning."

"Father got so excited," Novelle interjects. "He denied it later, but I know he thought maybe you'd decided to return."

Her words stab my heart. The truth is, I've never considered returning. It hasn't been an option, of course. It's not as if I can requisition a Satori starship to do my bidding. But I have to admit that, even were that not the case, I probably wouldn't have sought a homecoming.

"But soon it became clear that what we were observing was not a ship," Allegra continues. "For a start, it appeared to be stationary. We thought it might be a natural phenomenon of some kind."

"And then the Luz came," Novelle says excitedly.

"Who are the Luz?" I ask, confused at the sudden turn in the story.

"Buena Luz is a planet in our system," Allegra says. "We didn't know it was inhabited until they decided to make contact."

"Yes, we had no idea that planet had undergone a terraforming process or anything, " Novelle says. "The Luz say they came to the system once Sanctum was already settled, and our monitoring systems at that time must have missed them all together."

The Satori must have known they were there though. I repress a sigh at the knowledge of all the information they haven't thought to tell me.

"We did upgrade our monitoring systems with specifications provided by the Satori during their visit," Allegra says repressively. "Nothing like what they have, of course. But a material improvement."

"Sienna doesn't care about that," Novelle says. "The point is, the Luz had identified the anomaly as a wormhole, and they wanted to consult with their neighbors about what we ought to do about it."

"I see." Sanctum had been forced into relations with its planetary neighbors whether it wanted them or not. I can only imagine their chagrin at the necessity.

"As you can imagine, the Luz had trouble making much progress with us," Allegra says. "We'd been engaged in desultory talks for a few years before the To's starship traveled through the wormhole and arrived at our doorstep, so to speak."

"The To?"

"We've never seen them," Novelle says. "Even though we traveled all this way in their starship and everything. They have a robot they use to interface with humans. I think they're cute."

Allegra turns to glare at her. "I thought we agreed that I was going to explain everything."

"Sorry," Novelle murmurs. But she shoots me a little smile.

"The To are an alien species, and it's their starship that is currently in orbit around this planet," Allegra says. "Since Novelle is determined to tell things out of order."

My head is spinning. "So these…To aliens created the wormhole to come to Sanctum's system?"

"No, no, no." Allegra shoots Novelle a victorious glance. "See, I told you to let me handle things. The To were aware that a new wormhole had been created, although they say they aren't responsible for it themselves, and they came to offer their assistance. We don't know much about them, to be honest." She looks over at the Satori representatives. "We were hoping the Satori might have encountered them before."

But the man with the mustache shakes his head. "Assuming the validity of your claim, this will be the first documented instance of communication between humankind and an alien species. The Satori have never heard of these To, although it would be helpful if you could tell us more about them. Thus far, you and your colleagues have been decidedly vague."

"Not on purpose," Novelle protests. She looks wounded. "We've been as helpful as we can. But the To are rather…mysterious."

"They were willing to come here," Allegra points out. "We were the ones who suggested it. We were raised hearing all about the chaos when the Satori arrived, and it seemed like you would be better equipped to deal with the ramifications of a new wormhole arriving out of nowhere, followed by first contact with an alien species. Were we incorrect in our assessment?" She raises both eyebrows.

"We are honored in your trust in the Satori to respond to such a complex and evolving situation." This from a woman with a perfectly smooth bun sitting further down the table. "As we've said, we will do everything in our power to assist you and develop further relations with the To. And we were pleased to facilitate this reunion between you and your kin."

"I'm glad you're here, Aunt Sienna." Novelle leans forward as she speaks. "The To were very interested in our stories about the Satori's time on Sanctum, and in the role you played in particular. I imagine they'll want to learn more directly from you." She casts a glance down the table. "At the appropriate time, of course."

"You say these To claim they don't know the origins of the new wormhole in your system?" Diantha asks. I'd forgotten she was here, and I'm grateful I have at least one person I know in the room.

"That's right," Allegra says. "From what I've gathered, their civilization has been using wormholes for a long time. I think they might have a way to monitor the wormhole network. It sounded like they had received an alert about the new wormhole, and they came to investigate."

"And do they have any way of determining how the new wormhole was formed?"

Allegra and Novelle exchange glances before shaking their heads. "I have no idea," Allegra says. "I didn't think to ask them that. No one in our system has the science to really understand how the wormholes even work. Do the Satori know?"

It might be my imagination, but I feel a sudden tension in the room. I remember Ereni explaining to me how divided the Satori are on making use of the recently discovered wormhole technology.

"Yes, we understand how wormholes function," the woman with the smooth bun finally says. I wonder if Allegra and Novelle have noticed the awkward silence. "Or at least, our scientists know the theories behind the wormholes. We will be interested in learning more from the To. Do you know when they will be sending their own representatives down?"

Novelle shrugs. "There's no rhyme and reason with the To. They do what they want to do in their own time. They told us all the humans should have time to confer before next steps could be taken, and then the entire delegation from our system boarded the shuttlecraft and came down."

"As we've told you before," Allegra adds pointedly. "If we knew more, I promise we would share."

Her frustration must be apparent to everyone in the room. I quickly intervene. "Where will the delegation be staying?" I ask. " I would welcome the opportunity to be nearer to my niece and"—I realize I don't know what to call Allegra—"her friend. I don't want to inconvenience anyone, but would it be possible for them to stay in Seji?"

The man with the mustache frowns, looking on the verge of saying no, when the woman with the smooth bun says, "Of course. It's only natural you would want to be close to those from your own planet. They can accompany you back to Seji if that is what they wish. It is only a two-hour journey if they are needed here."

I hope I haven't overstepped. But when I look at the two ladies, they are both beaming at me. "We would love to go," Novelle says. "I've spent my whole life hearing stories about Aunt Sienna, and now I can finally hear them directly from the source."

"Then it's settled," Diantha says. "Let's arrange for Novelle and Allegra's rooms in Seji, and then we can travel back and get them settled. That is, unless there's anything else?" I notice she appears to be addressing the woman with the smooth bun instead of the man with the mustache.

The woman nods, and the man says, "That would be acceptable. Aside from any diplomatic business, I imagine we'll want to arrange for some visits with a cultural scholar who can make note of any changes on Sanctum since our last visit there, if the two of you would be amenable."

"You're only a few decades out of date," Allegra says with a frown.

"Of course," Novelle says at the same time. She turns to Allegra, a sheepish grin on her face, and I get the impression this is a pattern between them that has happened many times.

"We'll set something up," the man with the mustache says, taking Novelle at her word. Diantha rushes us out before the ladies can agree to anything else they might regret later.

Novelle and Allegra are assigned rooms in a hospitality house just a few blocks from my own. We arrive in the mid-evening, having dined on the train. As much as I want a full update of what has happened at home since my absence, I can tell both ladies are exhausted, and Diantha and I leave them in their rooms to get settled. "I'll come see you first thing tomorrow," I promise.

Allegra snorts. "Not too early," she says. "Novelle is not what I'd call an early riser."

Novelle is still batting ineffectually at her friend when we leave them.

"I suppose you need to get back to Theckla," I say to Diantha. "Since you didn't have to spend the night."

But Diantha shakes her head. "I'm going to let her have her overnight," she says. "Better to see how it goes when I'm close by so I can intervene if necessary. She'll contact me if there are any problems." She walks beside me for a block, frowning at her feet. The sun has almost completely set, and I pull on my jacket against the subsequent chill. "I'm interested to hear what Ereni thinks about what we've learned today," she finally says.

"You mean about the discovery of another sentient life form in the universe? I'm sure she'll be as excited as we are."

"No, about that rogue wormhole," Diantha says. "If the To say they didn't create it and they're telling the truth…then who did?"

I consider as we walk. "I don't know much about the creation of wormholes. Do they ever spontaneously form?"

Diantha stares off into the middle distance, checking her N-CAT. "It's technically possible," she says after a moment. "But natural wormholes tend to be highly unstable. They usually collapse fairly quickly. Whereas this wormhole was secure enough for the To to travel through. I assume they wouldn't have risked it if they thought there were much danger."

With my brain full of hermit aliens and mystery wormholes, we finish our walk and enter my own building. After dropping off my bag in my room, we continue on to Ereni's room, where she and Burke are waiting for us. "Sounds like you've had an adventure," Ereni says when we come in. She presses the appropriate button to heat up water for the ubiquitous tea. "How was Jundo? We didn't expect you back until tomorrow."

Burke pulls me into an embrace, kissing me lightly. "I, for one, am glad you're back early," he murmurs.

"Me too," I whisper.

"You could go to one of your own rooms, you know." Ereni shakes her head fondly at us before turning to her mother. "I didn't expect to see you either. It's been a while, hasn't it?"

I hadn't realized they hadn't been talking. But Diantha doesn't make any excuses, forcing me to remember yet again that Satori parental relationships are completely different than what I'm used to. "How are you finding your re-entry?" she asks.

Ereni shrugs. "I've been spending all my time catching up with everything that's happened in our absence, reconnecting with old friends and crèchemates who I expected to be long dead. You know, the usual." Not a hint of a smile cracks her deadpan façade.

"Yes, it's been a busy time." Diantha doesn't seem to notice Ereni's little joke. Instead, she launches right into business. "Tell me what you think about the current wormhole debate."

"I feel like when we were last here, it wouldn't have been a debate at all," Ereni says promptly. "The technology is out of the bag, so to speak, and so we might as well figure out how to make the best use of it. We have the resources to deploy wormholes more responsibly than most worlds, I imagine, and with foreknowledge we can put safety checks into practice that could help not just us, but humanity as a whole. It's our responsibility."

"And what would you say if I told you someone is already creating new wormholes, following an agenda of their own?"

"Is this true?" Ereni's eyes dart from her mother's face to mine. "Why would they summon you about wormhole technology?" The water in the kettle begins to bubble cheerfully, but she ignores it.

"They didn't." I grab my own mug from a rack on the wall and pour hot water into it. "They asked me to come because there were a few people from Sanctum on board the alien vessel."

Ereni's mouth forms a perfect "o." "That is unexpected," she manages.

Burke comes up behind me and squeezes my shoulder. "That must have been quite a shock," he says. "I don't suppose it was anyone you know?"

Leo, he isn't asking. He wants to know if Leo decided to follow me after all. I swallow a sudden stab of disappointment. I'm lucky to be reunited with someone with such a close link to Leo, after all. It's not something I ever dreamed of happening.

"Leo's daughter," I say. "And Gianna's daughter. The two of

them traveled here together. The rogue wormhole Diantha was talking about is in Sanctum's system. I got the impression the two ladies made the impromptu decision to represent Sanctum's interests, in spite of Sanctum's own insistence that they didn't want to get involved."

"That sounds like Sanctum," Ereni says with a wry smile.

"They didn't know I'd be here," I say. "They expected me to be on Arbor. But I'm glad I am here. They seem so…young."

Diantha makes a coughing noise. "They appear to be about the same age as Sienna." She keeps a diplomatically straight tone.

"Yes, but they've never met a single Satori," I argue. "This is the first new planet they've visited. And it sounds as though they had their families' support in coming here. It's not as if they had to escape their father's closet."

"Inexperienced then," Ereni murmurs. "But brave to come this far. It's only the two of them?"

"Them, and an entire delegation from the other habited planets in Sanctum's system," Diantha says. "The others are staying in Jundo, but we brought the two Sanctum girls back with us so we can keep an eye on them."

I wrinkle my nose. "Is that why you thought I invited them to live here? I thought I was acting like family."

"From the little of your culture that I've studied, aren't those two ideas quite similar?" Diantha asks.

I open my mouth to make a retort but have to shut it again when I realize she's correct. Burke gives me a sympathetic look. "So there's a rogue wormhole in Sanctum's system," he muses. "I wonder who would have done that. And why that system?"

"It might not be just that one system," Ereni says. "This is the first one we're hearing about here on Satori, but we have no idea how many other wormholes might be out there."

"Exactly," Diantha says. "We might not know the full extent of these actions for quite some time."

"Unless we create a wormhole in our own system so we can receive news more quickly." Ereni frowns. "This changes everything. We have to push both the Assembly and the Council to act quickly."

The Citizens' Assembly is a larger body than the Council, made up entirely of Satori who have been randomly selected to serve for limited terms. Ereni has done her best to explain the way the two bodies share governance, but my understanding is still hazy.

"You have useful contacts in the Assembly?" Diantha asks. "Because no one will return my calls."

"Burke and I have one crèchemate who serves in the Assembly now. I've spoken to him."

"Once," Burke interjects. "For five minutes."

"It's a start," Ereni insists. "After all, we've been gone a long time. We're expected to take some time to get back up to speed. No one will want to seriously consider what we say until we've been home long enough that they're sure we're as informed as we ought to be. But this is too important to honor that grace period. Surely everyone will understand that."

"Who do you think would create a new wormhole near Sanctum?" I ask. "Can you tell me more about the humans who discovered this technology in the first place?"

"They come from a civilization called Doctrina, spanning four worlds in the Nova F system," Diantha says. "It's nowhere near Sanctum, which makes this more interesting. It's a culture of scientist-clerics. They take their calling to advance the cause of science very seriously, and they were fascinated by the similar mission of the Satori, which they thought was complimentary to their own. We've established a permanent Satori community on one of their planets to assist in the exchange of knowledge between our two peoples. They'd be thrilled if we created a wormhole to facilitate that project even further."

"So do we think the Doctrina are traveling around the universe opening new wormholes?" I ask. "In the name of advancing their science?"

Diantha frowns. "I suppose it's possible," she says. "I'd gotten the impression they were more engaged in scientific theory than in pursuits of a more practical nature, but I imagine they have individuals amongst them interested in applied science. An expert in their culture could provide a sounder opinion on the subject."

Burke has been gazing off into the distance, catching up with his N-CAT. "Apparently we are not the first people with whom the Doctrina have shared this technology. They tend to be fairly free with their knowledge. It's part of their creed. And probably part of the reason why our two cultures get along so well."

"There's a third possibility," Ereni says softly. "The people creating the new wormholes? It could be us."

"What do you mean?" I ask. "The Satori can't even decide whether to create a single new wormhole in their own system, let alone begin deploying their own network. No offense."

She doesn't seem bothered by my words. She's pursing her lips as though she's thinking particularly hard. "But maybe some Satori aren't taking part in the debate. Maybe they got tired of it; it's been going on for a long time. Or maybe they didn't bother to participate in the first place. Maybe they decided it would be better to act first and ask questions later."

"You think a mission has gone rogue," Diantha says. "You think it's a group of Satori going around opening up new wormholes."

"It's a theory," Ereni says. "I don't *think* anything. We don't have enough information. But it is certainly as likely a possibility as the other ones."

"What about the aliens?" I ask. "They said they weren't involved with the new wormhole forming, but what if they're lying? They did arrive soon after its formation."

"We don't have enough information to form a solid hypothesis," Burke says.

"In a way, it doesn't matter who is making the new wormholes," Ereni says. "At least, the identity of the creators isn't as important as the fact that they're doing it at all. If anyone has decided to leverage this new technology, that means we have to act quickly if we want to be able to play a role in its development."

"You said it yourself," Diantha says. "We're too newly arrived. We won't be playing a role in this policy discussion."

But Ereni has a familiar glint in her eye. "We might not be invited to play a key role," she says. "But I have a good idea of someone who will be invited. Someone we'll be able to influence. Two someones, in fact." She looks at me expectantly.

"Oh, no." I shake my head. "No, no, you can't be serious." But I know her too well to believe that she isn't.

"Sienna, you're about to become the best aunt there ever was."

And just like that, I'm caught up in another of Ereni's schemes.

CHAPTER 12

The next day I take Novelle to visit Akari Park. I invite both ladies, but Allegra insists Novelle and I need family time. I message Ereni in case she wants to take advantage of Allegra being left behind to have a private conversation with her, and then Novelle and I set off for the park. It's a beautiful day, cloudless but not too hot, and Novelle asks to walk so she can see more of the city.

Novelle looks quite different today. Instead of her restrictive Sanctum dress, she has already obtained clothing in the Satori style, wearing a long, loose white tunic and stretchy blue pants along with practical sandals. Her hair is bound in a simple loose bun at the nape of her neck, no ribbons in sight, and she's baring an amount of skin that might cause a Napoleon lady to fall into a faint. "I see you're already adjusting well to the local culture," I say. She gives me a cautious look, almost as if she suspects me of making fun of her, but when I smile, she gives a shy smile back.

"Satori clothes are so much more comfortable." She gives a little skip as if to illustrate her greater range of motion. "I don't see how I could ever go back."

We settle into a companionable silence as she takes in the new world around her, seemingly interested in every little detail. I'm still becoming familiar with Seji myself: its smooth, terracotta red streets, all but the major thoroughfares of which share traffic with pedestrians, bicycles, and the occasional vehicle; its jumbled, colorful architecture, many of the buildings having shops on street level with apartments above; and its laidback atmosphere.

"It's so clean," Novelle marvels. "I never thought I'd see another city as beautiful as San Marco, but Seji is delightful in its own special way. It makes me feel like I've stepped into a different world."

"Well, that's because you have." I give a little sigh. "There's nothing like our canals back home, though. Not anywhere else in the universe."

"There isn't," she agrees. Then, a moment later, "Have you ever felt homesick?"

I repress a laugh. "All the time," I say. "Until you and Allegra arrived, I never thought I'd see another person from home. Sometimes I feel like a living time capsule, carrying memories of a Sanctum and a Napoleon that existed long ago. I know the Satori from the mission remember as well, of course, but it isn't the same. They saw our world with different eyes."

"I heard so many stories about them, but they're not really what I expected," Novelle confesses. "They have such a beautiful world, but they seem a little...." She hesitates.

"Conceited?" I suggest.

She gives me a grin. "I was going to say restrained, but conceited also works. For a people who have traveled so many places and pride themselves on their diplomacy, I expected them to be more charming. But they remind me of my nurse scolding me to eat my vegetables. I knew she was probably right, but the way she told me made me want to eat them even less."

"They were a bit different in Arbor," I tell her. "The Arborists are more technologically advanced than we are, and they've adopted a more egalitarian model for their society. I think the Satori see them as being on more of an equal footing."

"Is it really true that you can study anything you want here?" she asks. "Even as a woman?"

"It's really true." She gives another skip at the news. Another reader maybe? I'm finding myself liking my new niece, even though she doesn't remind me of Leo as much as I'd been hoping.

We stop for sweet frozen ices: Novelle selects a dark purple berry flavor, and I select lemon. We walk slowly to allow for our steady licking. Finally, I can't wait any longer. "I don't want to be rude," I burst out, "but I'm dying to hear everything about Leo. Your father. If you don't mind talking about him." I'm filled with a sudden sharp fear that as he got older, he somehow changed into a replica of our own father, stern and sometimes cruel. Novelle hadn't known the sweet youth I'd grown up with, after all.

But I needn't have worried. "Oh, Father is a darling," Novelle gushes. "I miss him terribly. He always spoiled all of us so much, and he could, of course, because of Mother's money. Mother said raising children should be a woman's domain, but he always laughed at her and insisted on spending time with us. When we got older, he told us we could always come to him with our problems, however small, and he actually meant it. He is such a good listener."

I love hearing such glowing praise from Leo's daughter. She's speaking as if there was a genuine love between them that had been missing between me and Leo and our father. "Who did he marry?"

"Oh, he married Vitalia Maccari. Do you remember the Maccaris? They're a grand old family, and very rich. They made Mother a very handsome settlement upon her marriage. Father says he couldn't believe they agreed to the match, not after all the scandal with"—she lowers her voice—"your father, and apparently it was quite a trial for Mother. She told me she had to embark on a year-long campaign to convince her father that marrying Father was the best path for her future and not a disastrous mistake."

I can hardly imagine any Neopolitan father agreeing to his daughter marrying Leo after our family disgrace, let alone Vitalia Maccari's father. I had known Vitalia; everyone in our circles had gone to the same events and parties. But I don't remember her very well, except as a quiet, well-mannered girl who had appeared to take to heart the adage that a young lady should be seen and not heard. That she would have taken it upon herself to wage a campaign against her family to marry Leo is deeply unexpected.

"Why did she take so much trouble for Leo?" I ask.

"Oh, well, you know Father. He's always been so dashing." Leo, dashing? "Mother said she liked how different he was compared to everyone else. She said when she spoke, he actually listened. And she liked that he cared about things besides money. Given she had so much, Grandmother used to warn her on a daily basis about fortune hunters. I think that made her a bit sensitive."

"Was it…a love match?" I would scarcely have dared hope for such a thing for Leo even before Father went to prison.

Novelle considers a moment before answering. "I would say so," she finally says. "Their love wasn't of the dramatic, passionate sort, at least not by the time I was born. But they do genuinely care for one another and support one another. I can't imagine one without the other."

I wouldn't want anything else for my twin. "And his art?" I ask. "Did he keep making masks?"

"Of course." Novelle stops dead in her tracks. "Had you already left when he apprenticed with Signor Gipetti?" I shake my head. Leo had been accepted before I left, although his apprenticeship hadn't officially begun.

"My father became a master in his own right. There were some families who looked down on us because of it, but he never cared. I have photos of all of his work if you'd like to look through them sometime. He did a whole series called "Ragazza d'Oro," which he said was inspired by you."

A sudden burst of emotion sweeps through me. "I would love to see," I say. "I'm so glad he got to live his dream. It wasn't at all a sure thing when I left, you know."

We resume walking. "He told me once that for the first year after you left, he wondered if he had made a terrible mistake not going with you. He felt responsible for you, you know, and also a little jealous, I think. You were going off to have a glorious adventure in the wider universe while he did the same old things at home. But once he began working harder with Signor Gipetti, I think his perspective changed. And then things heated up between him and Mother, and, well…it all worked out just as it was supposed to. That's something

Mother would say." Her smile falters. "It's hard to believe they're so far away now, and…." She trails off, not wanting to say what both of us are thinking. That they're dead.

We've reached the People's Arch while we've been talking, and I pause in front of it, letting Novelle admire the majestic red arch. "It's so different from home," she finally says. "My siblings and I spent our childhood pretending to be you. We play-acted adventures in planets all over the universe, and in the end, we always saved the day. But the reality of interstellar travel is quite a bit different from what I imagined."

I don't know what to say. I try to imagine a passel of nieces and nephews pretending to be their unknown Aunt Sienna and fail utterly. All the time I've spent sleeping while hurtling through space, I've been a hero in my family's eyes without knowing it.

We veer off to the right, away from the garden where Ereni and I had spoken about the wormhole technology, instead taking a path across a meadow to the lake closer to the center of the park. Novelle stops from time to time to look more closely at a particular flower, exclaiming with delight and taking photos on her qualpad. "I want to look them up later so I can learn more about them," she says.

We continue in this way until we reach the lake. A few small boats glide across the water, and a flock of birds gathers at the edge of the lake closest to us, squawking and shaking their wings. I wait until we walk past them to speak. "It must have been a difficult decision to leave," I say carefully.

"It was, and it wasn't." She looks down at her feet. "You know how Neopolitan can be. I doubt it changed much in the time between when you left and I grew up."

"If Leo was able to become a master, it must have changed at least a little."

She shakes her head. "Only because he was a man. A rich man. And his eccentricity didn't actually hurt anyone or even challenge them. He still got married, had a large family, enjoyed the proper entertainments, and generally did what was expected of him." She pauses. "Also, he's a very good artist. If he had been mediocre, he would have been mocked out of every drawing room in San Marco.

But people could see the real quality of his work. It helped them tolerate him. His masks became so popular, people would compete over their purchase."

More success than Leo had ever dreamed of. "I have one of his early masks with me here," I say. "The first Ragazzo d'Oro. He made it before people knew I'd been racing in his place."

"But once they found out you'd been racing yourself, they weren't exactly understanding, were they?" A shadow crosses her young face. "And it's not as if your example meant young ladies were suddenly allowed to have our own speeder bike races."

"No, of course not." I feel like I'm making a mess of this conversation. "Did you want to race?"

She huffs. "You're a very literal person, has anyone ever told you that? No, I didn't want to race. I fell in love with Allegra."

I stumble but catch myself before I trip. I hope she doesn't notice, but from the sidelong glance she casts in my direction, I think she did. "That came out very abruptly," she says. "I meant to work up to it more or maybe just not say anything at all. It's just...I want you to like me. I've been hearing stories about you all my life, and now here you are, and I don't know what to do or say."

She's acting like I'm a respected elder when we're the same age. I don't know how I can live up to the mythological figure she grew up knowing. "I do like you," I tell her. "It doesn't matter to me who you're in love with." The Satori treat same sex relationships as a matter of course. It had seemed odd to me when I first encountered the idea, but it's not as if Neopolitan mores have treated me particularly kindly.

Novelle gives a big sigh of relief. "And I hate those restrictive dresses too. I didn't want to shock you when we first met so I got all dressed up, but you weren't wearing one, and I never want to wear one again as long as I live."

I stop then and turn to face her. "You won't shock me," I say, holding her hand firmly in mine. "And even if you do, I'm sure it will be fine. It's not as if I'll die from it." I gesture around us. "You're on Satori now. I'm not going to say things are perfect here, but they are definitely different from what we're used to."

She bites her lip, and she suddenly looks vulnerable and very, very young. "My parents said they still loved me," she whispers, "but I could tell they thought there was something wrong with me."

I wince. Mightn't I have done the same if I were still living in San Marco and had never met Burke and Ereni? "There's nothing wrong with you," I say. "No one here will think there's anything wrong with you."

She takes a long breath. "That's what we hoped. That's a big part of why we decided to come. It seemed like the only way if we wanted to be together. Even though we had to leave our families behind, we thought it might be worth it." Hope shines from her eyes. "We didn't want to have to sneak around. And if we hadn't figured something out, eventually we would have had to get married to other people." She shudders. "But Allegra said you were supposed to have married some terrible boy or another and you had managed to avoid it, so we could too. When the alien starship arrived, it was like an answer to our prayers."

I'd assumed Novelle and Allegra had had an easy lifestyle, but they've had plenty of their own troubles. "From your point of view, coming here wasn't so much about representing Sanctum then? It was about finding the freedom to be who you really are."

Novelle rolls her eyes. "For me, yes, that was what mattered. But Allegra wants to save Sanctum from itself. She really does believe our planet deserves a voice in whatever happens with the wormhole. That is, if something more hasn't already happened since we left."

"I don't think the Satori know who is making the new wormholes," I tell her. "Or even if yours is the only one. Although Ereni has already come up with some theories."

"I bet she has," Novelle says. "Father told me about her too, you know."

I don't really know what Leo would have said about Ereni. He hadn't gotten to know her as well as I had. Or Burke, for that matter. But he knew they'd offered me a new life far away from the threat of the asylum, which is where I would have otherwise been sent to live out my days. "What did Leo—I'm sorry, your father—say about you and Allegra leaving?"

Novelle stares out at the lake. "He told me he'd always do everything he could to protect me. But he thought I should go. I could tell he did." She looks over at me, and I realize we're almost exactly the same height. "He told me once that I reminded him of you. It's one of the best things anyone has ever said to me."

The hero worship from this young lady is going to kill me. "I'm not so special," I tell her. "I only did what I had to do."

She looks at me in disbelief. "Aunt Sienna, you testified against your own father in the highest court on the planet. How many ladies would be capable of doing that?"

I think of all the women I've met since I left Sanctum. "You'd be surprised."

"Maybe, but you're the only one from Sanctum."

Enough. "You have to remember that for me, that all happened only a few years ago. Your father has lived a whole lifetime since then, and so have you. But I haven't. I'm still just trying to figure things out. I haven't been here on Satori very long at all, and I have no idea what I'm going to do next."

Novelle smiles shyly at me. "At least that's one thing we have in common."

We stare at each other for a minute, and then we both burst into laughter. "We have a lot more than that one thing in common," I finally say when I calm down.

"You know, you're not anything like I pictured you'd be." I tense, wondering if I've already managed to disappoint her. "But somehow you're exactly as you ought to be. I can see why my father spoke about you so often. He must have missed you very much."

"Just as I will always miss him," I say. My emotions threaten to overwhelm me. I still haven't gotten used to the idea of a niece who is my own age. "Let's keep going. I want to walk around the entire lake."

If I can't have Leo back again, Novelle is probably the next best thing.

CHAPTER 13

I am sitting by myself at a small round table in a teashop when I see Lyra enter with three people I don't recognize. Ereni insisted on meeting me here—she says it's one of the most exclusive meeting spots in Seji—but she's running late. In the meantime, I've been practicing reading the daily news in Kensho, resisting the urge to have my qualpad provide a translation.

I have a steaming cup of tea in front of me, a slightly gingery aroma wafting to my nostrils, as well as a small plate of cakes I plan to share with Ereni. Both had been delivered via conveyer belt a few minutes after my order. Burke has told me they don't have waitstaff anywhere on Satori, such labor having been automated sometime in their distant past.

I watch as Lyra and her friends choose a table and submit their orders, falling briefly silent to do so. They don't have to use their qualpads as I do but can communicate with the café's systems directly through their N-CATs. They lounge as they wait for their beverages, talking too quietly for me to hear but occasionally erupting into contagious hilarity.

Lyra looks so comfortable in her own skin, leaning back with a careless elegance I couldn't hope to emulate. She's slung a fancy-looking silver tote bag with a scaly texture over her chair, and she appears to be explaining something to her friends, who are hanging on her every word. Her black hair flows over her shoulders, the white streak in the center highlighted to dramatic effect. I glance at my qualpad and wonder how much longer Ereni will be.

Lyra and her friends order tiny cups of a popular stimulant drink, and they down them in single large gulps. Her friends then stand up and make for the exit, but before I can collapse in relief at avoiding an awkward encounter, Lyra catches my eye across the room and rises gracefully, shrugging her stylish bag over her shoulder and striding over. "It's Sarah, isn't it?" she says, giving me a charming smile. "Burke's little friend?"

I try to control the expression on my face. "Sienna," I correct her. "It's good to see you again." It's anything but, but I know what's expected of me. Burke has seen her a few times since our arrival, and he hasn't had anything but positive things to share about her.

"Do you mind if I join you?" She sits in the chair I've been saving for Ereni without waiting for my response. "I'm going to order another drink," she announces. "What's that you have there?"

I tell her the name of my ginger tea, and she looks a little baffled. "I've never heard of that," she says. "How quaint. I'll try one now myself."

I'm grateful for the sudden blankness of her face as she orders, but soon enough her attention is tightly focused on me. "Burke told me you saved his life," she says. "Your planet's culture sounds positively barbarous. Oh, I'm sorry, I don't mean anything by that. You can see why I never joined a mission myself, I'd be absolutely hopeless. In any case, I owe you a debt of gratitude for returning him safe and sound."

She speaks of him in a similar way to how I'd imagine she'd speak of a particularly prized pet, and I give silent thanks for my old etiquette training, which allows me to remain outwardly calm, maintaining a small, noncommittal smile on my lips that would have made Gianna proud.

"No thanks are necessary," I assure her. After all, I certainly didn't save Burke for her sake.

"Oh, but they are," she gushes. "You are quite the hero. Burke speaks so highly of you. I'm genuinely glad to get the chance to know you better."

Before I can think of a suitably vacuous reply, she holds up a finger and gets up to fetch her cup of tea from the conveyer belt at the front of the shop. I take the opportunity to frantically send Ereni a message. "Where are you???? Lyra here." I hope my multiple question marks are sufficient to convey my urgency.

Lyra returns with her cup and takes an experimental sip. She makes a little moue with her mouth before swallowing. "Charming," she says, but I assume she's lying because she doesn't move to take another sip. "Where were we? Oh, yes, an absolute hero. When I knew him before his mission, Burke tended to be quiet. He listened more than he spoke. Quite an admirable trait. But when you come up, he becomes positively chatty."

"I'm sure you two have a lot to talk about," I say diplomatically.

"So much," she positively gushes. "We've barely broken the surface. After all, so many consequential things have happened since his departure, and I've made it my personal goal to help him. I've always thought he was such a promising individual, and I've told him I won't rest until he knows absolutely everything he needs to know to fit back into life here. And he's making such impressive progress. There are so many opportunities for a young person like him."

I make a noncommittal noise and stare at her full mug of tea. If only I could spill it down the front of her salmon-colored blouse. I'm sure it would make a pleasing stain. I pick up my own mug and take another sip.

"It must be difficult for you to adjust to a new culture," Lyra continues with a sympathy that doesn't ring true. "From everything Burke has told me, Sanctum is quite…underdeveloped. I was quite shocked to learn that the people of your planet don't enjoy the basic genetic techniques we take for granted here. I thought all humans had learned to alter themselves by now."

My eyes narrow. I know an insult when I hear one. For all her superior genetic alterations, Lyra doesn't seem particularly enlightened to me. "I'm having a nice time here with Burke and Ereni."

The fake sweetness in my tone almost makes me gag, but Lyra doesn't react at all. I wonder if she even notices. "I was just telling Burke how generous he is to take you under his wing like he has," Lyra continues. Take me under his wing? Does she know we are romantically involved? A sudden uncertainty makes my heart race, and I grip my mug harder. "And you couldn't have a better guide than Ereni."

"What's that?" Ereni comes bustling up, wearing a flowing orange garment that arranges itself around her in impressive billows. "I thought I heard my name."

"Ereni!" Lyra pushes back her mug and stands up. "I was just keeping Sienna company until you arrived." So she does know my name.

"I'm terribly sorry I'm late, Sienna," Ereni says, settling herself down in Lyra's vacated chair. "It simply couldn't be helped, I'm afraid, but here I am. What a cute spot." She gives a tight smile in Lyra's general direction.

"Isn't it?" Lyra says. "The ambiance can't be beat."

Ereni's eyes go blank for such a short period of time, I'm left wondering how she could have ordered that quickly. "And how are you doing, Lyra?" she says, folding her hands on the table. "You keeping busy?"

"I should say so." Lyra gives a stuffy laugh. "I can see you haven't heard. I've decided to run for the Councilor position representing Seji. Everyone was surprised when the seat opened up, but then, you wouldn't know the whole story behind that, would you?"

"How exciting for you," Ereni says coolly. "I didn't realize you had political aspirations. Have you done a great deal of political work over the past three hundred years then?" She widens her eyes in interested innocence, which I only understand when Lyra shifts her bag uncomfortably on her shoulder.

"Oh no, I wouldn't say that." She keeps her voice bright and unconcerned, but her sudden absorption with her bag gives her away. "I've had other projects to occupy myself. But now the time is right, and I would be honored to serve our people in a position of leadership."

"I'm sure you would. I've heard it will be a tight race. Aren't several candidates already running?"

Lyra gives a careless smile. "That's true, but I believe I can muster enough support. And I have plenty of help, of course. In fact, I'm hoping to recruit Burke to work with me on my campaign. I'm sure his assistance would be invaluable."

Ereni tightens her jaw. "Burke excels at whatever he puts his mind to," she says.

"Although it's a shame you all came back in disgrace," Lyra continues blithely. "All three of you were ejected from your mission, weren't you? I heard you wouldn't have been allowed to return home if Diantha hadn't intervened." She licks her lips as if she's finding this vicious gossip to be particularly delicious. "Oh, don't worry. It's not like the story is common knowledge. But since I'm making it my business to help Burke, I needed to have all the details at my fingertips."

I shift uncomfortably, but Ereni doesn't bat an eye. "Oh, it wasn't as bad as all that," she says coolly.

If Lyra is disappointed by her calm response, she doesn't show it. "I was surprised when Diantha came home, I have to say. I'd always thought she was a lifer."

Ereni is a master at keeping her face expressionless, but she's leaning her body as though she wants to be as far from Lyra as possible. "She had a child while she was stationed on Zamavat," she says coldly. "She wanted to return so the child could be educated here on Satori."

Lyra's mouth shapes into a perfect "O" of simulated shock. "Will the scandals never cease? What do you all get up to when you're away on missions? It's almost enough to make me jealous." She says it in such a way that we both get the clear message she'd rather die than join a disreputable mission. "I suppose at least the child is safely ensconced in a crèche now where she belongs."

"On the contrary." A thin smile curves Ereni's lips, as if she's enjoying getting to tell Lyra she's wrong. "The child will receive an excellent education at a nearby crèche, but Diantha has decided to raise her herself."

Lyra stares at Ereni, seemingly rendered speechless by this news. I thank my blessings that Ereni has managed to halt her poisonous torrent.

Ereni's smile broadens at the reaction she's elicited. "Well, it was nice seeing you, Lyra. Don't be a stranger."

Lyra comes to herself with a shudder. "I wouldn't dream of it. I suppose I'll be seeing you both at the reception next week."

I look over at Ereni before I can stop myself. What reception? Ereni maintains a disinterested look, but I've given away my ignorance.

"Oh, have you not heard about it yet? Don't worry, I'm sure you'll be invited." Lyra smiles down at me as if I'm a small child. "All the delegates from your system will be there, including your two…relatives." Allegra isn't related to me, but I don't bother to correct her. The Satori who haven't traveled to other planets seem to get confused when it comes to family relationships. "It should be quite the affair. I've heard even the To are sending an emissary of some kind. What fun we'll have." With a little wave, Lyra swans out of the shop.

Ereni maintains her ramrod straight posture. "I can't believe she's running for a Councilor position."

I'm still staring at the front door, making sure Lyra doesn't suddenly return. "I can't believe she was invited to a party involving my own planet before I was." I make a disgusted sound. "But I suppose it doesn't matter as long as I'm allowed to attend."

Ereni makes a small puffing noise. "It feels like it matters, though, doesn't it?" She drops her head dramatically into her hand, coaxing a small laugh from me.

"In any case, I don't see why you're bothered," I say. "I thought you liked her. Weren't all three of you crèchemates together?"

Ereni peers down at Lyra's untouched mug with disgust. "We were. But she and I were never close. I thought she was boring. If I'm being honest, I never really understood what Burke saw in her. I doubt their romance would have lasted, even if Burke had decided not to join our mission." She shakes her head. "I don't like her sudden interest in politics though. Why now? It's such a crucial time for Satori. I feel like Lyra will say whatever asinine thing she thinks will be popular, whether or not it's the right path forward."

"I don't care about Lyra's politics." Impatience bubbles inside me. "I care about her and Burke. She couldn't stop talking about him. And now they're going to work together? What if…." I don't want to finish my thought. It seems disloyal.

"You should talk to him, Sienna." Ereni stands and gets her order from the conveyer belt: another mug of tea, this one a light peach color that matches her outfit. She sits down with a sigh. "You don't have anything to worry about with Lyra, but you shouldn't take my word for it. Remember how much trouble you and Burke got into by not discussing difficult things on Arbor?"

She has a point, as usual. "I'll talk to him," I say. "But I don't want him to refuse a good opportunity for my sake."

Ereni makes a dismissive sound. "Being Lyra's grunt worker is not a good opportunity for anybody," she says. "Now, are any of these cakes for me? Excellent."

She pops one into her mouth and begins to tell me about her visit with an old professor that morning.

I TAKE Ereni's advice to heart, and I speak to Burke that very evening. I tell him about running into Lyra, about her political aspirations, and about her suggestion that he work for her campaign. "Is that something you'd be interested in doing?"

"Oh, I don't think so." Burke looks distracted. He's obtained a large map of many of the nearby star systems, which he's tacked up on the wall, and he's staring at it now.

"You would get to meet a lot of important people," I press.

"Perhaps," he says. "I haven't really thought about it."

"And you'd get to spend a lot of time with Lyra."

This time he doesn't respond at all, continuing to look at his ridiculous map. After a moment, he shakes his head. "It's hard to believe any of those systems could already have an operational wormhole as we speak. Just think, because our system doesn't have one, it could be years until we find out."

Is that what he's thinking about? "You're not listening to me at all," I accuse. "I just ran into your ex-lover, and she's obviously plotting something, and I'm very upset."

Burke jolts to sudden attention. "Do you have to call her my ex-lover?" He makes an attempt at a smile. "It sounds so sordid."

But I'm not amused. "Did you tell her that the people on Sanctum don't have the same genetic makeup as people from Satori?" I feel sick at the thought. "Were the two of you making fun of us?"

Burke looks horrified. "No, Sienna, we would never do that. *I* would never do that," he corrects himself. "Lyra and I have barely discussed Sanctum at all. She enjoys reminiscing about her youth, that's all, and talking about how much has changed. She clearly wants to take on a mentorship role, making sure I find my footing again. It's kindly meant, but I want to take the time to make my own decisions."

"She wasn't very kind to me," I say.

Burke stands up and puts his hands on my shoulders. "I promise, Sienna, you have nothing to worry about. I don't know why Lyra is trying to stir things up, but I don't like it, and I don't want to spend time around people who don't treat you well."

I look down at the ground. "But she is your *first love*." There is an embarrassing desperation in my words, but I remember how bad it had been when we didn't tell each other how we felt, and I persevere. "I would understand if you still have feelings for her. Even if you… wanted to be with her."

"That is very generous of you." He presses his forehead against my own. "But I don't still have feelings for her. I left thinking I'd never see her again, and I made my peace with that. The fact that she's still alive doesn't change anything about my feelings for you."

"But she obviously still cares about you." Why else would she be involving herself in his life?

"She doesn't, not like that," Burke says. "There's a difference between nostalgia and love. She doesn't even know me anymore, and I certainly don't know her. She's had almost three hundred years of experience. Every time she speaks to me, I feel that difference as a vast gap, and I can tell she's affected by it too. She barely listens to a word I say, not that I get the chance to say very many. She sees me as some pliable, moldable child. Even if you weren't here, I wouldn't be interested in her in a romantic way." He pulls me closer. "But you are here, and that makes me a very lucky person indeed."

I push a hand against his chest. "I don't think I'm lesser than you because I come from Sanctum," I say. "Whatever Lyra might think." I have to believe that.

"Good," he says. "You aren't. I'm glad you know that." He slips a hand to my waist. "To be entirely clear, I don't care what Lyra thinks. She's different than I remember. Less substantial, shallower. You'd think hundreds of years would cause a deepening, but all our conversations have been so superficial. Maybe Ereni has been right about her all along." He mock groans. "She'll be thrilled to hear me admit that."

"Lyra will be at this reception she told us about." I can't help feeling a vague sense of dread at the idea of seeing her again. "She took great pleasure in discovering we hadn't heard about it yet."

Burke shakes his head. "You see what I mean? As if it matters in what order you receive an invitation. Caring about that sort of thing is petty."

I look up, meeting his brown eyes. "When she told us about it, I cared," I confess. "I cared a lot."

He makes an impatient noise. "That's because she was manipulating you into caring. But who cares if she'll be there at all?"

I know he's right. I'm eager to meet the other delegates and hear about life on the other planets in my system. I'm looking forward to spending more time with Novelle and Allegra. And I'm fascinated at the idea that the To are going to attend in some fashion.

"I thought the Satori were all supposed to be these generous, enlightened beings," I complain. "And now you're telling me this woman who is three hundred years older than me is manipulating me into feeling bad she got a party invitation before I did."

Burke makes a low groan. "We're all just humans, Sienna. That's the truth. The Satori aren't inherently any better or worse than anyone else. We're just people."

"It's kind of disappointing to find that out," I tell him. "But it's also much less intimidating to know you're not some kind of god-like person." I give him a playful peck on the lips.

"Are you sure about that?" He wiggles his eyebrows at me. "After all, I'd be your very own god-like person."

I bat at his arm. "You'd like that, wouldn't you?"

He draws me into his arms and kisses me until I'm breathless. "Maybe I'm just doing my best to keep up with you. Ever thought of that?"

I kiss him even harder.

CHAPTER 14

The evening of the reception, I am very excited. I have allowed Ereni to dress me in certified Satori finery, which consists of a gown almost as billowy as the one she'd worn to our tea date the other day. It's a deep emerald color with gold accents: nothing I would have ever picked for myself, and yet once I put it on, I'm spellbound by it, sweeping up and down my room ahead of time to practice flaring my skirts. The sleeves swirl as I move, long slits allowing me freedom in spite of the large amounts of fabric.

We'll all be staying overnight in Jundo since the party will go so late, and we get ready together in Ereni's room. Novelle wears a slightly more relaxed version of a Sanctum gentleman's attire, complete with intricately ordered cravat. Allegra wears a Sanctum gown that could have been worn during my time there except for its slightly narrower profile. Ereni is swathed in even more fabric than I am, and Burke watches us all preen from a chair in the corner, a smile playing around his lips. He's wearing a long formal jacket that goes down to his knees and particularly spectacular shiny red shoes.

When we arrive at the reception, I try to hide my surprise at how simple everything is. I expected the affair to rival our parties in San Marco, but instead, the party spans a plain series of large rooms.

They're fitted comfortably enough, with seating in various configurations, both regular chairs and small poofs closer to the ground, as well as tall graceful tables for placing food and drink while standing. But there are no decorations of any kind, as well as no musicians or other entertainments. Some soothing ambient music plays in the background, completely forgettable. There is a long conveyer belt in the largest room, where any ordered food and drinks emerge, but no waitstaff circulates with delicious hors d'oeuvres or flutes of champagne.

"Sanctum does surpass us in some ways, you see," Burke whispers into my ear. "I'd never been to the type of affairs you seemed to attend as a matter of course. My first event in your Capitol, I felt like every person in the place had to be staring at me as I tried to pretend I was perfectly confident."

"I, on the other hand, was actually perfectly confident," Ereni interrupts.

Burke mock scolds her. "What did the Mission Council tell you about eavesdropping, Ereni?"

"Oh, really!" She flounces towards the conveyer belt, but I can tell she's not really angry.

Novelle and Allegra hang back behind us, sticking close to one another and looking around with wide eyes. It doesn't look like this was what they'd been expecting either. We slowly move to the far side of the room where we have a good view of all the arrivals.

Lyra makes a grand entrance soon after, flanked by two people on each side. But Burke makes no move to greet her, and it's clear she has a networking agenda for tonight as she begins to work the crowd. I force myself to look away. It's none of my business what she does at this party.

It's not long before a short man, his dark hair marked with distinctive yellow stripes, slinks our way. My mother would have deplored his posture, but I have to admit his slouch gives him an insouciant attitude that makes him surprisingly attractive. "Good evening," he drawls, giving each of us the benefit of his smile in turn. "The delegates from Sanctum, I presume?"

Do we really look so out of place? I move closer to Burke and give an internal sigh of relief when Allegra flashes her smile. "I'm afraid you have us at a disadvantage, sir."

"My name is Aeson." Another grin. "I'm here as a representative of a group called the Unity. Perhaps you've heard of us?"

I exchange blank looks with Allegra and Novelle, but Burke interjects. "The group that wants Satori to create its own wormhole. How interesting to meet you." He says the words flatly. "Sienna and I have recently returned from a mission so we aren't entirely up to speed."

Aeson looks at me in delight. "Oh, really? I've heard about you. Returned from a mission only to be reunited with two of your relations completely by chance. How wonderful." He beams at all of us. "Tell me, Sienna, how are you finding our planet so far?"

For some reason this man is rubbing me the wrong way. I don't know if it's his attitude or simply the fact that I feel out of place in this large, echoey room. "Just lovely," I say with a false smile. "I've already received a complaint through the Superior Mission Council that's made me feel right at home."

Aeson's face falls. "Perhaps I can help you with that," he offers swiftly. "I am very well connected amongst the mission groups. I myself returned from a mission not so long ago."

At his quick offer of help, I feel ashamed for even mentioning it. "No, no, Ereni is helping me take care of it. There's no need to trouble yourself."

"Ah, but it wouldn't be any trouble at all," he declares.

Just then, a group of short, squat people enter, dressed in curious silver robes. I count at least twelve of them, and I have trouble telling them apart from one another, given their uniform clothing and height. They all have hair closely cropped to their heads and knee-high black boots. Their skin color ranges from pasty white to deep brown.

"Those are the Word," Novelle says quietly.

"You'll have to excuse me," Aeson says. "I've been waiting to meet them. It's been quite a pleasure speaking with you." He gives us all one last smile before approaching the group of the Word with a confidence I can't help but admire.

"They live on Veritas, on the far side of the system from the wormhole," Novelle continues. "They are honest to a fault. They will deliver a grave insult to you before they will lie to you, which I have to admit is a useful trait in a society with whom you're trying to negotiate. But they do not understand the principle of politeness in the slightest."

"Noted." I can't imagine never being able to tell even the smallest of lies. How would I have survived in my parents' household?

Several Satori come in at different times, with Burke whispering their names in my ear when he knows them, which is more often than I would have expected. He really has been studying.

I'm thinking of suggesting we all order some snacks when another group enters. It's all I can do not to cry out in delight because these people have tails. Actual tails, similar to a cat's, waving with arrogant disregard of all the stares they're causing.

"Finally," I whisper, and Burke smiles at me. When the Satori had first come to Sanctum, before I'd had a chance to meet them myself, I'd heard rumors they had tails and had been dying to see them. Imagine my disappointment when the Satori ended up looking like ordinary people.

But these newcomers are decidedly not ordinary. In addition to their tails, they have light violet-colored skin and many different shades of hair, some styled almost a meter high, so they all look taller than they really are. Their clothes, which involve bouffant skirts like flower petals, parted to allow for their tails, over thin pants, give off a noticeable glow, and they are all barefoot.

"The Luz," Novelle whispers. "They're the ones who snuck into our system more recently and made sure Sanctum never knew they were there. The Word knew though."

"Are they friends?" I'm fascinated by this intrigue I never knew existed.

Novelle frowns. "Not exactly."

"They appear to tolerate each other," Allegra adds. "They have a trading relationship that is mutually beneficial, and nobody wants to ruin that. But there's definitely a tension there."

"I think it's the tails," Novelle says. "I think they make the Word nervous."

"I think it's the Word's penchant for telling the truth in the most brutal way possible," Allegra says. "It makes them difficult to be around."

Novelle winces, and I wonder what the Word have said to her. "Point taken. I'd much rather deal with tails."

"Neither of them think much of us," Allegra says. "Although I don't think it's anything personal."

"They could have tried to reach out to Sanctum earlier," Novelle argues. "I think we would have come around."

But I'm sympathetic to the Word and the Luz. Sharing a system with an unpredictable isolationist planet can't be an ideal situation for either of them. And both of them have proved they can maintain harmonious relations with cultures very different from their own, a feat I'm not certain Sanctum will ever be able to match.

I will always love my home, but that doesn't mean I can't see its flaws.

"Can you introduce us to the Luz?" Burke asks. "I have a feeling Sienna has some questions she'd love to ask."

"I'm not going to ask them about their tails," I hiss, and both Novelle and Allegra break into laughter.

Still, a few minutes later, Allegra gestures for me to accompany her, and we approach two Luz who are talking to one another. "Teofila, Lucia, so wonderful to see you outside the ship," she says. "Would you allow me to introduce you to one of my fellow Neopolitans? Her name is Sienna Tascioni."

I wait for a cue as to how they handle greetings in their culture. Both individuals bow low from the waist until they're practically parallel to the floor. I glance over at Allegra, and seeing her begin to bend, I follow suit. We all hold our position for what seems like an eternity before the two Luz begin to rise upright once more.

"We are honored to meet your fellow Neopolitan," Teofila says, and for a horrified second, I think she is going to bow again. "But please tell us how this came to be. Your Sienna Tascioni was not on the To's starship with us, certainly we would remember. And Neopolitans do not possess the technology to travel here to Satori of their own independence. This has been the understanding of the Luz, we regret the error if we have misunderstood?"

"There hasn't been a misunderstanding," I say. "I left Sanctum some years earlier with the Satori, who had been visiting our planet. I've been traveling with them ever since, and when they ultimately decided to return to their home world, I came with them."

"That makes a certain sense," Lucia says, and she gives an additional tiny bow. "We thank you for your clear explanation."

"Your Gallo is quite good," I say. "May I ask how you happen to speak it, given the lack of diplomatic relationship between our worlds?"

Teofila's tail gives a visible twitch. "We benefit from an assistive brain technology not so different from that used by your Satori friends. It allows us to access many known languages."

"We don't recommend you try to have a complicated conversation with the Word," Lucia almost purrs. "They do not use such technology, and their Gallo is quite rudimentary. They have never bothered to learn our language at a high level of proficiency either, preferring to require us to speak to them in their native language in spite of the valuable nature of our trade relationship."

"They classify this behavior as efficiency, which is a highly valued trait in their culture," Teofila adds. "It is not meant as an insult." Her tail twitches again. "We would not mean to give you a misapprehension of the Word."

"Novelle tried to learn a few words in their language, but we've really only communicated with them with the help of the Luz and the To," Allegra says. "Assistance for which we are deeply grateful."

Both the Luz's' tails rise up at Allegra's words of appreciation. "You are too kind." Lucia is practically arching her back in satisfaction.

"It is our deep pleasure to be of some small assistance to the two Neopolitans who have taken on this mission with no official government sanction," Teofila says.

"We met some of your officials when we finally visited your planet in the wake of the wormhole's sudden appearance," Lucia tells me. "We regret to say they mostly met our expectations. But you, Signorina Allegra, and your bosom friend Signorina Novelle, we have found to be most courageous. And therefore, we welcome your acquaintance as well, Signorina Sienna."

Teofila taps her companion's arm excitedly. "We are curious to ask, Signorina Sienna, how you find our hosts, the Satori? It seems as though you have been living amongst them for some time. We would welcome your counsel."

"The Satori?" I try to buy myself some time. "I wouldn't be here without them, of course." Both Luz peer at me, as though trying to ascertain my deeper thoughts. I remember my recent conversation with Burke. "They are just as human as you or I," I tell them. "They have grand aspirations of what they believe and who they want to be. And sometimes they fall short."

If I were the Luz, with only secondhand knowledge of the Satori, I'd want to learn as much as possible. "They are not a culture that has experienced real hardship in recent memory," I say. "Perhaps your culture is similar?"

Teofila's tail ripples. "That is so," she agrees. "We are certainly far more scientifically advanced than your people. Although the To leave us in the dust."

"My guess is the Satori will have an easier time respecting you due to this similarity," I tell them. "It is easier to understand another culture when you have more in common, however much we may try to rise above such biases."

Both Luz nod gravely. "Thus far, the Satori have been all that is correct," Lucia says. "Because we use similar assistive devices, the communication between us has been all we could have wished. We hope this augurs an auspicious collaboration."

"I'm sure it does." The two Luz bow down to waist level again, and Allegra and I follow suit before retreating to a far corner. "I suppose it goes without saying that Sanctum won't be on the receiving end of quite such a warm welcome," I say in a hushed voice. "The Satori do not understand my resistance to having an N-CAT implanted, and they will doubtless pressure you and Novelle as well."

"I'm considering it." I blink at Allegra's surprising statement. "If, as you say, it is a trigger for prejudice from the Satori, we might be better served to blend in, so to speak. Especially if we decide we want to live here long-term. After all, there's no point in continuing to conform to Sanctum's mores, is there? It's not as if we plan to return."

"They shouldn't be pressuring us to adapt to their ways," I argue.

"No, they shouldn't," Allegra agrees. "But they are clearly going to do so anyway. And there's nothing inherently wrong with taking the path of least resistance, not when doing so won't harm anyone or compromise what I believe or who I am."

I shift my weight uncomfortably. "But how do you know having something installed in your brain *won't* change who you are?"

Allegra shrugs. "The Satori don't seem to think it will, and neither do the Luz. It will be a change, of course, but not as big a change as moving to an entirely new system where I don't know anyone."

Not having an N-CAT implanted has become such a defining decision for me. The fact that Allegra sees it differently makes me uneasy. "I don't want to lose who I am." I realize I'm talking more loudly than I should. A few people give us strange looks.

Allegra cocks her head as she studies me. "You shouldn't do anything you don't want to do, of course," she finally says. "We've had quite enough of that back on Sanctum. For me, I just feel like there's so much for me to learn here, and I wouldn't mind having a little assistance."

I open my mouth to change her mind, then close it. It would be hypocritical of me to try. She's completely correct that we've already experienced an absurd amount of judgment and pressure to conform. I shouldn't be adding to that now that she and Novelle have left Sanctum behind.

Allegra takes a big gulp of the drink in her hand. "Novelle said she told you about our relationship. I'll admit, at first, I was angry at her. I thought it was too soon. We had no idea how you'd react to the idea of our romance." She takes a breath. "She sees you as her hero, you know. She couldn't imagine you rejecting her the way her own mother did." She leans closer. "But I am not as idealistic. I could imagine it. And if you had hurt her, I would have never let you forget it." She tosses back the rest of her drink. "But I guess she is a better judge of human character than I gave her credit for. It seems like your time among the Satori has truly opened your mind, just as she hoped. When I first heard you were here, against all odds, I couldn't believe our bad luck. But I can admit when I'm wrong."

It's not exactly an apology, but it is a reminder. I hadn't even stopped to consider how Novelle and Allegra would feel about my presence here. I'd assumed they would be happy about it. "Novelle's mother rejected her?" I ask.

Allegra's mouth firms into a thin line. "She caught us once. Not even doing anything particularly scandalous, but it was enough to send her into hysterics. She wouldn't let Novelle see me for months. It took all of your brother's persuasion for me to be allowed into the house again. And Novelle was never allowed to come see me." Allegra frowns at her empty glass. "Novelle loves her mother so we don't talk about what happened much. But her mother wasn't part of the plan. She didn't know we were leaving Sanctum with the To ahead of time. Your brother kept the information from her."

I swallow. I wonder how his marriage had fared once his deception had been found out. Or if he'd kept it a secret for the rest of his life. "What about Gianna?" I ask. "Your mother? Did she know about your relationship?"

"Novelle's mother told her personally. I watched her come in, watched her be shown to the drawing room, waited while they spoke. Novelle's mother didn't even stay long enough for tea. I thought I would be in so much trouble." Allegra shakes her head. "My mother came upstairs to my bedchamber, and she said it had been all she could do not to take a good whack at Novelle's mother with the fireplace poker."

"She took your part?" I can't hide the surprise in my voice.

"I was as shocked as you are," Allegra says. "But she said no one had the right to judge her daughter. There was nothing she could do about the opinion of society, but she promised she wouldn't force me to marry without my consent. She said that kind of thinking was a relic from an earlier time when she was still a girl."

I try to imagine Gianna defending her daughter from accusations of impropriety. Perfect Gianna! The Gianna who'd been an admirable mother to Allegra is a completely different person from the young lady I'd once known.

The din in the room suddenly quiets, and as I crane my head to see what's happening, a shiny blue robot rolls into view. It stands a bit more than a meter tall, not quite reaching my height, and it looks something like a large rabbit, with long ears sculpted back against its head, large shiny eyes, and a facsimile of a nose that moves from side to side as I watch. It has two arm-like limbs attached to its torso, complete with articulated fingers, but no legs: its body tapers into a kind of pedestal, underneath which I assume there are some sort of wheels that allow it to move.

Altogether, it is a most uncanny…creature? Object? I realize I'm not sure if it's sentient.

"Ah, Milo is here." Allegra sounds pleased.

"Its name is Milo?"

"Novelle and I named it upon its request. On Sanctum it was referred to as the 'To Robot,' but we found that rather awkward when engaging in conversation."

Novelle finds us in the crush and squeezes my arm. "We must introduce you to Milo." She claps her hands in excitement. "It was with us when we learned you were present on Satori, and it expressed great interest in meeting you someday."

I look dubiously at the little robot. "Is it…alive?" I ask awkwardly.

Novelle puts her hands over her mouth. "Oh dear, we never explained things to you. I'm sorry. The robot is a conduit. The To speak through its mouth. To be honest, I've never been entirely clear as to whether we're always speaking to the same To or whether they rotate their use of Milo."

"We saw a few other robots on the ship," Allegra volunteers. "They were differently formed. One of them even looks like a glassy-eyed human, but we told the To we found that one rather disquieting. Our favorite has always been Milo."

"It was the first one we met too, and always so kind to us," Novelle says. "Come on."

She tugs on my arm until I follow her to the circle surrounding the robot. "Milo!" Novelle cries. The robot swivels around at its name. "I'd like you to meet my aunt. This is Sienna."

The robot advances a short distance. "Pleased to make your acquaintance, Sienna Tascioni." Its voice is smooth, androgynous, and somewhat monotone. While it has a facsimile of a mouth, its face doesn't move when it speaks, aside from the twitching nose. Its large black eyes are fixed on my face, its head tilted slightly upwards.

"It's a pleasure to meet you, Milo," I say. "I must thank you for your care of Novelle and Allegra. They say you have been very kind to them, and I know they wanted very badly to come here to Satori." It feels awkward to be speaking to this blue bunny, but I do my best to pretend I'm thanking a respected colleague.

"We were glad to have them on board," Milo says. "Sanctum deserves to have representation, as we told its officials repeatedly. Allegra and Novelle have shown a great care for their people by agreeing to come." I wonder if it knows the real reason of their departure, and then it says, "Even if they were not always shown great care in return."

"Indeed." I have an answer to my question. "I must admit, I have been very interested to meet you."

"And I you," the robot says. "Come, let us talk further." Without waiting for my reply, it lurches forward and rolls towards the corner I'd been previously occupying. I pause, but when no one else makes to follow, I hurry after it.

"Please to tell me which other planets you have visited since leaving Sanctum?" Milo asks.

I blink at the strange phrasing, as well as the abrupt introduction of a new topic. For the first time, I wish I was standing in the same room with whichever member of the To is currently speaking through the robot. I suppose if the To are physically different enough from humans, body language might not give me much of a clue of their thoughts and feelings, but with the robot, I have absolutely nothing to guide my understanding.

"I accompanied the Satori to Arbor." I keep my voice even. "After

Arbor, we traveled to a planet called Zamavat, and then we came directly here."

"We know of Arbor," Milo says. "But Zamavat is unknown to us, at least by that name. Perhaps the Satori will be willing to share its coordinates."

"Perhaps." I have no idea how cooperative the Satori are inclined to be towards the first alien species encountered by humanity, but I'm certainly not going to make any promises on their behalf. "I wonder if you would mind answering a question."

"We welcome open communication," Milo says. "It gives us more data about humanity."

I swallow at the implications of that statement, but then I realize the To might not be so different from the Satori, who are also obsessed with collecting data. "I've been wondering how you came to travel to Sanctum's system," I say. "I have gathered it's not a central system nor is it considered particularly noteworthy."

"Perhaps among humanity that is true," Milo says agreeably.

"Why not come directly to Satori?" I press. "It seems like they would be a logical choice if you wanted to open communications with humanity, given their varied experience."

Milo moves its nose back and forth in an uncanny way. "Our primary goal was not to open communications with humanity," it said. "We had no particular intention to do so. We traveled to your home system to investigate the new phenomenon that had appeared there. I believe you call it a wormhole."

"But that isn't the first wormhole that has recently appeared in human space," I press. After all, the Doctrina must have tested the technology.

"That is the case." Milo nods its head stiffly. "But upon investigation, it was the first time it appeared as though the system's inhabitants hadn't been directly involved in a new wormhole's establishment. This is a cause for concern, is it not? We believed it to be sufficient reason for further involvement."

"You've known about humans for a while then." Whereas we have only just learned about their existence.

"That is so," Milo confirms. "We have been familiar with you since the time you were all living on a single planet. We have watched you with great interest, always through the proper channels, of course."

What the To consider to be proper channels is a mystery not only to myself, I suspect, but to humanity in general. But I'm sure the Satori have already been asking questions, and I have no idea what might offend my alien companion. Better to leave our conversation on a positive note. "I appreciate you deciding to get involved at this time." I don't know how the wormhole issue will be resolved, but I do know that without the To, I wouldn't have ever received any news from home.

There is a pause while the robot stares glassily at me. "Thank you for your appreciation," it finally says. "We are happy to have met you. Your young family member was very excited when she learned of your presence on this planet."

With that, it rolls back into the crowd, and Ereni immediately approaches me. She'd obviously been keeping an eye on the interaction. "I want to know everything that robot said to you," she says without preamble.

I fill her in without delay.

CHAPTER 15

Soon after we return to Seji from the party, Diantha asks me to come to her residence for dinner. "Certainly," I message her. "I'll just check with Ereni and see if she wants to walk over together."

Diantha messages back right away. "No, just come yourself." She provides no explanation.

I walk at a more rapid pace than usual, wondering why Diantha couldn't have invited Ereni too. I don't think I'll ever get used to the vagaries of their relationship. By the time I walk up two flights of stairs to Diantha's flat, I'm breathing heavily and almost wishing I hadn't agreed to come.

When I knock on the door, it immediately opens and Theckla comes barreling out, throwing her arms around me so hard I stumble a few paces backwards. "Sienna!" she says with enthusiasm. I think this is the first time I've heard her use my name.

"Hello, Theckla," I say to the top of her head. "How are you doing?"

She doesn't answer me, instead opting to run back into the flat. I follow, closing the door behind me. The room I enter is cozy, with colorful curtains already drawn even though it isn't yet dark, several lamps with multi-colored shades lighting the space. Diantha is standing in the kitchen area off to one side, doing some last-minute chopping. Theckla points to a round table in one corner, already set with utensils and purple cloth napkins. "I did that," she tells me solemnly.

"Welcome, Sienna." Diantha doesn't cease her chopping. "I'm so glad you could come. Theckla has been looking forward to seeing you again, haven't you, Theckla?"

"I have to finish my math practice first." Theckla giggles and runs down a short hall and out of view. Diantha sighs and sets down her knife. "Can I get you something to drink?" she asks.

"Whatever you're having."

She takes a bottle of bright red liquid and pours some into a clear goblet. "This is Theckla's favorite Satori beverage."

I take a sip of the sweet liquid and look around the space. I recognize a few of the handmade rugs on the floor, and Theckla's inexpert artwork has once again been tacked on one of the walls. A large Satori seascape painting dominates another wall. Diantha notices me looking at it. "My one nod to being an adult here," she says with a rueful laugh. "Theckla was very dubious about it at first, but she told me last week that she guesses it's okay."

I glance towards the hallway. "How is she doing?" I ask in a lower voice.

"She's made two friends at her crèche, thank goodness, which is making things much easier for everyone." Diantha glances down the hallway herself. "But there are still difficulties."

"Is she homesick?" I feel real sympathy for the little girl, being relocated so far from the only world she'd known. If I'd found it hard at age seventeen, how much harder would it be at age seven?

"She was at first," Diantha admits, wiping her hands on a towel. "But she is proving to be remarkably resilient."

I hear singing from the other room. "She doesn't seem unhappy," I venture.

Diantha sighs again and drops into one of the chairs around the table. "The children still tease her for having a mother," she says. "The new friends have helped, but the children still find Theckla odd.

They don't understand why she doesn't stay with them all the time. And she misses out on so much of the social time the other children spend together."

"That doesn't sound easy." I join her at the table, still sipping my juice.

"No. And the adults are even worse. They call me in almost every week to discuss their concerns about Theckla, which is really just a thinly disguised attempt to pressure me into having her stay at the crèche full time. They don't even want me to have special visiting rights! If I do as they say, I might only see Theckla a couple times a year." Her face crumples, and she puts her head in her hands for a long moment before looking back up. "I apologize. They are constantly telling me how selfish I'm being, how Theckla will be so much better off adhering to the normal Satori upbringing now that she's home. And maybe they're right. Maybe I am being selfish. I honestly don't know."

She looks at me entreatingly, and suddenly I understand why she asked me to come over instead of Ereni. She could never have this conversation with the daughter who did have a normal Satori upbringing. It would be a cruel and unthinking thing to do. But me, on the other hand…I've known what it is to have a family more in the style of the relationship she has with Theckla.

"Have you asked Theckla what she wants?" I ask.

She looks down at her hands. "I have. So far, she's been very clear that she wants to stay here with me. She had a great time spending the night at the crèche when we went to meet your fellow Neopolitans in Jundo, but she wouldn't let me out of her sight the next day."

"Then I think you have your answer," I tell her. "It's not going to be perfect, and things that are different sometimes make people uncomfortable." I think of my own lack of N-CAT. I can't imagine not feeling the need to be defensive about it. "But if Theckla wants to stay with you, I think that should hold a greater weight. Someday when she's older, she might change her mind. But tearing a child away from their family when that's not what they want…." I shudder at the thought. "Sanctum might be backwards in a lot of ways, but even so, most people there wouldn't support such a course of action except in extreme circumstances."

She gives me a wan smile. "Every society has its strengths and weaknesses," she says. "Even Sanctum. I hope you know that we don't expect you to hate your home."

I shake my head, trying to sort through my own confusion. "I don't hate my home," I say slowly. "I hate a lot of the ways we think at home and a lot of the things we do. But that doesn't mean we're all bad. It can't mean we're all bad or there's no hope for me either."

"Your mission group did a real number on you, didn't they?"

"They actually lodged a complaint against me with the Superior Mission Council," I tell her. "I haven't heard anything since the initial hearing, so I have no idea how it will be resolved." I keep waiting for some official communication, but thus far there has only been resounding silence.

She rolls her eyes. "Who knew Irisa would be so vindictive. I know she feels terrible about the mission's failure under her watch, but a formal complaint isn't going to solve anything." Diantha gets up, grabs a towel, and pulls a large dish out of the oven. Her N-CAT must have informed her when the food was ready. Delicious smells waft from the dish, and I suddenly realize how hungry I am. "Theckla, dinner is ready!"

During the meal, talk turns to Theckla-related matters. She and I discuss the pleasures of Akari Park at length, and she mentions her upcoming boating lessons with real excitement. From time to time, I catch Diantha watching Theckla while she talks, a small smile playing around the corners of her mouth. A mother's relationship with her child is such a given on my world—however troubled such a relationship might sometimes be—but I realize that here, it is in its own way as subversive as my desire to race speeder bikes as a woman had been on Sanctum. The Satori are a bit more tolerant of difference than my fellow country people had been. But Diantha is testing the limits of that tolerance right now.

When I finally get up to leave after enjoying a piece of delicious spice cake Theckla helped to bake, I'm glad I came. "I want to try more of your baking experiments," I tell Theckla at the door.

"You're always welcome here," Diantha tells me. "Come again soon."

Theckla gives me another vigorous hug. "I'm going to make you your very own picture," she tells me with enthusiasm.

"But not tonight," Diantha intercedes. "It's almost time for bed."

Theckla runs off at this statement, whether from a desire to start on her art regardless of her mother's wishes or to get some last-minute energy out of her system, I'm not sure. "Thank you," Diantha says quietly. "It's good to talk to someone who understands."

We share a moment of eye contact. "Yes, it really is," I finally say. We clasp hands, and I leave her home feeling like I have a new friend.

A FEW DAYS LATER, Kuusta and I go on our second speeder bike expedition. This time we decide to venture further, choosing as our destination a small island where other people actually live. Ereni has told us it's an arts colony where a group of serious glassblowers practice their craft, uninterrupted by the distractions of the city. I marvel at the freedom of choice the existence of this island implies. Leo would have thrived here, free to pursue his mask making with the full support and approbation of society. In comparison, I almost feel like that scope of freedom is wasted on me.

We speed across the water, my fear much reduced given our successful first attempt. I haven't started to learn to swim, in spite of Burke's repeated encouragement, but I feel confident in the life preserver around my torso. And even more, I believe in my piloting abilities.

Kuusta keeps pace with me, and we fly side by side. I've pulled up a map on my console, and I navigate towards the island I've marked. Once we're out in the open water, we push our speed to the max, the wind rushing through my hair. My cheeks feel numb from the chill, but I never want to stop.

I'm disappointed by how quickly we arrive at our destination, but I dutifully slow my speed and ride my bike up the beach and onto a paved area where a few other bikes are parked. Kuusta follows my lead. "That felt like no time at all," he says as he removes his life vest.

"I'm not even tired," I reply. I place my life vest and helmet in a bag attached to the bike. Burke has assured me no one will steal them, which still feels strange to me. But I suppose on a world in which you can decide to devote your life to art and move to a beautiful little island at will in order to do so, there wouldn't be any need to resort to thievery.

There's no one else on the beach, but once we walk further into the settlement, we see several artists hard at work in studios that are open to the air. When I look more closely, I see they have retractable walls so they're still comfortable in inclement weather. We stop to watch the first artist at work as she blows a glass object, turning it carefully in the fire. Eventually it becomes clear she is making some kind of large vase.

We slowly walk down the row of studios. In addition to the glassblowers, we see a mosaic artist hard at work placing pieces of glass onto a large wooden board and another artist shaping wire as he creates jewelry that incorporates glass objects.

We stop in front of the jewelry maker, who doesn't give us a second glance. "What do you think of Satori so far?" Kuusta asks in an undertone.

"Sometimes it seems like they have everything figured out," I admit. "It makes me feel like maybe they were right to look down on me for being from Sanctum."

Kuusta snorts. "There's an important distinction between acknowledging difference and ways to do things better and being sanctimonious about it."

"That's easy for you to say. You're from Arbor, a planet they respect. It's not really so different than it is here. Wise Ones aside."

"Do you have any idea what you're going to do?" Kuusta asks. "I've applied for the next semester at the university in Seji. My understanding is that all applicants are automatically accepted, which, I will point out, is both unlike the way we do things on Arbor and probably preferable. We are none of us perfect."

I know he's trying to make me feel better, but he's never been to

Sanctum. He can't really understand. Sanctum will shape my view of the universe, for better or for worse, for the rest of my life.

"What will you study?"

I expect him to say politics or economics, but he surprises me when he says, "History."

"History?" I almost ask why he'd bother to study that before remembering to hold my tongue. But he seems to sense the incredulity behind my question.

"Yes, history," he repeats. "I want to understand why things are the way they are. What forces are important, which seem important but are actually insignificant. I want to know what we've seen repeat over and over again, and what we've been able to learn from. The university in Seji has a strong history program that involves cross-study in cultural anthropology and the Satori's accumulated knowledge from other human-settled planets. I can't think of a better use of my time."

He speaks with a passion I recognize from back on Arbor when he would give public addresses as an Arbor representative. I've known he feels strongly about both public service and dirt bike racing, but his love of history is something new to me. "Did you study history back home?"

"A bit. Not as much as I wanted. History scholars on Arbor really only had the choice of studying Arborist history or ancient history. There was one course giving an overview of the history of other human-habited planets in our sector. Only one course! The level of scholarship I can pursue here is of another order entirely. And here there's no pressure to go after a clear path to utility and fame in order to secure a Second Life. I am free to follow my heart."

That Kuusta would have chosen a different career path if it hadn't been for the existence of Second Life had never crossed my mind, but it makes sense. That feeling of restriction had been part of why my friend Pilvi had been so adamant that Second Life should be available to everyone on Arbor instead of the few lucky ones. "Do you regret losing your chance at Second Life?" I ask him curiously.

"Earning my Second Life has been a focus for me ever since I can remember," he tells me. The jewelry maker strings a large black bead, which I assume is made of glass, onto the necklace he's creating. "I have always tried to push my achievement levels with that end in mind, even as a small child. But now I've utterly and completely failed to achieve that goal." He shrugs. "I have to admit, it's surprisingly liberating."

"It probably doesn't hurt that the Satori have unlocked the secret to a much longer human lifespan themselves," I point out. "And one that doesn't require transformation into another physical form."

"Yes and no," he says. "I can see how it would seem that the chief allure to Second Life is the extended lifespan, but becoming a Wise One is about a lot more than that. I wanted to be chosen to transcend humanity, not simply live a longer life. To be connected in such an intimate way with my fellows...." His voice trails off. "It's not that I don't mourn the loss of my guiding motivation in life. It's that any such dream comes with an intense pressure. It is the pressure I don't miss."

This I can understand. I don't miss the reality of my life in Neopolitan as the daughter of an eminent and wealthy politician, but I have sometimes missed the fairy tale fantasy of it all. I'd grown up with very little choice, limitations I'd chafed against constantly. But with little choice comes little responsibility, along with the sense that others will take care of you for the rest of your life. Even when I'd left Sanctum, the Satori had provided me with the goal of becoming a member of their mission. Now that I can do whatever I wish, with no specific path laid out in front of me, I have no idea what I should actually do.

Instead, I drift through my days, exploring Seji, practicing my Kensho, spending time with Burke, getting to know Novelle and Allegra. I've been looking into wormholes in a desultory fashion. But I don't have a clear goal in mind, not like Kuusta's plan to continue his education.

As if he can read my thoughts, Kuusta asks, "What about you, Sienna? What are your plans? We've been here long enough to get our bearings, and your Kensho has become quite good." He grimaces. "Much better than mine."

I don't want to admit I have no idea what I'm doing. He's right;

we've been here long enough to make some decisions. The fact that I'm so utterly lost isn't one I want to admit, not even to a friend. "I've been learning more about the new wormhole technology," I say brightly. Perhaps I can distract him from his original question. "It's not an instantaneous process, you know. It takes some time to create a new node in the wormhole network. And not only time, but a rather large amount of energy as well. Aside from the problem of correctly gauging the location of the wormhole opening, the process needs to be carefully harnessed in order to avoid any damage to surrounding space time."

"What does that mean?" Kuusta asks.

I shrug. "The technical aspects are beyond my current knowledge, but that's what both the Satori and the Doctrina scientists say. After studying it at some length, I do think it makes the most sense for the Satori to be actively expanding the network. They'll be able to do so in a safe and responsible manner. We don't want surprise wormholes popping up all over the universe without the permission of a system's inhabitants, let alone destroying entire planets or moons."

"I don't disagree," Kuusta says, "but even if the Satori take on such a massive endeavor, it won't stop whoever is already out there from creating wormholes as they please."

"No, but it will establish a baseline and set of best practices about how such a process ought to be carried out." I warm to my topic. "We don't know who is deploying the technology or why, but it's possible they will improve their own safety measures if the Satori develop and demonstrate a proven process. Besides, as more worlds learn of the existence of this technology, some of them will want to deploy it themselves. This will force neighboring worlds to cooperate on an entirely new issue, and more powerful worlds will do their best to assert their will over the future of their systems. We have an obligation to at least try to ensure all involved worlds have the proper information to know what decision they're making."

"You said we," Kuusta observes. "You're thinking of yourself as one of the Satori."

I immediately feel silly. "Well, I'm not. And they'll never let me forget it."

Kuusta begins walking away from the jeweler still hard at work, and I follow him. "I didn't mean that as a criticism," he says. "We're going to have to adjust one way or another, now that we're here. That doesn't mean we have to change everything about ourselves, but it's good for us to feel like we're a part of something."

I think about what he's said as we stroll past the last few studios. I tried so hard to feel part of the Satori mission on Arbor, I'm hesitant to take another risk that might end in disappointment. But I can't pretend that I don't care about the wormholes. And I'm indelibly tied to the Satori through my connection with Burke and Ereni.

"I can still do good work even if I'm not a Satori," I finally say.

"I don't think that's in question," Kuusta replies. "It's just a matter of what kind of work you'd like to undertake." He says it as if knowing the answer should be easy.

"It's frustrating that the Satori themselves don't see how important this moment is." We've reached the end of the line of studios, but we continue walking to the edge of the bluff, where we have a view of the sea. "Here we are in the middle of an important election of Councilors who will work and decide on these sorts of policy questions, and not a single Seji candidate has made a strong statement in support of developing and expanding the wormhole network. It's as if it's either completely inconsequential or not even happening at all. Lyra"—I frown at her name—"gave an interview a few days ago where she was asked a question about the mysterious wormhole. She giggled and said we should leave it in the hands of the scientists before turning it into a question of practicing diplomacy with the To. I understand that humanity making our first contact with an intelligent alien species is deeply important, but that doesn't mean the wormholes don't matter. Besides, they're the reason the To are here in the first place. If we refuse to engage, won't that impact our ongoing diplomatic efforts with them?" I stamp in frustration. "But I'm just an uneducated girl from Sanctum, so what do I know about anything?"

Kuusta gives me an amused look. "It sounds like you've found something important to you," he observes. "And it's not as if you're on Sanctum anymore. So what are you going to do about it?"

As if anyone on Satori would ever listen to me. It's not as if I have the technical expertise to help develop protocols. All I have is the willingness to work hard and a stubborn spirit.

And my friends. "Ereni should run for Councilor," I say in a sudden burst of inspiration. "The Satori might find excuses to ignore me, but they'll listen to her." I know it's a wild idea, but when I say it out loud, I find myself warming to it.

"She's a bit young," Kuusta says. "And wasn't she ejected from your mission in disgrace just like you were?"

"That simply shows how principled she is," I say. "Although if the Satori have a penchant for electing leaders who are at least three hundred years old, that might be a problem."

Kuusta and I both pull out our qualpads, but from a cursory search, it looks like the Satori have elected leaders of all ages. "And you know how charismatic Ereni is," I tell Kuusta.

He makes a face. "I know *you* think she has a certain presence. But you're not exactly the average Satori voter."

"It's not just me," I say. "Look at the importance of her assignment on Sanctum. Ereni's problem is that she tends to be overconfident. But in a political campaign, I don't know if that's much of a drawback. In fact, it's probably an asset. No one will vote for someone who doesn't seem confident."

"As a former candidate myself, that sounds right." Kuusta laughs before descending back into seriousness. "But we don't know anything about Satori elections, Sienna. We have no idea what's important and what isn't."

I refuse to be dissuaded from my new idea. "But Ereni does," I say. "I'm not saying I want to be her campaign manager. I just want to persuade her to apply for the job."

"She'll say no," Kuusta says. "She'd have to be out of touch not to."

But I've made up my mind. It's Ereni's decision, of course, and I'll abide by whatever she says. But I'd be remiss for not suggesting it.

After all, that's what friends are for.

CHAPTER 16

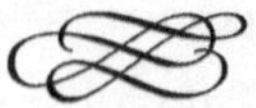

*E*reni says no.

In a calculated move, I make the suggestion while the two of us are spending time with Evander, who seems to be enthusiastic about everything. Granted, he doesn't seem to be particularly discerning, but I'll take any support I can get.

We're sitting on an outdoor patio, the open air above our heads strung with colorful papier-mâché sculptures hanging from wires. Evander has insisted I try a special kind of cheesy pastry for which Seji is famous, and I wait until Ereni has finished hers before suggesting she run for office. Evander immediately claps his hands and looks as excited as I was hoping, but Ereni remains cool and collected.

"I'm flattered you think I could do it," she says, smoothing her hair down as though someone might be watching us. "But I've returned so recently. No one would think I can have an accurate pulse of what the Satori community is wanting in this moment. I wouldn't be a serious candidate."

"You've been doing nothing but catching up since we arrived," I argue. "And it's not as if you lack connections. Every day you're meeting some old friend I've never heard of."

Ereni is markedly different from Burke in this respect. Burke has a few old friends, including Lyra and Evander, but Ereni seems to know everyone. She flits from person to person and from invitation to invitation. She reminds me of my Tio Roberto, Gianna's father: the foremost politician in Napoleon until his murder.

"She does have a point, Ereni," Evander chimes in, and I give him a warm smile.

"And you've been saying the Satori have become out of touch," I remind her. "Who better to remind them of who they are?"

She makes an exasperated sound. "That's exactly my point. If I think they're out of touch, I'm the last person who should run to represent them. Clearly I don't sufficiently understand their perspectives."

"Well, what better way to learn than through a campaign?" I don't want to let this idea go. "You'll never be able to persuade them of the importance of the wormhole technology if you don't understand them."

Ereni pauses, and for a moment, I think she might be seriously considering it. But then she shakes her head. "It's out of the question." There's not a hint of uncertainty in her voice. "I could consider such a thing in ten years or so, once I'm well established on Satori again. If I choose to stay that long. But not this cycle."

"Wise, wise," Evander murmurs, and I look over at him with annoyance. He is not being as staunch a supporter of my idea as I'd hoped. "It would be difficult to beat Lyra in any case. She's remarkably well connected."

I stab my pastry with my fork. "Then what's your bright idea for convincing the Satori that it's imperative to create a wormhole here in their home system? That we need to be further tied to the rest of the universe if we want to help humanity through the transition of this new technology?"

Ereni eyes me before saying, "I don't have any plan. We can't control everything, Sienna. I'm still figuring out what I want to do next." She must notice the distress on my face because she reaches out and puts a hand on mine. "You know I'll do whatever I can to help your niece. But I don't get the impression she's here primarily to advocate for Sanctum concerning wormhole policy. I think she was looking for a means of escape, and she was lucky enough to find it."

I pause. "You know this isn't about Sanctum," I tell her. "When the human diaspora is suddenly so much closer to one another, everything will change, for better or for worse."

"We'll be pushing to make things better," Ereni says. "But I don't think me running for office right now is the way to accomplish that. We should take some time and figure out a game plan."

"I suggest you discuss this with Lyra," Evander says. "I know she can be a bit…off-putting at times, but she isn't entirely unreasonable. She might not know very much about the topic, which means she could prove to be persuadable. And it's not as if she's a stranger."

Ereni sighs. "That's not a bad idea," she agrees. "We can arrange a meeting and make sure Novelle and Allegra are there as well. She probably hasn't had a chance to talk with any of the delegates who have been directly impacted by the new wormhole. They could offer her a new perspective."

Evander beams. "I'll help you set it up," he says. "I know just how to get Lyra to agree."

I still think it would be better for Ereni to run herself, but I suppose if we're able to persuade Lyra to our point of view, that would be simpler. "I'm sure Novelle and Allegra would be willing."

"That's our plan then." Ereni leans back in her chair and closes her eyes. "In the meantime, I know I should go ahead and accept one of the policy positions I've been offered."

"Too many opportunities," Evander jokes. "A good problem to have."

"What's holding you back?" I ask.

"My hubris has been my downfall," she says with a little laugh. "I'm trying to compensate by carefully weighing my decision this time around. Perhaps that can be a start towards mending my bad habits."

I can't imagine the Ereni I'd met back on Sanctum ever admitting to having bad habits. It makes her seem more human. "I saw Diantha the other day," I say casually. "And Theckla."

I watch her closely to observe her reaction, but she doesn't open her eyes. "That's nice. How are they doing?"

"Theckla is beginning to adjust to her new circumstances." I don't want to talk to Ereni about the troubles Diantha is having in that regard. "She's learning to swim and sail, and she's made a few friends."

A small smile plays around the corners of Ereni's mouth. "That sounds about right."

"Do you mind?" I blurt out the words before I can think better of them. "That Diantha is raising Theckla herself?"

Ereni does open her eyes at this rather intrusive question, and she and Evander exchange a knowing look. "Not particularly," she says. "I have to admit, it was a bit of a shock to learn what Diantha was doing on Zamavat. You have to understand what an unusual decision it is for a Satori to bear and raise their own child. I can't imagine what her colleagues must have thought. But now that I've grown used to the idea, I'm fine with it."

"But she's your mother," I say softly. "And she chose to have you raised in a crèche, but she's raising your sister herself."

"Are you imagining yourself in my place?" Ereni asks. "Would that be considered an upsetting scenario on Sanctum?"

"Yes." It doesn't bear thinking about it.

"But you do understand that here on Satori, it's entirely different?" Her question is not unkind. She's cocking her head, focused intently on me. "I know your own mother's behavior was not all that could be hoped for by Sanctum standards. But I've never seen Diantha in that kind of role. She didn't make an exceptional choice in having me raised in a crèche. Almost every child here is raised in that manner. It is a thoroughly normal and boring thing to happen. It was nothing personal about me. She would have been notified when her egg was successfully fertilized, but she might not have given it much thought for years after that. I certainly didn't think about her. And when our paths did cross, we knew we were biologically related, but it honestly didn't matter to me. I don't think it did to her either."

"But isn't everything different now?" I ask, trying to understand.

"Maybe for her," she replies. "I don't know how she feels. But it's not different for me. I never felt like I wanted for anything as a child. I always had the love and attention I needed. I'm still in touch with my favorite of our crèche carers. I didn't expect they'd still be alive upon our return, but I'm delighted they are." She interlocks her fingers, tapping them against one another. "It's important for you to understand that I don't feel like I've been treated poorly. If anything, after observing societies with strong familial structures like Sanctum and Arbor, I feel lucky. On Sanctum, if your family happens to be difficult or cruel, you have very little recourse. That was your experience, wasn't it?" I push at my pastry. "I never had to worry about anything like that. That could never happen here."

Evander is nodding. "That's right. We developed the crèche system for a reason. Not to say there's anything wrong with other ways of doing it," he adds hastily. "We just found something that works well for us."

I think about what they're saying. It's still difficult for me to understand, but I can't argue that Ereni received a better outcome from growing up in a crèche than I did growing up with my family, even as wealthy as they had been.

"I support Diantha's choice," Ereni continues. "And I can't imagine making it myself. Unlike on Arbor, there aren't the same support structures in place for someone who wants to raise their own child here. That will make things more difficult for her. But I support her." She pushes back her hair. "If I'm being honest, I'm just so relieved we're back on Satori at all. There was a time when I thought we'd be stuck on Zamavat for the long term. I know Diantha had something to do with how things worked out for us, and I'm grateful to her, as I would be to any older colleague who went out of her way to help me."

"So you wouldn't mind if I went to visit Diantha and Theckla from time to time?" I ask.

She gives me a mystified look. "Mind? Why would I mind? By all means, you should go visit them if you'd enjoy that. I imagine it would be good for Theckla to be around someone else who doesn't fit into the Satori status quo."

"Now why don't you actually try that pastry you've been defacing?" Evander says with a laugh. "I promise you, it's delicious."

After taking my first bite, I can't argue with him.

IN SPITE OF MY RESISTANCE, Burke continues to insist I learn to swim, and eventually I capitulate. I know he's looking out for my safety, and I want to continue riding the Satori speeder bike over the water. While I think my life preserver is sufficient, I can't fault Burke for his concern.

Accordingly, I find myself at the beach with Burke, dressed in one of the more modest Satori bathing costumes. I still feel like I'm baring a shocking amount of flesh, the small flared skirt scarcely covering my bottom and the back plunging in surprisingly daring fashion, but at least it is all one piece, unlike one of Ereni's bathing costumes. The sun beats down on us, and I'm glad for the sunglasses I remembered to bring.

We both smell faintly sweet from the sun protection Burke has insisted we wear. Burke is wearing a similar costume that zips up the front, covering his chest while accentuating the breadth of his shoulders. It is rather revealing in the groin area, and I blush and look away, adjusting my own costume.

Now that we're here, I feel a strong resistance to walking into the ocean. Burke takes my hand and leads me to the edge of the surf. The water is a deep blue capped with white, and a few Satori are playing further out. Two small groups are spending time on the beach, laying out on colorful towels, but the area isn't very crowded. The sand feels hot under my bare feet, uncomfortable but not burning, and I can feel its tiny grains rubbing between my toes.

I stand just out of reach of the water, staring at it with uncertainty. The waves lap in and out several times as I watch, making strange crashing sounds. The violence of it alarms me, even though the Satori in the water seem undisturbed. Eventually Burke steps forward and allows the water to rush over his feet.

"See?" He looks over his shoulder at me. "It doesn't hurt. And it's nice and cool."

I sigh and step up beside him, allowing the water to engulf my own feet. He's right; the water feels refreshing on such a warm day.

My feet sink in the sand, and I curl my toes at the unfamiliar sensation. I allow the waves to gently rock me several times.

"Ready?" Burke holds out his hand, and I take it. Together we take several steps forward until the water is up to our knees. My grip tightens as the waves crash into my legs, but the force is relatively gentle. Burke has told me this beach is known for good swimming for that reason.

He leads me deeper into the ocean, slowly and steadily. Whenever I experience a second of panic, I look over at him. He's always watching me with a care I find reassuring. Burke isn't going to let me drown on his watch.

Once the water reaches our shoulders, Burke teaches me to float, holding me as I bob up and down with the waves. I find it surprisingly easy to relax with the reassuring touch of his hand on my back. I let the water buoy me up, and for a time it's almost as if I live in another world, one delineated by the heat of the sun, the embrace of the water, and the steady roar of the surf. I can see why Burke loves it out here; it feels like we're removed from our normal life.

When I finally come out of my float, I'm grinning, and I don't care what my wet hair looks like or whether my bathing costume is showing too much skin. I'm simply happy to be here, in the water and with Burke. He smiles at me before leaning down for a kiss. His lips are salty, and I know mine are too, but I continue the kiss anyway. The water rushes back and forth against us as we lose ourselves in each other.

Finally, Burke pulls away with a laugh. "Let me show you how to tread water," he tells me. "It will be easier if we go a bit deeper."

He indicates that I should grab hold of his back, and he swims out, towing me along as easily as if I weighed nothing at all. When he stops, I look back the way we've come. The shore looks further away than I would have guessed.

"If anything happens when you're taking out a speeder bike and you end up in the water," he says, "your life jacket should keep you floating. But I want to show you what movements to make with your body to keep you floating even without the jacket. Look at what I'm doing right now and try to copy me."

I balance on my tiptoes on the ocean floor, and as I watch him move his arms in seemingly random patterns, I suddenly feel almost unbearably fond of him. He's been swimming since he was old enough to walk, but here he is giving up his day so I can learn as well. I gyrate my arms and legs like he's doing, although since I'm able to touch the sand with my feet, it's hard to tell how effective my efforts are. But Burke beams at me as if I'm the cleverest new swimmer he's ever seen.

"Keep going," he encourages me. "You're doing great."

All this motion of my limbs makes me tire surprisingly quickly. I haven't been exercising as much since leaving Arbor, not without a goal to motivate me. But if I want to become a decent swimmer, I'm going to have to practice in much the same way I did to become a better dirt bike rider.

Burke tows me further out into the ocean until I can't touch the bottom. I let go of him reluctantly and begin my treading practice once more. I haven't practiced long before a sudden bump against my ankle makes me momentarily panic. "What was that?" I look down into the water, trying to see. I look back up at Burke, who is definitely too far away to have accidentally hit me with his own feet. "Something touched my foot," I tell him.

Before he has time to respond, I feel a bump against my other calf. "What is that?" I can't ignore the fear rising in my throat.

A large creature suddenly bursts out of the water between Burke and I, chittering excitedly. It is a sleek blue-gray, with bright, intelligent eyes, a narrow snout, and a dorsal fin. "A dolphin!" Burke exclaims. He doesn't sound frightened. "Hello there," he says directly to the dolphin. "It's a fine day for swimming, isn't it?"

The dolphin chirps its agreement.

"This is my friend's first time in the ocean," Burke continues. "She is learning to swim."

The dolphin swims in a circle around us before suddenly taking off across the water. "I take it dolphins are friendly?" I ask weakly.

"Very." Burke has a wide smile on his face. "I'm sorry it startled you. It was just curious about us. The Satori would consider it a lucky sign that you met a dolphin."

"Is it common?" I ask. "And when you were talking to it, did it understand what you were saying?"

"There's a large pod that lives in these waters at this time of year," Burke says. "And yes, it understood. Or at least, it understood in part. It's never been entirely clear exactly how precise an understanding the dolphins have. They don't care about the same things that we do, you see. They've made it clear they think we are very silly to live lifestyles that don't allow for the volume of freedom and play they enjoy."

"I see," I say, even though I don't think I do.

"We've lived in harmony for generations," Burke continues. "The original settlers from Earth brought frozen dolphin embryos in order to save the species, and since they've settled into Satori's oceans, they've evolved a bit."

I'm about to ask more when a dolphin zooms up beside me, followed closely by a second dolphin. "It's brought a friend," Burke says in delight. The first dolphin bumps him with its nose. "Would you like to learn to ride? That's obviously what it wants. I think it's excited this is your first time swimming. It usually only sees children who are learning."

"It wants me to…ride?" I can't help feeling taken aback. All my experience is with riding and driving mechanical vehicles, not living creatures. "Is that a good idea?"

"People do it all the time," Burke says. "Only when the dolphins offer, of course. But they tend to think it's great fun." He turns to the first dolphin. "You have to remember that Sienna doesn't know how to swim," he says sternly. "You'll keep her safe, won't you?"

The dolphin bobs in apparent agreement, turning its head to look at me expectantly. "I don't know how…."

In spite of my hesitation, or maybe because of it, the first dolphin swims right up to me and nudges me cheerfully in the chest. It swims around, presenting me with its smooth back. "You can use the dorsal fin to help you," Burke says. "Don't worry about hurting it, it's quite sturdy."

The dolphin swims back around to nudge me in the chest again.

"Okay, okay." Its obvious enthusiasm makes me laugh in spite of my nerves. "But let's go slow to start, okay?"

The dolphin chitters at me before again presenting its back. This time I clamber on, using the dorsal fin to pull myself into place. Before I'm quite ready, the dolphin begins to swim forward, and I throw my hands around it and hold on for dear life.

It takes me a moment to realize we're not actually going very fast. It only seems that way because of the adrenaline pumping through my veins. I look over to see Burke riding the other dolphin beside me. When he sees me looking, he lets out a whoop, and his dolphin starts swimming faster.

"We can't let him get the best of us, can we?" I murmur to my own dolphin. It bucks slightly in response before increasing its own pace. Burke's dolphin falls back beside us again, and I can tell Burke is keeping an eye on me, making sure I don't fall off.

Swimming with the dolphin is entirely different from anything I've experienced before. It's fast just like riding a speeder bike, but on the bike, I'm the one in control. This time I'm merely along for the ride, and swimming through the water is a completely different sensation from flying through the air. The dolphin keeps my head above the water—mostly—but there's nothing it can do to protect me from the spray.

The speed feels familiar, however. Once I realize I'm not about to abruptly slip off and have learned to gauge when I need to take a quick gulp of air, I begin to truly enjoy myself. This is a kind of abandon—and trust—I've never known before. Every aspect of my safety is in the control of the dolphin underneath me. As someone who clings to whatever vestiges of power I'm given, the need for me to hold on and trust a creature I've only just met is both terrifying and exhilarating.

When the dolphin finally pulls up, I fall off its back and remind myself to begin to tread. It takes me a moment to orient myself and realize we've returned close to our original starting point. Burke drops into the water beside me and swims over to take me in his arms. The two dolphins do a little dance across the waves before leaving us with two flips of their tails. "What did you think?" Burke sounds a little breathless.

"Did you know that was going to happen?"

He grins and shakes his head. "You never can tell when a dolphin will show up wanting to give you the time of your life." His smile fades as he searches my face. "Are you okay? It wasn't too much for you?"

I deliberately pause before giving into an earsplitting grin of my own. "When can we go again?"

CHAPTER 17

The meeting with Lyra takes place in a pleasant co-working space, bright morning light pouring through its tall windows. Lyra is there before us, and she opens the door to greet us, garbed in a spotless white outfit with no discernible seams. I wonder how she manages to keep it so clean.

Lyra has provided the Satori version of coffee and two boxes of muffins, which Novelle instantly dives for, Allegra looking on in amusement. I hang back with Ereni, watching Lyra coo sweetly at my niece and wondering if this was a good idea. Even though the room is huge, there is no one else present.

Lyra leads us to the back of the room, where a circle of comfortable chairs has been set up. As soon as I sit down, the structure of the chair encourages me to lean back, but I don't want to relax. I awkwardly perch on the edge, but my friends all make themselves comfortable.

"What a wonderful idea to set up this little meeting," Lyra is gushing to Ereni. "When Evander suggested it, I said yes right away. After all, who would have thought my beloved crèchemates would end up keeping such interesting company?"

Ereni looks poised even in these awful chairs, and I can't tell if Lyra's words have put her on edge the way they have me. I realize Lyra has taken the one normal chair, and my tension increases. But I keep my mouth firmly shut. It's clear Lyra doesn't have any respect for me, and I'd prefer for the meeting to go well.

"Novelle and Allegra, I'm eager to hear from both of you directly," Lyra continues.

Novelle looks guilty as she brushes muffin crumbs from her lap, but Allegra is ready. "We're very pleased to meet an old friend of Ereni," she begins. "We've come a very long way to ask the Satori for their assistance, and we're hoping you might be willing to advance our cause."

"I'm always happy to do what I can, of course," says Lyra, suddenly vague. "Do go on."

"We're hoping the Satori will be willing to investigate and help us discover who is responsible for creating the wormhole in our system," Novelle says. "But we understand this endeavor would probably necessitate the Satori creating a wormhole in your own system to facilitate the travel such an investigation would require."

Lyra sends a look toward Ereni that I can't interpret. "I think it's so brave that the two of you left your home and everything you've ever known to travel here," she says sweetly. "And without any support or mission team. It really is remarkable!"

Her lack of answer is lost on none of us. "I understand the idea of a wormhole in our system is still quite controversial," Ereni says. "But we're hoping you might espouse it during your campaign, and then hopefully continue to champion the cause going forward. What are your thoughts?"

"Well, it would certainly be a major change for us here on Satori, wouldn't it?" Lyra lets out a small, tinkling laugh, but nobody joins her. "I don't think we should get ahead of ourselves. Before we embark on such an irrevocable course of action, we need to do our due diligence. We would need to test the technology thoroughly ourselves, and then we'd need to engage in intensive dialogue about what exactly this change would mean, both to Satori society and to our mission work. I'm not saying we should never have our own wormhole, but I believe the decision-making process should be measured and deliberate. We mustn't be in any hurry, not for something this important. Now, in the fullness of time, would I support such a plan? It's possible."

"How exactly would you define the fullness of time?" I'm sure I'm not the only one who catches the edge in Allegra's voice.

"It's hard to say." I want to scream at Lyra's deliberate vagueness. "We need to act responsibly and ensure that every voice is heard before such a transformative decision could be made."

"That's Satori politician-speak for 'it's never going to happen,'" Ereni says. "We were hoping you might be persuaded by the urgency of the cause. These wormholes are already being created, and we don't know the extent of the issue."

"Well, the harm's already been done, hasn't it?" Lyra gives a graceful shrug. "I don't see any particular urgency now. The two of you"—she gestures to Novelle and Allegra—"are very welcome here, for however long you'd like to stay. And I know we're all eager to open more formal diplomatic relationships with the To. This is a truly historic time for the Satori. A thrilling time to be alive."

I can already tell Evander's idea to get Lyra on our side isn't going to pan out, but I can't give up so easily. "I can't help thinking the Satori mission to Sanctum might have played a part in the new wormhole appearing in the Promise B system. It seems like a big coincidence that it should have appeared soon after your visit. It's a big universe, after all, or so they tell me." Lyra doesn't smile at my attempt at a joke. "I wonder if the Satori somehow drew attention to the system through their presence there."

"I don't think we need to resort to wild conjecture," Lyra says. Her tone has shifted to be condescending. "Sometimes a coincidence is just that."

"We won't know until we look into it," Ereni argues. "The right thing to do is to start a proper investigation. But beyond that, we should be considering the greater implications. If the Satori don't have our own wormhole and several other systems do, we're going to be bypassed when it comes to making important decisions that affect all the connected systems. The Satori could step up and play a critical role in organizing the new status quo. Otherwise, the rest of the human diaspora will pass us by."

"I hardly think that's our responsibility, Ereni." Lyra gives her a patronizing smile. "When you've lived as long as I have, you begin to understand that we're not the center of everything. We should focus on our own problems."

"This might become one of your problems," I say quietly. "As long as we don't know who is creating these wormholes, you might get your own surprise wormhole right here."

"Nonsense." Lyra's voice sharpens. "That could never happen here." She turns her smile back on Novelle and Allegra. "I'm sorry there isn't more we can do right away," she says. "But I like to say that patience is a higher calling."

"I'm afraid our people on Sanctum don't have the luxury of patience," Novelle says. "They're having to deal with the ramifications of the wormhole as we speak. And they've been doing so for decades at this point. Who knows what challenges they might have already encountered?"

"And would your people be so quick to help the Satori, should our places be reversed?" We're all silent. Sanctum hadn't even wanted to send delegates to Satori, let alone have anything to do with any other planets, and we all know it. "That's what I thought." Lyra stands up. "It was a true pleasure to meet both of you," she says gaily. "Do let me know if there's anything I can do to help make your stay more pleasant."

The dismissal is clear, and the rest of us stand. Novelle and Allegra seem eager to leave, but Lyra holds Ereni back, and I linger behind.

"I'm surprised you're taking up the wormhole cause," Lyra says quietly. "A word of advice, my dear. The Unity and other aligned fringe groups aren't taken seriously here. Not by the people that matter. You would do better to steer clear and devote yourself to work that's actually useful."

"This isn't the first time you and I haven't seen eye to eye," Ereni replies. "But I appreciate the information."

"Any time." Lyra shrugs. "You've always been so independent. That's one of the things I've admired about you. You and Burke could both go on to do great things if you'd only learn to compromise."

"Is that why you're trying to mentor Burke? To help him learn to compromise?"

"I'm simply trying to be helpful, my dear, like I always am. I have a practical army of protégés at this stage of my life. And Burke is capable of so much if he ever decides to realize his potential."

"As long as you remember that's *his* decision," Ereni says.

"Well, he always has you to look after him, doesn't he?" Lyra notices me watching them and waves Ereni away. "Always a pleasure, Ereni. Have fun with your little…project."

Ereni doesn't rise to the bait, but she does give a huge sigh once we leave the building. "Lyra hasn't changed as much as I would have thought," she says. "Three hundred years and she's just as petty and bossy as she ever was."

Lyra isn't quite done with us. The next day, she publishes an opinion piece that is run by a popular local outlet, calling herself a champion of the Satori way of life. She writes against what she calls a growing movement of people embracing the traditional family structure from humanity's troubled past.

Burke, Ereni, and I discuss it over dinner. "She's just trying to get attention," Burke says. "Everyone knows it's vanishingly rare for Satori to opt out of the crèche system. This comes up every ten or twenty years, and it always blows over."

"It's certainly about attention," Ereni says. "And it's disgusting. I honestly wouldn't have thought she'd stoop to this kind of intolerant slop. She actually says that being off-planet for the length of a mission erodes the Satori identity."

"No one will take her seriously," Burke says, but he has a worried look on his face.

"I wouldn't be so sure about that," Ereni says flatly. "She clearly believes these positions will be popular with the public. And given what I'm seeing, she might be right. There's such a push right now for people to go on missions, given the population pressures. And this right here? This might be the backlash."

I stare down at my food, my appetite suddenly gone. Trying to acclimate to Satori, for all its positive points, has taken a toll on me. I haven't forgotten that most Satori, however unconsciously, think they're better than me. How I can fit in when that's the case is a problem that doesn't seem to have a solution.

And now it appears that the Satori are going to shove the entire delegation from my system into the shadows while trying to cozy up with the To. And if the To object, they'll simply pretend to be doing more than they are. In some ways, this place is no better than Sanctum."

"Don't worry." Ereni has a strange smile on her face, and I'm suddenly worried about what she's going to say next. "We're going to fight back."

"How?" My exasperation is getting the better of me. Just like Arbor, Satori appears to be plagued by its own unique set of problems. Humans, it seems, carry troubles wherever we go. Even genetically improved humans like the Satori. They might not resort to physical violence, but there are other ways of causing harm.

How can it be that I've now lived on four different planets, and I still don't feel like I belong anywhere?

Burke reaches out across the table and takes my hand. His skin is warm, and I let the reassuring pressure comfort me. "We'll figure something out," he says.

I take a few slow deep breaths. I may not belong to any one planet, but I do belong with my friends. With Burke and Ereni, with Diantha and Theckla, with my budding relationships with Novelle and Allegra, even with Kuusta. Things between us may not always be easy, but we keep finding our way back to one another.

"When I first met the two of you, I thought the Satori were these magical beings," I whisper. "You knew so many things that I thought I would never understand. I assumed you had all the answers if only I worked hard enough to learn them. It felt like there were light-years between us." I pause. "I wish I hadn't been so wrong."

Burke reaches out and puts his other hand on mine. "I think sometimes we like to believe we've solved all our problems. But we haven't. I don't know that we ever will. We just have to keep trying."

"That's exactly right," Ereni says. She puts her fork down with decision. "And that's why I'm going to challenge Lyra and run for office myself."

CHAPTER 18

The day of Ereni's campaign launch dawns bright and clear, with a small but vigorous breeze that she declares to be absolutely perfect.

I've been helping manage her calendar for the past few weeks: interviews, photo shoots, strategy and messaging meetings, and most importantly, individual conversations with a huge number of people: current and past elected officials, distinguished teachers and artists, subject matter experts. Anyone and everyone who might decide to contribute to the word of mouth around Ereni's campaign.

All our efforts will culminate today with the official launch, the first time Ereni will be speaking directly to the people she hopes to represent. In order to do so, she has insisted on throwing a traditional boat party, a decision I have spent considerable effort arguing against.

"People need to see you," I've told her. Repeatedly. "They need to be in the same room with you. They need to feel special, like you know who they are."

I feel like after watching my father campaign, and then Pilvi's father on Arbor, I know a thing or two about strategy.

But Ereni feels no qualms about ignoring me, and once I see the boat party for myself, I understand her point. Her party has taken over an entire docking area, all the boats attached to one another so people can roam at will from boat to boat. The various boat hosts have arranged for food and drink so the guests can explore, trying different treats and delicacies. As a result, everyone feels a certain sense of ownership over the event.

I allow myself to be swept into its ambiance: the slight bobbing of the deck underneath my feet, the briny smell mixing with the delicious smells of roasted protein, the muted roar as everyone talks at once. The boats have been decorated by their hosts: some boast colorful flags, while others feature wreaths of twinkling lights that I can tell will be enchanting once full darkness falls. Even now in the dusk, I can look down the row of boats and see various sculptures crafted from the lights. Down at the end, I think I see one representing a dolphin.

Whether from regret that his idea to reach out to Lyra backfired so stupendously or genuine support of Ereni, Evander is sponsoring his own boat for the party. His vessel is practically afire with lights, and I see him talking a mile a minute to several people while they savor the special truffles he ordered specially for this event. He sees me watching from the next boat over and gives a little waggle of his fingers, not missing a beat in his pitch.

I stay close to Ereni, who hops from boat to boat, chatting, trying the different snacks, accepting full glass after full glass. She looks like she's glowing from within, and even though I know her N-CAT is assisting her, it's impressive watching her work the crowd, addressing everyone by name and asking them questions about themselves. I can see people visibly leaning into her, as though attracted by her inner light. Maybe this idea of mine, that Ereni can run for office and *win*, isn't so absurd after all.

I'm hanging back as Ereni talks to a few people I don't remember when someone pokes me on the shoulder. I whirl, startled, only to see a familiar smile and hair decorated with yellow stripes. "Oh, Aeson, isn't it?" I summon up a polite smile.

I haven't seen the man since the night of the party where I met the To robot, and I can't help thinking I hadn't made the best impression on him. I'd completely forgotten him since then, but a detail from our first meeting emerges from my mind. "You are in favor of wormholes," I blurt out.

He gives me a mischievous smile. "I see you possess an excellent memory in addition to your refreshing candor."

I almost choke on my drink. "I'm so sorry—" I begin, but he interrupts me.

"Which has allowed me to help you," he says. He pulls a sheet of paper from his front pocket and hands it to me. "I printed it out since I hear you don't have an N-CAT."

I look from him to the paper in some confusion before unfolding it and taking a look. It is an official-looking document from the Superior Mission Council saying the complaint against me has been dismissed. I stare up at him, forcing myself to close my mouth. "You remembered?"

His grin widens. "I told you I had connections. And it really was the least I could do."

"I can't thank you enough." I look back down at the paper, overcome by relief. I've been busy with Ereni's campaign, but the worry of the complaint has remained lodged in the back of my mind. "How did you know you would find me here?"

He glances at Ereni, who is still speaking with her supporters behind me. "You mentioned Ereni when we met," he says. "I figured you would be here. And I'm supporting Ereni's bid for Councilor. It probably won't surprise you to learn that she and I have very similar opinions when it comes to wormholes, and I appreciate how she's been making that an issue in the campaign."

"You should meet her." I'm eager to help this person who has gone out of his way for me. "I can introduce you right now."

"She seems somewhat occupied at present," he says with an easy smile. "However, the Unity, the group I represent, would be pleased to have a private meeting with her. At your convenience, of course."

I pause. Perhaps his assistance on my behalf hasn't been so selfless after all. But on the other hand, how much harm can a meeting do? "I'll help you set something up," I tell him. "She'll be so pleased we don't have to worry about the Superior Mission Council anymore."

"Like I said, it was my pleasure." He appears to catch sight of someone beyond my shoulder because he presses my hand lightly before making his goodbyes. "We'll be in touch soon, I trust."

I can't help looking down one last time at the paper. One less obstacle for me to face.

Once it's full dark, Ereni makes her way to one of the largest boats, which has an area set up for her to speak, spotlights at the ready. While she will be speaking out loud, no amplification is necessary; she will broadcast through her N-CAT. Since all the Satori have N-CATs, I'm the only one who needs to be on this boat to hear her speech.

I wish Kuusta had opted to come so I wouldn't feel quite so alien without my N-CAT, but he graciously declined my invitation. "I've attended enough political events for one lifetime, I think," he'd told me. "And for this election, I don't even have a vote." And when I'd pressed him: "Heaven forbid I get bit by the political bug a second time around. No, I'm sitting this one out."

I can't blame him, but I still wish he were here. Burke is on another boat whose host is respected in political circles, wooing her into hopefully throwing her support behind Ereni.

Ereni stands tall, chin up, hair flowing loose down her back. There is a camera present to provide a visual feed through the N-CATs along with the audio. To me, Ereni looks like a star. She's wearing a floor-length silver dress with long sleeves that shimmers softly in the dark. But when the spotlight turns on her, the shimmer turns into a dazzling sparkle. She raises her hands over her head and holds them there, basking in the attention from everyone in the living mass of boats around us.

"Friends," she says, her voice perfectly modulated. She beams at the camera, all her considerable focus on this one task of persuasion. "What a beautiful evening for a party."

Cheers sound from the surrounding boats, and a few boats blink their lights on and off to indicate their excitement. Ereni lowers her arms and smiles engagingly at the camera.

"Now, I know when I first told many of you that I was going to be launching my bid for this Councilor position, you were surprised.

Shocked, even. Delia, I truly thought you were going to fall on the floor in disbelief." She pauses as laughter swells in the air. "I know I'm freshly back from serving on a mission, and I know I've been gone a long time. And I have to say, as I've been spending my time catching up on everything I've missed, I am so impressed by everything you have accomplished in my absence. I have never been so proud to be from Satori."

The wind picks up, and I shiver in my short sleeves. It feels like the future of Ereni's campaign depends on this moment.

Ereni shifts her tone. "I wanted to serve on a mission all my life, and I'm so happy to have realized that dream. Being far away from my home made me see clearly how truly special our values are and how far we've come in achieving our original vision, stretching all the way back from our original flight from Earth. And having caught up on all you've done, I've come to realize how much I'd like to offer my own service to the people of Satori, doing my part to ensure that we continue along the path we started to travel so long ago.

"To that end, I intend to strengthen our support of both mission programs and our research. The Satori should remain on the forefront of human progress in the sciences, the humanities, and the arts. And we should continue to excel in our mission of acting as a wide repository for human knowledge. I intend to be a champion for the unity through respectful difference that has characterized serious Satori thought since our arrival on this beautiful planet."

The crowd cheers.

"I'd like to stand firm in protecting Satori: our environment, our values, and our way of life. Because make no mistake, change is in the wind." As Ereni says the words, the wind picks up even more, her skirt swaying in its wake, her hair flowing away from her face. I whisper a small prayer that the direction doesn't shift, pushing her hair into her mouth.

"Humanity has discovered a new foundational technology—how to create wormholes and form them into a travel network—and the change that will arise from that fact is inevitable. We can either pretend not to recognize this fact, pushing our heads into the sand and hoping to ignore reality for as long as possible, or we can prepare. I want the Satori to be an integral part of shaping the future course of humanity. The truth is, we've been preparing for this moment for generation upon generation. Now is the time for us to show our integrity, our compassion, and our leadership as humanity grapples with a huge shift in our paradigm, and the universe becomes both a lot smaller and a lot more connected."

"Humanity will move on in its evolution with or without us," Ereni continues forcefully. "I say let's not only be a part of that change, let's help shape it as only the Satori can do."

A chill rolls down my spine at the implied power in Ereni's statement. Even if the Satori choose to get further involved, that doesn't guarantee a positive outcome. I know as well as anyone that the Satori have flaws.

But as I stare at Ereni's face, bright in the spotlight, I know nothing as groundbreaking as this new technology could ever be simple and straightforward. And the Satori are not a united front; they have differing viewpoints and expectations and values, just as the people on Sanctum did. I can't wish for them to exclude themselves from this matter because they're as flawed as everyone else.

Whether we like it or not, all the human-settled planets are in this together.

ERENI'S CAMPAIGN launch is considered a grand success by Satori standards. People keep comparing her to an old firebrand politician, 'Evangeline the Erudite,' from almost five hundred years ago. Ereni leans into the compliment. She begins to wear bright red lipstick and dress in oversized jackets just like Evangeline did. She has her nails done with little stars that glow in the dark to symbolize that she is the candidate in favor of opening the universe. She does not, however, cut her hair short as Evangeline's had been, which I find reassuring. Ereni can market herself all she wants, but I don't want her to entirely reinvent herself.

I do what I can to help her, but I can't help feeling like this campaign has taken on a life of its own. It suddenly seems like everyone is talking about Ereni, wanting to meet Ereni, inviting Ereni to every event imaginable. Her calendar, which I manage, is full to bursting with everything from meet-and-greets to elaborate galas celebrating various disciplines, institutions, and individuals. It seems like Satori is actually one never-ending celebration of what they're able to achieve with the freedom they've achieved.

I can't say I blame them. But my own lack of purpose stands in stark contrast to all the success they seem to take for granted. I can't help thinking many of the Satori seem to be more enchanted by the vision of Ereni as a trailblazer of the universe rather than serious proponents of the ideas she's espousing.

The longer I spend time on Satori and the more people I meet, I notice that some of the Satori who have chosen to stay on their home world seem a bit different than their counterparts who opt to go on missions to other planets.

In a word, they seem…decadent.

It's not as if my own lifestyle in San Marco as the daughter of a leading Senator hadn't been luxurious, but it isn't opulence I'm noticing now. Indeed, my surroundings in Neopolitan had been much more sumptuous than anything I've seen here on Satori. And it's not the easy Satori appreciation of pleasure either. Or at least, not just that.

It's more that they can take the ease of their lives for granted. They have never known hardship, nor can they imagine that they ever will. They have never had to sacrifice, not to get something they want and not to realize a higher ideal. They are content and healthy and educated and quick to laugh, and sometimes I sense a certain softness of character that makes me uneasy.

As much as I like Evander, he is a case in point. Everything seems to come easily to him, and his philosophy, as far as I can tell, is to do his best and not worry. It's innocuous enough, but it doesn't ring true with my own experiences. His steady calm is pleasant to be around in the chaos of the campaign, but I can't help thinking it's because he has nothing at stake.

I can't imagine bringing this up with Ereni, who is already run off her feet, or with Burke, who doesn't have a hint of such softness himself. But one day I do broach the subject with Novelle. As Ereni has been engulfed by her social obligations, I've been spending more and more time with Novelle and Allegra. There is something fundamentally comforting about speaking Gallo and being around people who understand where I've come from.

This evening Novelle and I visit an art show featuring several up-and-coming Satori artists. Novelle is an artist herself, taking after her father, although she doesn't make masks. Instead, she loves to paint. Already the walls of her room are covered with many small paintings —experiments, she calls them—and she has just been granted space to work in a nearby art studio. I've taken to inviting her to attend various art functions around Seji, welcoming an obvious way for us to bond.

Sometimes she reminds me so much of Leo that it physically hurts, a peculiar ache in my upper chest that I almost welcome. Leo has receded so much from my awareness in the months following my departure, a loss in and of itself, and I like being more regularly reminded of him. I want my twin to continue to live, even if only in my own memory.

This latest art show is in a large warehouse-like space with lofted ceilings and simple design. It's clear that all that matters here is the art itself, displayed on the walls and on carefully placed plinths throughout the space. The lighting has been very deliberately done, and I can tell that whoever organized this event has an admirable eye for detail.

Novelle and I stand in front of a painting, taller than I am, of one of the famed racing yachts Burke has told me so much about. It is riveting in its accuracy and detail, the yacht captured mid-race. With its hydrofoil extended, it looks almost like it's flying through the air. Its sail appears to shimmer in the light, and the surrounding spray reminds me of my recent dolphin adventure in the ocean. "What do you think?" I ask.

Novelle shrugs. "It's technically impressive," she says. "That describes most of the art I've seen here."

"But you don't like it?" I prod.

She twists her mouth as she stares up at the painting. "It's not that

I don't like it," she finally says. "It's a good example of what it is. But it's hardly innovative, is it? I suppose it must mean more to the Satori who view it. I understand these races are an important cultural event."

"That's what Burke tells me." I look around the crowded space, wondering if there are any more of the cute little cakes I see some people eating, but Novelle tugs my arm and gestures towards another painting further down the wall. I temporarily give up my quest for cake to follow her to another canvas, this one depicting the vastness of space. It focuses on what I've learned is called a nebula, a gorgeously colored gaseous cloud that almost looks like it's on fire, limned as it is with orange and red filaments.

"I like this one better," Novelle says. "It's also outside my experience, but even to me, it possesses a sense of scope. I can imagine the team of Satori scientists who originally worked together to photograph this phenomenon, and it reminds me of all the mission groups that set off from Satori to learn everything they can about the universe and our place within it." She stands in admiring silence for a moment. "This artist went on a mission, you know," she adds. "He spent several decades in service before he returned. I wonder how much that influenced his choice of subject."

"Do you think his life experience makes for a better painting?"

Once again she is slow to answer. "I don't know about better," she says. "We'd have to define what that means. It certainly makes for a different painting. How could it be otherwise? We bring a part of ourselves into any art we create, don't you think?"

I shake my head. "I haven't really thought about it. Leo was always the artist, not me."

Her mouth curves upward. "I think he'd agree with me. I'm sure you won't be surprised to learn he always supported my painting. Gave me the use of a bright attic room with plenty of windows and a skylight, made sure I had all the materials my heart could desire, obtained the best art tutors to help me study. Mother went along with it. A young lady perfecting a talent in art is respectable enough, even if I approached the pursuit with an unseemly zeal." I can only be in sympathy with her on that front, having possessed my own unladylike enthusiasm. "Father was the one who understood. He told me once that he saw his own mask making as an outlet to say everything he wanted to say but wasn't allowed to. I think he hoped my art would prove to be a sufficient outlet for me as well."

"And was it?"

She smiles wryly. "Well, here I am, so clearly not. But it did help, especially when I was younger. And before I fell in love with Allegra. I wish I could have taken Father's path. I know he was disappointed that I wanted to leave."

"We each have to find our own way," I say to her. "And I know you were not your father's first disappointment." That dubious distinction most likely belongs to me.

I catch sight of more cakes coming out on a conveyer belt to the side, and I cut the conversation short to obtain my share before they're all gone. Novelle laughs at me, but I notice she takes her own chance to snare a few of the sweet little cakes. She may appreciate the art more, but our priorities aren't so very different.

It's only when we step out of the confined gallery space into the freedom of the night that I share what I'm really thinking. And even then, I wait until we've walked a few blocks and are alone. "Sometimes I feel entirely alien here," I admit. It's easier to say in the dark when I can't see her face. "I know the Satori aren't perfect, I've learned it through firsthand experience, but sometimes it all seems so flawless." I gesture aimlessly around us, as though to encompass the whole of Satori. "Even coming from the wealthy Tascioni family, we had our share of problems. But the Satori seem to have conquered so many of the difficulties I take for granted. Imagine being able to do whatever you most wish to do, without complication or obstacle."

Novelle's voice is low beside me. "I don't think it's quite that simple," she observes. "Yes, they are able to pursue art for art's sake, scholarship for scholarship's sake, sport for sport's sake. And the crèche system appears to lend itself to more resilient community ties. No one in Satori is truly abandoned." Coming from a planet where so many people are abandoned on a regular basis, without anyone so much as blinking over the state of affairs, this difference in the status quo is noteworthy to both of us. "But that doesn't mean there are no problems," Novelle continues. "The Satori still suffer just as we do."

"I suppose." I know she's right. I've seen my Satori friends struggle, after all. "But even when they suffer, they seem…somehow insulated. Does that make sense?"

"Yes, they've succeeded at creating something rather wonderful. And now we get to take part in it as well." Novelle frowns. "There is no nobility in suffering more than necessary, Sienna."

"But they are untested as a result," I argue.

"Do you really think we are somehow better than them because we come from a place where life is harder?"

"No…." But I trail off because her words do bear a relationship to what I'm trying to say, only phrased in a way that makes it obvious how silly it is. "Are you telling me you're happy with how they're brushing you off over the wormhole issue?"

Novelle stops walking. "Of course not," she says. "But the authorities on Sanctum were no better. In fact, they were worse. They all agreed that isolation was best. There wasn't even any discussion that maybe we should consider participating in meaningful dialogue with our neighbors. They are going to be forced to deal with the humans beyond our planet at some point, whether they like it or not. But at this rate, they'll burn through a lot of goodwill before they get there. And for what? The wormhole is already there, and the To have told me there's no way to close one once it's open. We're stuck with it."

"They're unlikely to back down," I say, remembering all too well.

"Exactly. The Satori might not be acting with the urgency that seems appropriate to me, but this is a lot for them to take in. Their entire way of life could be changing irrevocably. And some of them seem to want to ignore the problem, just like so many on Sanctum. But opinions on Satori differ, and they have a robust culture of discussion and debate. They'll work it out eventually."

"That's…surprisingly sanguine," I say after a long pause.

She shrugs. "Our people have made their bed. We can't expect other planets to come to Sanctum's rescue just because. And Allegra and I got what we wanted, against all the odds. I'm willing to give the Satori the benefit of the doubt." She begins to walk again, and I keep pace with her. "It was different for you, meeting the Satori the way you did. But they're not so different from us, not on an individual level. And humans are messy. They'll just keep disappointing you if you keep them up there on that pedestal."

I don't know how I feel about my niece giving me this sage advice. Isn't it supposed to be the other way around? But as I think about what she's said, I have to admit she has a point. The Satori have worked hard to make the improvements they've made, but that doesn't make them geniuses or saints.

All this time, I've been focusing on all the differences between us. But maybe the similarities matter more.

CHAPTER 19

$\mathcal{E}$reni and her fellow candidates are preparing to do a speaking tour of every neighborhood of Seji, and I am helping her as much as I can.

When we're beginning to plan, both of us staring up at the white board she's permanently propped in her room, I ask why the candidates can't simply do a few big events. Ereni laughs in a slightly fatigued way. "You have to understand, if I'm to be elected, I won't get to make any big decisions by myself," she tells me. "It's not like the Arborist government here. My job will be to communicate with everyone who lives in Seji, help them reach consensus as much as possible, and then represent their viewpoints at the Greater Conclave when any planet-level decisions must be made."

I gape at her in horror. "But a large number of people will never agree."

She nods her assent. "But we spend an awful lot of time talking everything through to get as close as we can," she says. "For some issues, most of Seji won't care overly much, and they might entrust me to do the necessary research and consult with enough people to make an acceptable decision. But for anything that's a hot topic, everyone will want to weigh in." Like around the question of whether to create a wormhole in the system, she doesn't have to add.

"So this tour is kind of like an audition," I say slowly. "So they know how you communicate and conduct yourselves."

"Exactly. If I were to win, I'd be doing events like these constantly. Sometimes through my N-CAT, sometimes in person. Accountability is very important in Satori government."

I muse over what she's told me. "Do the N-CATs help with all the discussion?"

She nods. "If there's a real division, we use our N-CATs to share our final position. Majority rules, at the end of the day, but it is the Councilor's job to make that decision as palatable as possible for the minority and address any concerns that may remain." She sighs and pulls her hair back from her face. "It's a big job."

"You can do it," I assure her. But secretly I think that's a lot of pressure to put on any one person.

I feel guilty when I leave her a few days later to travel back to Jundo. But Novelle and Allegra have invited me to attend a meeting they are having with the other delegates from our system, and I don't feel like I can miss it. Ereni insists I go. "I have plenty of help," she tells me. I eye her dubiously. Allowing others to help her is not one of Ereni's many strengths, and more often than not, I'm doing tasks before she asks. I can't force her to ask other people while I'm gone.

But Burke promises to keep an eye on her in my absence, and I trust him to do his best.

This time when I'm traveling with Novelle and Allegra, they hold hands openly, and from time to time they whisper in one another's ears. When I'd lived in San Marco, I might have felt excluded by their behavior, but now I simply feel happy for them. They appear so much more comfortable than they had when they'd first arrived, laughing with each other and reaching out to touch each other.

The steady movement of the train lulls me into a light sleep, something that would have been embarrassing on Sanctum but seems perfectly acceptable here. I wake to Novelle's hand on my shoulder. "We're here," she says happily. "Come on, sleepyhead. We need to drop off our things. We're meeting all the delegates at a bar for some social mingling before the more serious discussions tomorrow."

When we arrive at the bar, it's packed with people, an excited din immersing us as soon as we step inside. Allegra leads the way to the far corner where the other delegates appear to have claimed a few tables. The two planetary delegations are completely separated by table. The Luz look as flashy as ever with their violet skin and glowing clothing. I eye the Word warily; there are six of them here now, all dressed in the same silver robes they'd worn to the party. I remember what Lucia said about their poor grasp of Gallo and wonder how we'll manage to communicate at all.

I recognize the two Luz I met at the welcome party—Teofila and Lucia—amongst their delegation, and I present myself to exchange the expected deep bows. After we've finished the formalities, Lucia pushes a green-colored concoction in my hand. I take a tentative sip and try hard not to gasp at the subsequent burning sensation.

It's so loud I can only hear two words out of three, so I sit down and watch as Allegra and Novelle settle themselves further down the table, falling into immediate conversation with a Luz man I haven't yet met. While the Luz all talk amongst themselves, I can't help noticing the Word are sitting fairly quietly, methodically munching on finger foods from big platters in the middle of their table. I try not to keep an obvious eye out for the Luz's fascinating tails, which only become visible when they stand.

When Lucia leaves the table, presumably to obtain some more of the terrible green liquid, Teofila turns to me. "We were glad to hear you were able to attend our little gathering," she says politely. I have to ask her to repeat herself, and she practically screams the words into my ear, her highly sculpted hair shaking in rhythm with her speech.

I nod over to the adjacent table of the Word. "Are they not having a good time?" I shout into Teofila's ear. It's loud enough I don't have to worry that any of the Word will overhear.

Teofila laughs and shakes her head. "That's just how they are," she shouts back. "They don't enjoy engaging in small talk. They have told us several times how sacred they find language, and how they believe words should not be squandered. I think"—she leans closer to me, a mischievous smile on her face—"that's their way of politely asking us to get to the point."

I look over at the Word with renewed interest. As a proper young lady, I'd been raised to speak only when necessary and appropriate. Men like my father, on the other hand, were encouraged to expound at length, their words considered to be wise and valuable by default. Neopolitans certainly engage in our fair share of small talk, which is often the only topic deemed appropriate for ladies. I appreciate that the Word don't want anything to do with that kind of social lubricant. I almost wish I could join their much quieter table.

I slowly sip at my shocking drink, never growing accustomed to the strong burning sensation it produces. The conversations ebb and flow around me, and I feel like the eye of the storm, invited but not quite belonging within the socializing taking place. Even sitting still, the heat begins to become oppressive, and when I realize no one will notice, I slip away and outside onto the back patio where I can cool down.

Only a few small groups are sitting at circular tables outside, and I lean against a decorative railing that separates the eating area from a small fountain hewn to look like the water is erupting from natural stone. The fountain's musical tinkle soothes me as I examine the profusion of green plants surrounding it. Some of them feature bright pink blossoms that smell like sweet sugar, and I wonder if the petals might be edible.

Someone comes alongside me, and at first, I assume it must be Novelle checking on me, but when I look over, I see a woman with dark skin and wide shoulders and hips dressed in a silver robe. She doesn't smile at me, but she does give me a friendly enough nod. "Greetings to you," she says in heavily accented Gallo.

"And to you." I look behind her, but I don't see any of the rest of the Word coming to join us.

"Is loud, yes?" She points to her ears, and I nod. "But here is nice." She gestures towards the fountain. "Full of...peace."

"Yes, I like it," I tell her. "Inside I don't quite know where I fit in."

I don't think she'll be able to understand me, but she nods as if she does. "My Gallo, not so good," she says. "I hear, I understand, better than I speak. You see?"

I do see. Like her, I often have an easier time understanding someone speaking a language I'm learning than coming up with the correct vocabulary and grammar myself. "My name is Sienna Tascioni," I say slowly. "What is yours?"

She gestures at her chest. "Abril Pacis."

"It is good to meet you, Abril Pacis." I'm grateful for the effort she's making to communicate with me in spite of the difficulties.

"Yes, is good," she agrees. She wrinkles her nose as she thinks of the words she wants next. "You not on ship?" she finally asks.

It takes me a moment to understand what she wants to know. "That's right, I wasn't on the To's ship. I left Sanctum earlier with the Satori. They invited me to go on a mission with them." I pause, watching her forehead wrinkle at my words. I don't know how to explain a mission in a way she would understand. "I was in danger from my people," I finally say. "I needed to leave."

She nods vigorously to show she's understood. "We know Sanctum to be violent," she says.

I blink at her bluntness and open my mouth to protest before realizing I agree with her. After all, my parents tried to force me to marry someone I didn't wish to marry. My father locked me up in his closet. My supposed fiancé tried to assault me. And I'd had to flee my planet forever or be locked away in a mental institution. All of this had been violence of a brutal sort. "Yes," I say instead. "It is very sad."

She looks at me seriously for a moment. "The Satori can be violent too." She states the words almost as a question, as if not certain how I'll react.

I remember my conversation with Novelle at the art show. "Yes." It is a painful agreement to make. "Although not like Sanctum."

"Not like Sanctum," she agrees. "But Sanctum…stays put. The Satori, a problem for all."

I want to defend my friends, but she has a point. "The Satori travel all over the universe," I say. "They think they are doing good things, and I think sometimes they are. But it's so easy for things to get complicated."

"Not always good." She gives an emphatic nod.

"Not always good," I repeat.

She takes my hand and gives it a firm pat. "Sienna Tascioni," she says. "Good talk."

I watch her return inside the restaurant, a bit mystified by the conversation we just had.

THE DISCUSSIONS the next day are conducted in both Gallo and the Word's language, and no one seems to have anything particularly important to say. The other delegations are even more in the dark than we are, given my connections with Ereni and Burke. I share what I can to help them develop a better understanding, but I can't help feeling how powerless we all are.

If the Satori won't help us, I wonder if the To might once again intervene on our behalf. But no one brings that up as a possibility. When I ask Novelle and Allegra about it on the train ride back to Seji, they exchange a look before replying. "I don't know about that," Novelle says vaguely.

"But they've already helped us once," I argue. "And unlike the Satori, they helped us in a way we actually asked for."

"Oh, we're in favor of the To," Allegra assures me. "They've done us a real service, no question. But this is what they agreed to do: bring us to Satori so the humans can work things out. I've gotten the feeling they don't wish to become more directly involved."

"But they're already involved," I say. "If they truly didn't want to be, they didn't have to enter our system through the new wormhole in the first place."

"And do you think telling them that would go over well?" The irony in Allegra's words hangs heavily between us.

I give a frustrated sigh. "No. But there must be a way to convince them to help us."

Novelle leans her head against Allegra's shoulder. "It is a human problem, though, isn't it?" she says. "Besides, even if the To would help us, they certainly aren't going to create a new wormhole here without Satori permission. We'd have to spend years traveling to the nearest wormhole. And without the Satori diplomatic connections, I don't know that we'd have any chance of figuring out who's going around creating new wormholes on a whim. The To are more advanced than any of us, that seems clear, but it's not as if they're omnipotent."

She snuggles into Allegra's side and closes her eyes, and it's clear the conversation is at its end. But I'm still feeling frustrated when I join Ereni at a community meeting that evening. I sit in the audience and watch her work her usual magic, talking with familiarity about bringing more educational opportunities directly to Seji, about planet-wide environmental policies she supports, about the Satori responsibility to the rest of humanity. I know it's good the community is having all these important conversations, but I can't help wondering if it will be enough.

Lyra sits right next to Ereni, smiling smugly and name-dropping with almost every answer she gives. But I have to admit she knows the issues at play as well as Ereni does. And she's spent so much more time here in Seji. As the event wears on, I begin to slouch in my seat, a wave of exhaustion overtaking me. Burke, sitting beside me, squeezes my hand. "You okay?" he whispers.

I nod, even though I'm not sure of the answer.

After the event, Ereni has to stay and shake hands and talk to anyone who wants to speak to her. I eventually duck into the restroom to gain a little respite, but I'm annoyed to find Lyra at one of the sinks, washing her hands. "Sienna!" she says with faux enthusiasm. "I thought I saw you out in the audience. How *are* you?"

As if she really wants to know. "I'm great." I lie through my teeth. "I just got back from Jundo earlier today."

"Oh, that's right." Lyra rubs her hands together under the water. "I heard you delegates were having a little meeting. Was it good to be reunited?"

She knows I wasn't on the To starship with the delegates, doesn't she? Because how else would I know Ereni and Burke? But I realize

I'm either beneath her notice or she's trying to rattle me, and it doesn't really matter what I say in response. "We had a nice time," I say noncommittally.

"I'm glad you're beginning to find your place here on Satori. It can be difficult for newcomers to adjust." She walks over to the hand dryer. "And given that Burke's leaving soon, everyone must be relieved at how well you're doing."

Before I can process what she's said, she thrusts her hands underneath the dryer, which turns on with a loud blast of cool air, precluding further conversation. I try to cover my confusion by moving to wash my own hands. What does she mean, Burke will be leaving soon? He certainly hasn't told me any such thing.

Lyra is playing her own game here, that much is clear. But I can't help but remember in Arbor when Burke announced his sudden departure from Ojanla, where we'd been living in neighboring cottages, to accept a work assignment across the continent. Has he made another such decision, again without discussing it with me? I thought we'd become closer since then, but has that been wishful thinking on my part?

Lyra pulls her hands from the dryer, but the room is still filled with the sound of the water running. I'm hoping she'll just leave, satisfied with my confusion. But she comes to stand beside me so I can see her reflected in the mirror behind the sink. "He didn't tell you, did he?" She murmurs the words directly into my ear, easily audible above the water. "He's been offered a prime spot on the Makala 5 for the Prime Cup, one of the vessels highly favored to win. He'll have to leave soon to start training with the rest of the team. It's a great opportunity for him." She gives herself a self-satisfied smile in the mirror. "One I might have had a hand in setting up."

I think of how Ereni would handle the indignity of this situation and try to keep my face from giving any clue of the turmoil Lyra's words are causing me. But it does take me a beat to come up with an appropriate answer. "Burke is a talented person," I finally say. "I'm always very proud of him."

"As am I." Lyra smiles at me in the mirror. "It's been my pleasure to mentor him. After all, we can't allow him to languish in obscurity.

The crew of the Makala 5 will bring out the best in him and allow him to begin to truly thrive here. This is right where he belongs."

I realize what she isn't saying: that she doesn't believe I bring out the best in him. I abruptly pull away from the sink and use the hand dryer just as she had earlier, precluding any possibility of conversation. She waits until I finish to pat me sympathetically on the shoulder. "I'm sure you're going to miss him so much," she says. And with that last word, she exits the restroom, her picture-perfect smile pasted to her lips.

I take several deliberate breaths in front of the dryer. So what if Burke has accepted a position on the Makala 5? I know how much he loves racing. This is a natural thing for him to do. And if we're apart for a long time, well, we've managed to be apart before. Only this time, I'm determined to do things differently. The physical distance doesn't have to become such a gaping emotional distance.

I just wish he would have told me before Lyra let the news drop. I never have the advantage with that woman. She might not be interested in a romance with Burke herself, but she certainly doesn't want him wasting his time with me.

When I find Burke out among the remaining audience members, I smile and let him hold my hand. It's not until we return to our lodgings, him collapsing face first onto my bed, that I bring up what happened.

I tell him what Lyra told me in the restroom. "It's not that I don't want you to do what you want to do," I assure him. "But I would have preferred to hear about the racing team from you, not from Lyra. I don't know if you've noticed, but she isn't my biggest fan."

He rolls over to raise his eyebrows at me. "You don't say. That's why I stopped spending much time with her."

I sit down beside him on the bed. "I don't exactly wish that the Satori hadn't found a means to extend everyone's lifespans, but in this case, it is a little inconvenient."

He smiles at me. "Tell me that in three hundred years, and we'll see if you've changed your mind."

He's trying to charm me, and it's working, but I can't let him push me off track. "But really, why didn't you tell me?"

He sighs. "I didn't tell you because I turned down the team's offer."

I gape at him in surprise. "You did what?"

"I turned them down," he repeats. "So it didn't matter. Although in retrospect, I should have mentioned it. There's been so much going on, and I only got the offer a few days ago. It happened right before you left for Jundo so we've barely had any time alone since then."

"You gave them a fast answer."

He stretches his arms out over his head. "It was an easy answer. I didn't want to keep them waiting. They'll need time to put together the best possible team."

I stare down at him, but his face gives nothing away. "Why would you turn them down?" I ask. "I thought you loved to sail. And you were telling me the Prime Cup is one of the biggest races. Isn't this the opportunity of a lifetime?"

"Not to me," he says. "Not right now." Perhaps sensing my growing frustration, he sits up and grabs my hands. "Listen, Sienna, I understand why you're concerned. But I meant it when I said this was an easy decision. I'm not going to leave you behind when we've arrived on Satori so recently, and I'm not going to leave Ereni behind when she needs our support. I love racing, but there will be other races. This is the only time you'll be trying to adjust to an entirely new planet, and we can only hope Ereni doesn't take it into her head to run for office again any time soon."

I shake my head at him, tears pricking my eyes. On Sanctum a woman's needs are supposed to be entirely subsumed to those of men, whether her father, her husband, or even, yes, her brother. My father took every opportunity he was given without even a superficial consultation with my mother. And she did her best to support him, even when it meant leaving our country house, which she loved with all her heart, and resettling in San Marco for his political career. I never heard one murmur of protest from her.

"What are you feeling?" Burke asks me.

I shake my head again. "Are you sure about this decision? It might not be too late to change your mind."

He gives me a strange look. "Of course I'm sure. Like I said, there will be other races. The team that approached me understood I need more time to settle in. It's all set."

I fling my arms around his neck and hug him tight. I might have trouble imagining a world in which a man will consider the needs of others when making his own plans, but clearly Burke is already living there.

He hugs me back, but when we pull away from one another, he's frowning. "I don't know why Lyra approached you about this in the first place," he says. "I suppose she's angry I turned the offer down after she went to the trouble of setting it up."

"She can't be happy Ereni is running against her either," I say. "And I am spending a lot of time helping with the campaign." I allow myself to voice one of my worries. "I'm honestly not sure if Ereni can beat her."

Burke reaches out to take my hand again. "It's going to be close. But we'll see it through to the end."

CHAPTER 20

The next time Diantha invites me over for dinner, I bring Kuusta along. As far as I know, I'm still his only friend on the planet. He has just begun his course of study at the university, but when I ask him about his classmates, he shrugs. "They're nice enough," he tells me, but he refuses to elaborate any further.

Theckla has no qualms about meeting a new person. Once she's finished running into my arms and giving me an aggressive hug, she turns and stares up at him. "I know you," she says, a delighted expression dawning on her face at her recognition.

"The surprise child," Kuusta says in passable Kensho. "We meet again."

Theckla studies him for a long moment before flinging herself at his legs in greeting. Kuusta takes a startled step backwards, and the pair of them almost fall over before he reaches for the wall and steadies himself."

By the time we're finishing dinner, Kuusta and Theckla are chatting away as if they're old friends. They've discovered they watch the same cartoon program. "What?" Kuusta responds to my shocked face with an injured air. "I'm serious about practicing my Kensho." They discuss the plot twists at some length while I tell Diantha about my latest trip to Jundo.

When we finally prepare to leave, later than I'd planned, Diantha beams at us both. "Theckla has something to ask you, Sienna."

I turn to Theckla expectantly. She has become suddenly shy, looking down at her feet and twisting her hands in her skirt. "Will you come speak to my class next week?" she mumbles in a rush.

I look to Diantha. "What's this about?"

Diantha gives Theckla a fond smile. "It's a class assignment. Everyone is supposed to invite an interesting adult to be interviewed by the class. Theckla has been talking about you ever since she first heard about it."

"You'll be the most interesting person to come," she says. "Because you're from another whole planet." She puffs out her chest. "Everyone will be so jealous." Then she deflates, as if suddenly realizing I haven't agreed. "Please, will you come?"

I'm strangely touched at the invitation. "Of course I'll come," I tell her. "I wouldn't miss it."

She turns to Kuusta. "You should come too," she announces. "You're from another different planet, right?"

His ears turn red, and I wonder if he's embarrassed. "Oh, I don't have anything very interesting to say," he says, waving his hands in dismissal. "Sienna is an excellent choice."

Theckla's face falls. "You don't want to come?"

Kuusta gives a quick glance at the door. "I don't want to bore your classmates."

"Can't you just talk about Wise Ones for five minutes and give everyone a thrill?" I say.

"Please." Theckla clasps her hands together and starts wiggling around as if she can't contain her excitement.

I give Kuusta a look, and he sighs. "I would be honored to attend," he says.

It's not until Diantha has given us all the details and we've said our goodbyes that Kuusta gives me an exasperated look. He waits until we get outside the building to make his complaints. "My Kensho is nowhere near good enough for something like this," he tells me in Truncish. "I'll have to spend hours practicing."

I snort. "And yet your language skills are magically good enough for your university classes?"

"I have to spend hours practicing for those too," he retorts. "At this rate I'll be busier than I ever was on Arbor."

But he doesn't actually look unhappy. I can't help thinking that having interesting things to do will be good for him, even if he won't always be free to go on speeder bike adventures.

I'VE FINALLY SET up the meeting between Ereni and the Unity, and at the specified time, Aeson shows up by himself. We've set up a temporary campaign headquarters in a co-working space down the street that used to be a training gym. A few stray pieces of exercise equipment still grace the space, and its earthy aroma reminds me every time I enter that this building was grown from mushroom stock. I usher Aeson into a corner where we've set up several of the distinctive Satori curved chairs while Burke gets him the bitter drink he's requested from the kitchen area.

Ereni finishes the discussion she's having with several volunteers and joins us just as Burke arrives with the mugs. I wrinkle my nose at mine until I see he brought me tea instead of Aeson's requested beverage, for which I haven't acquired a taste. Aeson smiles broadly at the three of us. "You've all seen each other through a lot, haven't you?"

Ereni raises her eyebrows. "We're good friends," she says. "Sienna tells me you were able to get her complaint dismissed from the Superior Mission Council. Thank you for that. I was beginning to think they were deliberately ignoring me."

She tosses her hair, and I realize she's taken a dislike of Aeson, although I'm not sure if it's because he helped me when she couldn't or for another, less obvious reason.

"It was my pleasure," Aeson says smoothly. "It was a simple

matter to address, and we all need to look out for each other, don't we?"

"We've been looking forward to speaking to you," Burke says. "It seems there is major alignment between Unity's goals and the values of the campaign."

"Yes, we've watched your discussions about the new wormhole technology with great interest," Aeson says. "We've been starting many similar conversations for decades, of course, and we've learned that talk will only get you so far. But we always welcome allies."

Ereni's eyes narrow. "What do you mean by that, exactly?" She is enunciating her words particularly crisply. "Discussion, consideration, and consensus whenever possible are keystones to Satori governance. That is certainly the lodestone of every one of our Councilors."

"Of course." Aeson's smile remains steady. "And becoming mired in process can also ensure that nothing ever changes and no difficult decisions ever need to be made. These ideas can both be true."

"As long as we remember our ideals." The way Ereni says it, it almost sounds like a warning. "What does the Unity see as a desirous next step?"

Aeson looks from me to Ereni. "We'd like to see more support for scientific research on the wormholes," he says. "Knowledge is power, after all. Ideally, we'd send some scientists to Doctrina to study the technology in more depth before returning home to instruct others. We need to develop our expertise."

"That sounds very reasonable." Ereni speaks slowly, as if reluctant to agree. "That is something I'd be able to support."

"I'm pleased to hear it." But his voice lacks warmth. "We'd also like to see an increased investment in Unity-sponsored missions."

Ereni blinks a few times, the only indication she has been caught by surprise. "Surely our investment in the Superior Mission Council is already sufficient," she says. "I've checked the most recent numbers, and they looked to be within the parameters I expected to see."

Aeson shakes his head. "No, no, you misunderstand me. We want direct investment in the Unity instead of becoming mired in the bureaucracy of the Superior Mission Council." He gives me a little nod. "I think we've all seen how their methods can be less than desirable."

There is a long pause. "That is a highly irregular request," Ereni finally says. "All missions have always been registered with and funded through the Superior Mission Council. Proper oversight is not a corner to be cut, even if it sometimes creates inconveniences."

Aeson shrugs. "These are irregular times, and the Unity is ready to meet the urgency of the moment. Meanwhile, the Superior Mission Council has become weighed down by process and improper politicking. Things have changed in your absence."

I wince, knowing he has made an error in his approach. "I can assure you I am up-to-date in my information," Ereni says stiffly.

"With greater investment, the Unity can increase the number of missions we send out for both research and data collection purposes," Aeson says. "We're ready to ensure the Satori continue to play an active role in the human diaspora. And if you're willing to publicly commit your support to us, we are prepared to put our organizing apparatus at your disposal for the length of your campaign. I'll send over some specifics of what that could look like right now."

Burke's eyes glaze over, and I know he's looking over the proposal Aeson just sent via N-CAT. Ereni nobly resists the temptation and simply stands with a decisive nod. "We'll consider what you've said," she says. "And we'll get back to you soon."

"I can't ask for anything more than that." Aeson turns his bright smile onto me. "And of course, I must offer my gratitude to Sienna for arranging this meeting in the first place."

"It was my pleasure." I murmur the empty words, not sure how I feel about the man or his offer.

After several more platitudes, Aeson finally leaves, and the three of us look at each other. "Well, I have to confess, that didn't go the way I thought it would," I say.

Ereni shakes her head. "I don't like that man's smile," she says. "He's an operator through and through. I don't trust a word he says."

"I can look into his claims," Burke says. "But it does look like the Unity has a strong ground game they could deploy here in Seji. A lot of their people would be from out of town though, so it's hard to say how effective they would be at swaying people's opinions."

"I don't like what he's asking for," Ereni says frankly. "It might well be true that the Superior Mission Council is no longer what it once was. But that doesn't mean I want to commit to funneling significant resources to an organization with no public accountability mechanisms in place."

I'm beginning to wish I hadn't set up the meeting in the first place. "I don't like how he helped me with my case in order to make me feel like I owed him," I admit.

"The whole thing leaves a sour taste in my mouth," Burke says.

"Then we're in agreement," Ereni says. "However much the Unity can help us with our campaign, the price is too high. I'll wait a few days, thank them, and tell them I can't commit at this time."

That night, I dream of Aeson's strangely fixed smile, and I worry about the campaign more than ever.

Kuusta and I present ourselves to Theckla's class at the appointed time. Kuusta, who has recently taken to wearing more colors, has reverted to the Arborists' color palette and is dressed in black pants and a brown tunic. I'm wearing Satori clothing, having abandoned Sanctum's confining dresses long ago. I still have one dress tucked away, but I can't bring myself to wear it, not even for an educational opportunity.

When we enter, I'm immediately hit by a wave of smells: peanut butter and chocolate from snack time, paint, and a hint of some strong cleaning product. Light fills the room from a panel of windows on one wall, and tables have been arranged in a partial circle. The walls feature several large pictures in bright colors, the paint still wet. Twenty or so kids are playing some kind of game in the center of the room, and I catch sight of Theckla standing stone still, three other kids capering in front of her until her façade breaks and she begins to giggle.

"You're out!" one of the kids shrieks, pointing at her. She dutifully joins another throng of kids in front of another kid emulating a statue, and it's only a few more minutes before the game comes to its raucous conclusion with only one frozen kid remaining.

A teacher steps out from where she's been observing in the corner. "Well done, everyone. Well done, Despoina." The little girl who succeeded at the game twirls around in excitement. "And now it looks like your Interesting Guests are here, Theckla. Would you like to introduce them to everyone?"

The children slowly move to sit behind the tables, chatting loudly with one another. Theckla's face splits in a nervous grin as she joins Kuusta and I at the front of the room. We stand for another minute before the children settle down. Theckla gestures at me. "This is my friend Sienna. Sienna Tah-seee-ohhh-ni." She pronounces my last name very carefully. "Sienna is from the planet of Sanctum. We sent a mission there, and she joined them when they left. She's the most interesting person I know." Her little smile at this statement tugs at my heart.

"And this"—she gestures up at Kuusta—"is Kuusta Elo. He is from the planet of Arbor, where we had another mission. He is Sienna's friend, and that's how I know him. He is the second most interesting person I know."

With that amusing introduction, Theckla scampers to join her classmates, choosing one of the closer tables. The teacher smiles at us. "Welcome to our class. We've never had people from other planets visit us before."

Except for Theckla, I don't say out loud. The fact that she has a Satori mother seems to make all the difference.

"All right, class, who has a question for Sienna and Kuusta?"

One boy immediately sticks his hand straight up, as if he's been waiting for his chance. "Yes, Kon?" the teacher says. "What is your question?"

"Do you remember traveling through space?" the boy asks enthusiastically. "What's it like?"

Kuusta indicates I should go first. "I was awake for a limited time on a few different voyages," I begin. "Being on a starship traveling through deep space is different than being on a train or a speeder bike. It's difficult to tell how fast you're going from the inside. Space is very, very big, and it's also very empty."

The boy looks expectantly at Kuusta. "Being inside a starship isn't so different from being in this classroom." Kuusta speaks slowly, choosing his words carefully. "Except there's no sunshine pouring in the windows. You have to exercise every day to make sure to keep your body healthy in space, and when I was awake, most of the other passengers were asleep, so I had a lot of the ship all to myself."

A girl shouts out, "What about cryosleep? What's that like?"

"Ana," the teacher interjects, "would you like to raise your hand before asking a question so everyone can see it's your turn?"

Ana doesn't seem cowed by this direction, shooting her hand upwards before saying, "Cryosleep?"

"I don't remember my dreams from cryosleep," I offer. "I've read the process doesn't induce REM sleep so the entire time you're asleep, you don't dream. You simply exist in suspended animation until it's time for you to wake up again."

"When you wake up, you're covered in slimy gunk, and it's hard to breathe," Kuusta says. The whole class laughs. "But if you want to skip a boring decade or two, I recommend it." They laugh again.

"Were you on a mission?" another girl asks. "What was it like?"

"Yes, I was. On Arbor, where Kuusta is from. That's where we met." I pause, collecting my thoughts. What do I have to say about the Arbor mission to a class of seven-year-olds? "The thing that surprised me about the mission was how complicated it felt. When I studied the philosophy and the rules around missions, it all seemed so easy and straightforward. But once we landed, I learned that our mission goals were not always aligned." I remember that I'm talking to kids and try again. "What I mean is, sometimes one mission goal might make it hard to do a different mission goal. Does that make sense?" A few of the kids nod.

"What are the goals of most missions?" I ask the class. "You don't have to raise your hands, you can just shout out your answers."

"To collect knowledge and save it," a boy shouts out.

"To work well with others," someone else says.

"To make friends with people on other planets," a third child chimes in.

"To help people and make things better for them," Theckla says. I know she's repeating what Diantha has probably told her time and time again.

"To explore!" another child shouts. "And go far, far away!"

"Those are all good answers," I say. "In the case of the mission I was on, the goals of collecting and storing knowledge, establishing diplomatic relations with Arbor, and helping the people who lived there were all important. And sometimes they got in the way of one another."

There is a pause. I'm not sure I've explained things in a way the children will be able to understand. Then—"What about the aliens?" a child shouts out.

"Have you met them?" another one asks.

"Have you been on their starship? Is it the same as ours?" another asks.

"What do they look like?" another asks.

"Children!" the teacher says, raising her hands in the air. "One question at a time, please. You know how these interviews work."

A little boy with a bowl cut raises his hand. "What do you know about the aliens, please? Why did they come here?"

"Will they hurt us?" I can't tell who adds that question.

"I don't believe the aliens will hurt us, no," I say, relieved to have an obvious place to start. "They seem to have peaceful intentions, and they have already provided assistance to the humans from my home system who wished to travel here but wouldn't have been able to do so on their own."

"Sienna and I traveled here on a different starship," Burke adds. "We haven't been on the To's ship."

"The To use a robot to communicate with humans," I say. "I don't think any human has seen what the To actually look like or communicated with them directly. But I have spoken with the robot, and we were able to have a good conversation."

"I heard the new wormholes are the aliens' fault, and they're putting them into systems without asking." The girl raises her hand in the middle of her sentence.

Kuusta and I exchange a glance. If seven-year-olds are hearing this kind of opinion, what hope do we have?

"We have no evidence that the aliens are responsible for the new wormhole in Sienna's home system." Kuusta speaks slowly and deliberately, and I'm suddenly aware that I'm standing next to a former politician who is used to being asked difficult questions.

"The To say they don't know anything about the new wormhole," I say. "They expressed concern that an unknown party is creating them. The delegates from my system are asking the Satori for their help in investigating the matter more thoroughly." I leave out the depressing truth that it doesn't seem likely we're going to receive the assistance we're asking for.

Theckla raises her hand and waits for the teacher to call on her. "The Satori are one of the only human societies that regularly travel between many systems," she says in her clear voice. "My mother says most humans remain in their own systems, but the Satori are different because of the goals you talked about earlier: to collect human knowledge and help people." Several of her classmates shift uncomfortably at the mention of her mother. "Since we collect so much human knowledge and travel so many places, shouldn't we already know who is making the wormholes?"

If only it were that simple. "Perhaps someone from Satori does know," I tell Theckla. "Perhaps one of the missions far away from here have already solved the mystery. But since the Satori don't have a wormhole of their own, it could take a mission with information to share a long time to return to tell us about it."

Theckla nods as if satisfied with this answer, and another boy raises his hand. "What do you think the aliens *really* look like?" he asks.

Kuusta and I field another twenty minutes of questions about the To and our respective planets before wrapping things up. The kids seem particularly fascinated by the idea of Wise Ones and the fact that humans can be transformed into tree-like beings. The teacher is able to share photos of Wise Ones through the children's' N-CATs.

When we're leaving, she announces the children will all be making drawings based on the interview, and I imagine a row of pictures of strange-looking aliens, starships, and magical trees.

Kuusta looks thoughtful as we walk home. "Thank you for including me," he says. "It's good for me to become more a part of things here."

"It was Theckla who wanted you," I tell him truthfully. "I think the kids were really interested in talking with us."

"Although they would have been happier if we'd actually met a To in person." He laughs. "Do you think this is going to make Theckla more popular?"

"I hope so." But I'd seen the looks on some of the kids' faces when she'd mentioned her mother, and I'm not so sure. "Are you having dinner with me and Burke tonight?"

Kuusta shakes his head and looks vaguely embarrassed. "Believe it or not, I'm taking your advice," he says. "I've joined a study group of fellow students, and our first meeting is tonight. We're going to have food while we work."

I give him a look of mock shock. "Don't tell me you're actually making Satori friends!"

"Don't get too excited. It's only a study group."

But he can't hide his smile, and for the first time, I can actually see a future for him beyond the mistakes he'd made on Arbor.

CHAPTER 21

It's only a week before the election when the storm breaks.

The tragedy of it is that everything has been going so well. Ereni has been making real headway in her campaign as she makes deeper connections with people throughout Seji's many neighborhoods. Novelle has been happily painting, and she's decided to submit a few of her new works for a gallery showing. Kuusta seems to be genuinely enjoying his studies. I am making progress with my swimming. And Burke has begun speaking more seriously about returning to school as well.

I'm too engrossed by Ereni's campaign to consider my own future deeply, but I'm beginning to feel more at home in Seji. It's become easy to see why Ereni and Burke love it so much and to imagine living here for the foreseeable future. Burke even suggests the three of us, and maybe Novelle and Allegra, apply for a more permanent residence together.

I've begun taking a morning swim in the sea most days before I begin my tasks for Ereni. Burke has taught me two strokes, which I dutifully practice before lying back and floating, bobbing up and down with the waves. When I'm in the water the human world shrinks to a pinpoint in my mind, and I can focus on the sensations of the warm, buoyant water, the salt tinging my lips, and the dull roar of the surf. I've been visited by the dolphins a few more times, although my duties mean I can't always take them up on their offer of their joyous traverse.

I arrive back to my room, my wet hair slicked back, wearing a light dress over my still-damp bathing costume. I'm already running through my list of tasks for the day, planning to start as soon as I take a quick shower. But when I open the door, Burke is sitting at my little table, a grim expression on his face. He stands up when he sees me, and my heart plummets in my chest. "Is everyone all right?" I ask quickly. "Novelle, Allegra? Ereni?"

"They're all fine." He takes my hand and leads me outdoors to the balcony, where we can sit side by side.

"What is it?" I'm very aware of my wet bathing costume under my clothes and how I still smell of seawater. I sit gingerly on the edge of the chair, gazing longingly over my shoulder at the robe hanging on a hook on my door.

"You know Ajax's Insights?

I gaze at Burke blankly. Ajax is one of the most popular commentators on Seji, and we've been trying to get Ereni on his show Ajax's Insights for weeks. "Has he finally come around?" I ask. "Ereni is ready, even if we don't have time to prep. Just give me ten minutes to shower, and I can do whatever needs to be done."

He catches my hand in his before I can stand up. "No, it's not that. He's done an entire show about Arbor. He tracked down a few people from our mission who returned to Satori with us. He looked at all the mission records, what happened on Zamavat. All of it."

None of us have talked much about the mission on Arbor since our arrival on Satori. Not publicly. Ereni doesn't bring it up unless asked. "Well, that's unfortunate, but it's not as if our time on Arbor was any kind of secret. Ereni has always been honest when anyone's asked her questions about it. I think we're fine."

He swallows. "We're not fine."

"What do you mean?" I smooth my dress over my thighs. "Where's Ereni? We can figure it out."

He grimaces. "Ereni is with Evander. They're busy doing damage control."

"Well, I can go help her." I stand up. "Do I have time to change? Or does she need me right away?"

"Sienna. Ajax's show attacks you specifically. You and Kuusta."

I'm still not understanding. "What does Kuusta have to do with anything?"

"You remember when you and Kuusta went to meet Theckla's class? Well, somehow Ajax obtained a video of that conversation."

I frantically try to remember what I'd said during that visit. In front of a class of seven-year-olds, I couldn't have said anything too shocking. "Kuusta didn't talk about why he'd decided to leave Arbor." Of this point I'm certain. "We didn't talk about the fire at all."

"No, Ajax found out about that all on his own. But he uses clips from the classroom visit to cast allusions on your character." I shake my head, feeling like this entire conversation is something out of a nightmare. "He says Kuusta is responsible for all of the Wise One deaths, and that in spite of him being a mass murderer, the two of you are still close." He winces. "He implies you're very close, if you take my meaning."

The shock is catching up with me, and I'm suddenly glad I'm sitting down. "Kuusta and I have never—" I begin.

"I know," Burke interrupts me. "It's ridiculous. Ajax shows the clip of you talking about being torn between preserving knowledge and helping people, and then explains how all three of us were ejected from the mission because of that dilemma."

"All three of us…." My heart sinks. Ereni has been drawn into it then. Which makes sense. Why bother having an entire show about how shocking Kuusta and I are, unless it's to get at her? And right before the election too. "I assume it's not a sympathetic treatment?" Burke just looks at me. "Right."

"It gets worse," Burke continues.

"How could it get any worse?" I shake my head. "I honestly can't remember saying anything awful to those kids. And how did they get a recording of it anyway?"

"Any of the N-CATs in the room could have recorded it," Burke says matter-of-factly. "We can try to analyze it and see if we can figure out which angle it came from. But does it really matter?"

I blink. "I suppose not." I can't believe I've never considered the broader implications of everyone carrying an automatic recording device *inside their brains*. But even if I'd realized, I would have accepted the invitation to visit Theckla's class. How could I have known what I said would be taken so wrong?

"Ajax talks about the complaint the mission filed with the Superior Mission Council, and he says it was dismissed under mysterious circumstances. Basically, he's implying Ereni had something to do with it."

"She didn't," I say hotly. "That was all Aeson and the Unity's work."

"Well, I don't think they're going to admit to that publicly, do you?"

He's right. Aeson didn't get what he wanted during his meeting with Ereni. He has no reason to help us now.

"Ajax says you're accusing the Satori of being the ones responsible for the new wormhole in your system," Burke says. "He's making you out to be a bitter failure and social misfit who sows discord wherever you go. And now that the Satori have been kind enough to allow you here, he says you're trying to tear us down too. It's all completely ridiculous and untrue," Burke adds hastily. "No one who knows you would believe it for a second."

"I don't understand." This feels like it's happening so quickly. "I've never said the Satori created the new wormhole. I've never even thought it."

"They have a clip of you saying that it's possible a Satori mission might know."

I do remember saying that. Theckla had asked a particularly good question. "Well, everyone knows that's true. There are enough missions out there, one of them may have already stumbled onto the truth. But we have no way of knowing one way or another."

"Ajax twisted your words. He made it seem like you were

implying the Satori were responsible, that maybe you even believe there's some kind of vast conspiracy." Burke pauses. "And he made a big deal about how close you and Ereni are. There's a reel of photos of the two of you together in public."

"Because I've been supporting her speaking tour." I look around for where I've left my qualpad, wondering if I should see exactly what Ajax has said for myself. "This is absurd."

"No one can deny you and Ereni are good friends," Burke says softly.

"Of course not. But I can strenuously deny that I'm somehow filling her head with bizarre conspiracy theories." Besides, it was Ereni who had suggested the Satori might be responsible for the wormhole, not me. But she's certainly never said such a thing in public. "Surely people won't think…." But what do I know about how the people living in Seji will think? If we were talking about the people of Napoleon, I know they'd believe the worst.

"The race is close," Burke says. "This could be the boost Lyra needs."

Which answers another question: namely, why Ajax would attack me like this. But given the harm his accusations might do to Ereni's chances, it all makes too much sense. "I can refute everything," I say. "I can go public and speak to everyone, tell them what happened and what I actually believe."

"But a lot of what Ajax said is the truth," Burke says. "It's the truth told in a nasty way, but now people have been primed to think about it that way…."

He doesn't have to finish. "Oh no," I breathe. "What about Kuusta? Have you spoken with him yet?"

By the time Burke shakes his head, I'm already scrambling around the room, looking for my qualpad. I find it under my pillow, and I call Kuusta without hesitation. I just hope he isn't stuck in a classroom and unable to answer.

There's a pause, but then I hear his sleepy voice through the speaker. "Sienna, it's early," he complains. "I was up half the night finishing a reading assignment. Can we talk later?"

"I'm coming over right away," I tell him.

Burke and I hurry to Kuusta's room, and when we barge in, he's wearing a simple rumpled shirt and shorts, his golden curls sticking up every which way. He gives me a once-over, a small smile creeping onto his face. "Just get back from a swim?"

I hate to be the one to break the bad news, but I'd hate even more for him to hear it from anyone else. "Ajax did a show all about us," I tell him. "Do you know who Ajax is? I haven't had time to watch it yet, but apparently he uses clips from our interview at Theckla's school to make some terrible insinuations about us both. And"—I take a deep breath—"he also gets into your past. He talks about what happened at the Forest of the Ancestors."

Kuusta blanches. "The fire?"

"I think so, yeah." I turn to Burke for confirmation, and he nods. "We can watch it together if you want. I didn't want you to hear about it from anyone else."

Kuusta rubs his face, scrambling to keep up. "Yes," he finally says. "But give me a few minutes to get myself together. I haven't had anything to eat yet today."

"You might as well take a shower, Sienna," Burke says. "It's not as if this news is going away."

If only it would.

Less than an hour later, the three of us sit side by side at Kuusta's table and watch the entire show. When it finishes, I want to either lay down and cry or go hit my head against a hard surface. Ajax has gone out of his way to make both myself and Kuusta look bad, and he's good at his job, I'll give him that.

Lyra makes a brief appearance as well, given that she grew up in the same crèche as Ereni. She looks directly at Ajax as he interviews her, speaking slowly and sincerely. "What's clear to me, both from the records of the Arbor mission and from conversations I've had, is that, while Sienna undoubtedly tried her best, her Sanctum upbringing and lack of a formal Satori education crippled her in the field. She clearly doesn't understand the way Satori do things. We always strive to work together, collectively deciding what is the best way forward in any given situation. But Sienna remains guided by an unruly individualism I can only assume is the norm on her world, and where she led, Ereni was willing to follow."

I want to scream, either at the qualpad or out the window or preferably at Lyra herself. She makes me sound so unfit for mission work, for anything related to the Satori, really. Even worse, I'm not confident she's completely wrong in her assessment of me. On Sanctum, I couldn't trust anyone but myself and Leo, and I know I've brought that habit with me off-planet.

But never in a million years did I think my own trust issues would be used against Ereni.

Kuusta stares blankly forward. "I left my family, my planet, and everything I knew to leave this behind me. And it's still not enough." He shakes his head. "It will never be enough, will it? There are some things you just can't come back from."

"That's not true," I argue. "Everyone deserves a second chance. And it's not as if you started the fire on purpose." That would have been impossible for me to look past. But in Kuusta's case, he'd been careless and foolish, but not murderous. Surely that distinction matters to more people than myself.

"The last thing I want to do is relitigate the whole nightmare here on Arbor," Kuusta says. "Maybe the best thing I can do is disappear."

That doesn't sound promising. "What do you mean, disappear?"

He shrugs. "I don't know. Leave public life entirely. Quit my classes, not go anywhere, not speak to anyone. Maybe eventually I can take another starship out and try again, although"—there is a painful pause—"I don't have a lot of hope that would do any good in the end."

"Absolutely not," I say, and Burke chimes in, "That won't be necessary. The Satori believe in taking accountability. Not as a way to punish people, but as a way to allow everyone to move on."

"I've taken accountability," Kuusta says. "Before I left, I met with every family of a Wise One who died in that fire who wanted to meet with me. And it was most of them. I listened to everything they wanted to say to me. I heard every shred of grief I had caused them. I will carry their pain with me forever. And in every meeting, I apologized again and again, knowing it would never be enough. And then I removed myself from their sight forever. What more could I do that would wipe me clean in Satori eyes? They weren't there. They don't know. They aren't the people to whom I owe everything."

I didn't know he'd done that. He'd never mentioned it, not in all the time we'd spent together on Zamavat, on the voyage to Satori, and now here in Seji. I try to imagine what it would be like, meeting with family after family who had lost a beloved Wise One because of my actions. I try to imagine it, and I fail.

"This is my fault," I say. "I should have realized how heated this campaign was becoming. I should have never accepted that invitation to speak in the classroom. I should have figured out a better communications strategy—"

"It's not your fault, Sienna," Kuusta interrupts me. "It's simply the way things are. I have to live with my actions, whatever that looks like now. That I don't like the way it looks is not because of you."

"Just give me a moment to think." I spring up, hoping I'll think better standing. "I'm sure I can figure something out."

But Kuusta looks up at me with sad eyes, and Burke is shaking his head. "Ereni doesn't want you to involve yourself further," Burke says. "Not because she blames you or thinks this is your fault. Because she wants to protect you. And I do too."

My mind jumps from possibility to possibility, trying to reject what Burke's telling me. It takes me a moment to hear what's beneath his words. "Ereni doesn't think there's anything I can do that won't make things worse," I finally say. I know I'm right because Burke bows his head. "You can't just expect me to give up."

Burke stands up and pulls me into a hug. "You're not solely responsible for everything, Sienna," he says into my ear. "Let Ereni do what she can. The election is only a few days away, and you've already helped so much."

I look over his shoulder at Kuusta, who is staring blankly ahead. I say the only thing I can think of that might make things even a fraction more bearable. "Want to go on a little trip?"

Kuusta and I leave within a few hours. We reserve two speeder bikes and obtain the necessary supplies to survive on one of the little, uninhabited islands until after the election is over. Burke will stay and help Ereni as much as he can, but I can help the most by stepping aside.

And if Kuusta wants to disappear, I can at least make sure he doesn't have to do it alone.

CHAPTER 22

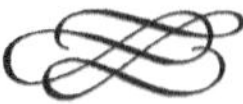

"You're really lucky," Kuusta tells me. It's the second night of our self-imposed exile, and we're both lying on top of our sleeping sacks, staring up at the stars. We brought compressible pads to cushion the hard ground. The weather is balmy, a slight breeze rustling the palm fronds overhead. In other circumstances, I'd call it an idyllic setting.

"Please spare me," I tell Kuusta. We've been mostly silent since our arrival late yesterday. Today we spent most of the day out on our speeder bikes, pretending we could outrace the ocean. After all, what is there to say? What I don't want is for Kuusta to get all sentimental after we've eaten from our utilitarian food pouches.

"No, I mean it," he says. "You have people who care about you, who want to help you when you need it and want to celebrate you when you don't. That's something worth having, don't you think?"

I think of how tightly Burke had hugged me before I'd left. "I'll be waiting for you to come home," he'd whispered into my ear. The supportive messages from Ereni, Novelle, and even Allegra. The horror in Diantha's messages, worried that she too had played a role in our downfall. Yes, Kuusta is right. I am lucky.

We've turned off our qualpads here on the island, trying to

achieve a modicum of peace since there's nothing we can do to affect the outcome on Seji. It's not really working. No matter how hard I try, my thoughts keep returning to Ereni's campaign and how it's going without me.

"It was hard on Arbor," I say into the night. "Burke had left for Lahti, and Ereni and I weren't speaking. I felt so betrayed and alone."

"But you forgave them." It isn't a question. Kuusta can see as well as anyone how close the three of us have become. "How did you do it?" There's a plaintive note in his voice.

"I don't know," I say honestly. "It took time. I didn't really trust them, and sometimes I still felt really angry. But both of them kept their word to me. They were obviously trying to improve things between us. And I knew I had to work to improve things too, or the whole effort would fall apart."

"It sounds like you built something together," Kuusta says. "But didn't it feel like a big gamble?"

I consider his question. "Yes. But everything that's been worth having in my life has come with a risk." I think about my joy speed bike racing in Leo's place, my efforts to prove Burke's innocence, my desire to marry someone of my own choosing, and more recently, my part in our collective decision to release the Second Life data to all Arborists. "I didn't know if we'd be able to build something new. But I did believe both Burke and Ereni were sincere in wanting to try."

Kuusta takes in my words. "I don't know why anyone would ever decide to forgive me," he finally says.

"You're so hard on yourself," I whisper.

"How could I not be?" he throws back. "I'm doing my best, but I've been fooling myself to believe I could leave the past behind. I don't deserve that kind of grace."

I prop myself up on my elbow so I can look in his direction. I can barely see his shadowy figure in the moonlight. "Maybe you can't leave it behind," I say, "but that doesn't mean you don't deserve a future."

A pause. "I don't know what that would look like," he finally says.

"Neither do I," I admit. "But that doesn't mean it's not possible. It just means we have some work to do."

"The first time I met you, I thought you were arrogant and disrespectful."

I give a rueful laugh, remembering how I insisted on competing in an all-levels scramble that was above my skill level, and how adamant he'd been that I was making a mistake. In the end, he'd been right, and I'd injured myself.

"But really what I was seeing was that you refuse to give up." Kuusta's not wrong about that. "I'm glad I met you, Sienna Tascioni."

I'd thought he was arrogant as well, and look at us now. "And I'm glad I met you, Kuusta Elo."

He chuckles. "I never would have guessed someday we'd be together, sleeping outside on a faraway planet."

"It's a good example of how we never know what might happen," I say. "That's why I never want to give up. Because of everything we don't know."

"To uncertainty," Kuusta says.

"To uncertainty," I repeat. But it takes me a long time to finally fall asleep.

WE RETURN to Seji as scheduled without checking the news first. I wish I could postpone learning whether Ereni won forever. This way I can pretend everything has turned out exactly the way I want.

There are no clues as to the outcome of the race on our walk back to the hospitality house. At least nobody looks at us strangely after our unwelcome time in the spotlight, but Kuusta keeps a hat pulled low over his eyes until we get inside. We go straight to Ereni's room.

She and Burke are laughing about something as we come in. They're both holding bright red fruit smoothies, and they look more relaxed than I've seen them in a long time, maybe even since we arrived on Satori. My heart sinks, even as I cling desperately to hope.

"How was your trip?" Looking alarmingly cheerful, Ereni takes a big sip of her drink.

"It was fine," I say. Kuusta doesn't respond at all. "How was the election?"

"Well, we lost," Burke says. My hope is punctured so rapidly, I feel unsteady on my feet. "But we put up a good fight."

"We didn't do so badly," Ereni adds. "I came in a strong second, if I do say so myself. But Lyra's longstanding connections were always going to be tough to beat. I congratulated her personally, of course." She doesn't even wrinkle her nose when she says this.

"I feel like this is all my fault," I tell them.

"Nonsense." Ereni stands up and begins to pour two more glasses of the fruit drink. "I did what I set out to do, and I think we did an excellent job. Yes, I would have preferred to win, but the real point of the exercise was to get more people talking about the wormhole technology, what we owe to humanity at large, and what's at stake around creating our own wormhole, and in that endeavor, we were extremely successful."

I hear the truth in her words, but I'm so tired. The personal and yet very public attack against me and Kuusta, which I suspect was orchestrated by Lyra herself, has broken something inside me. My own people hated me when they realized I'd been posing as a boy and when I refused to let my father get away with murder, but I never expected to face something even remotely similar here on Satori.

I'd tried to cheer Kuusta up, but the truth is I'm feeling just as lost as he is. I have people who care about me here, and that means so much to me, but I don't know what I'm doing. I have all this energy that I want to put into service helping people, but every time I try, I become embroiled in complications.

The Satori obviously don't need my help. And I'm tired of trying to convince them to help others, a goal we ostensibly share. It's clear if anything can be done about the new wormholes, it won't be the Satori leading the effort.

I accept a drink from Ereni and sink into a chair, taking sips to have something to do with myself. Ereni is speaking excitedly about her prospects for being offered a job at the Seji Association, running analysis about land use in the city. Evander is personally advocating for her receiving the position.

I don't know how she can be so upbeat after losing her race, but I appear to be the only one taking the news hard. I know Novelle and Allegra hadn't been particularly hopeful of the outcome even if Ereni were to win. She'd be just one of a large number of planetary representatives, after all, and that's without factoring in the even larger Citizens' Assembly with randomly selected members, at least some of whom would have needed to get on board.

Still, I'm relieved when Burke and I make our escape and return to my own room. He waits until we close the door behind us before pulling me in a tight embrace. "I'm really sorry, Sienna."

"We did what we could." My words are muffled against his shoulder. Even Burke's closeness doesn't lift my spirits. "I'm tired," I tell him, struggling not to start crying. "That show about me was so awful. It feels like everything is always a fight, and I hate having to pay such a high price, over and over again."

He gently rubs my back, and I try to modulate my breathing. "Why don't we get away for a while?" he suggests.

Sudden hope surges inside me. "Could we?"

"I don't see why not." He continues to trace circles on my back. "We don't have any real commitments here. We could give up our room allotments, and I bet we could borrow a boat. Go sailing wherever our hearts desire."

I like the idea of me and Burke out on the water, doing as we please. "But wouldn't that be irresponsible?" I whisper.

"No one will care. And we both deserve a break. How will either of us be able to figure out what we want to do next when we're both so worn out?"

He makes a valid point. Thinking about the future feels overwhelming. I feel further than ever from knowing what I'd like to do. Perhaps I should give up my greater ambitions and choose something simple and easy. I don't know what that would look like here on Satori.

"What about Kuusta?" I ask. I don't want to abandon my friend.

"Ereni's going to talk to him about some distance learning programs," Burke says. "Now that the election is over, I truly don't think anyone will give him a hard time, and hopefully he can resume his studies as planned. But there's no harm in having some backup options."

Why am I wavering? Burke is offering me a respite from everything that has been troubling me, something that would have been impossible in my life on Sanctum. This could be exactly what I need to gain clarity.

"Let's do it." I say it more decisively than I feel. Maybe if I ignore my old doubts, embracing the new will become easier. Maybe.

Burke squeezes me tighter. "I have to admit, I could use some time too," he tells me. "It's been uncomfortable seeing how three hundred years have transformed Lyra, and not for the better. I can't help wondering who I'll become in another three hundred years. What if that's a long enough time to lose sight of what I really care about?"

In a strange way, it's comforting to know I'm not the only one struggling with doubts right now. And not the only one who would welcome leaving them behind.

Why do I care so much about the mysterious wormholes anyway? For all I know, the only new one that's been created is the one in my system. Perhaps the damage they're causing is limited.

But one thing is clear. Going forward, any new wormholes will be someone else's problem.

"How soon can we leave?" I ask.

CHAPTER 23

*L*ife is very different on a boat.

I spend my days outside in the sun, wearing my few bathing costumes and little else. Burke begins to teach me how to handle the boat, and we continue my swimming lessons. My skin gets darker, my arms get more toned, and the salt water frizzes my hair, which I keep pulled back the majority of the time.

Sometimes we stop and chat with other people living on boats as we're doing, and we have a regular shore schedule in order to pick up much needed supplies. But mostly Burke and I are left to ourselves. I'm finally able to use the cooking skills I illicitly learned back home, although I'm making much simpler meals than my parents would have ever accepted. We read, and in the evenings, Burke plays me Satori music and sometimes we dance together, recalling our time on Sanctum soon after we'd met.

We don't talk much about the past, and we don't talk about the future at all. We talk about which fruits are ripe, when we're going into port, what we're reading, and how beautiful the stars are in the evening sky. I fall asleep every night with Burke curled up against my back, holding me in his arms.

After weeks of this, something deep inside of me that I wasn't even aware existed begins to release. My body relaxes. I've been living with dread for so long, at first I don't know what to do without it. Instead of looking for bad things beyond every corner, I slowly learn to follow the easy rhythm of the days as they unfurl.

I didn't realize it was possible to live this way.

In the beginning we check in with our friends every day, but as time passes, every day slips to every few days, slips to once a week, slips to whenever we happen to think about it, which isn't very often. Having spent my life trying to live up to the expectations of everyone around me, I love being unmoored. Burke asks very little of me, beyond my help with the basics of our life and my company.

I spend hours laying on the deck doing nothing but listening to the sounds of the ocean. Sometimes I think it's trying to speak to me, but I have no idea what it's saying. I think a lot about Leo. It's hard to believe he's dead now; he'd been my everything for so much of my life. I wonder what he'd make of where I am now, that I can laze around on a boat wearing all too little clothing and just *be*.

He probably would have lasted two weeks at most before he would have been desperate to return to an art studio and make the masks that were his biggest joy. But I am not so easily distracted. The weeks pass and turn into months. Burke's dark hair gets shaggier, and I get used to the smell of salt overhanging everything, the movement of the boat beneath my body, the way days string together into one long extension of unbroken time.

I keep thinking I might get restless or bored, but after everything that has happened, the sense of peace I feel living with Burke on the boat feels like everything I've ever wanted. The simplicity creates more space to breathe, and I take pleasure in the little moments: eating a freshly caught fish, lightly sautéed in oil; reading a particularly interesting passage in a book; how strong my body feels moving cleanly through the water; the way Burke's lips quirk upwards right before he makes a ridiculous joke.

Once, when we are cooking together in the tiny kitchen, I run into Burke, sending an entire bowl of seeds scattering across the space. Burke and I look at the mess, and then we both burst into laughter. "I love you," I tell him. Finally, after all this time together, I feel safe with him. I'm able to say the words without holding anything back.

"I love you too," he tells me. "So much, Sienna. So very, very much."

I clasp my hands around his neck, my fingers getting tangled in his apron strings. I press my body to his, and when our lips touch, it's pure magic. I never want to pull away.

I might never have to.

Sometimes, late at night, right before I fall asleep, Burke's warmth enveloping me, I wonder if this might be enough. Maybe we can remain like this forever. Maybe we can just be happy.

But even as I hold these hopes as I drift into sleep, I feel like they might be too good to be true.

I'M SUNNING out on the deck after my morning swim, a large hat shading my face. Guitar music is playing softly, and Burke is doing alternating sets of sit-ups and push-ups. Any moment now I'll start reading the tomb of Satori history I'm currently consuming. Kuusta will be so proud of me—that is, if I can manage to finish. We just stopped at a small town yesterday so we have fresh bread and cheese and berries for lunch.

The intrusive sound of my qualpad chiming interrupts the serenity, but I adjust the brim of my hat and ignore it. Five minutes later, it comes again. I look over at Burke, but he's launched into a series of stretches. If his N-CAT is pinging him, he's not showing any signs.

I sigh and look at my qualpad just as it chimes for the third time. It's Ereni. I frown at my qualpad until it falls silent and navigate to my history book.

I've finished a chapter and made good headway into the next by the time my qualpad chimes again. I make an annoyed noise, but then I see it's Novelle calling. I haven't heard from her in weeks, and she *is* my niece. I answer the call with a sigh. "Novelle!" I try to make my voice bright. "How are you doing?"

I hear something in the background, and Novelle says, "See?"

before she begins addressing me. "Sienna, hello. I was wondering if I'd be able to get in touch with you. Busy day?"

"Not really," I say honestly. "I just finished a swim, and I'm reading this history book Kuusta recommended to me. Have you seen him lately?"

Novelle makes a little huffing noise. "Why, yes, I am keeping an eye on your friend, just like you asked me to. He just finished his current load of classes, actually, and he's on a break for a couple weeks."

"So he was able to complete his work?"

"That's right," Novelle said. "I guess his classmates decided to be civilized about things. At least, he didn't mention any problems. He's keeping to himself a lot though."

"I knew he would." I lay back in my chair. "Maybe we can come pick him up and have him on the boat for a few days before his new classes start."

"About that." Novelle pauses. "I think it's a great idea for you to come back."

I give a little laugh. "I guess we can stay in port for a day or two if you miss us."

"Hmm." Another pause. "Actually, we could use your help."

I sit up straighter in my chair, and Burke looks over at me and slowly comes out of his current stretch. "Oh? Is everything okay?" I ask her.

"The To have asked that you be present at a meeting in Jundo. They are delaying until your return."

A flicker of interest pierces my detachment. "I'm sure it's nothing you and Ereni can't handle."

"All the delegates will be there," Novelle says. "But they've asked for you personally. By name. And Kuusta." I don't respond. "I would consider it a great personal favor if you'd come back for this," she finally adds.

I want to say no. This may be the first time I've been really, truly happy, and I don't want it to end.

If nothing else, these last few months have taught me how unimportant I truly am. The world of Satori has continued without me.

The world of Sanctum was happy for me to be gone. In the wake of immovable forces, perhaps all one person can do is look for a modicum of personal happiness and try to insulate oneself from the chaos of it all.

Burke walks over from where he was doing his stretches and sits on the chair across from me, leaning his elbows on his knees. I mute my qualpad. "It's Novelle," I tell him. "She wants us to come back to Seji. The To have requested my presence."

"I suppose when the first alien species to make contact with humanity asks to see you, you usually say yes." Burke reaches out and takes my hand. "But I'll support your decision either way."

I don't want to leave our boat. It has become the ultimate security blanket since we first came aboard. A part of me has been secretly hoping we could just stay here forever.

I don't know what I owe to the Satori. Our balance sheet has become strangely complicated. Or what I owe to Novelle, my own brother's child. Or what I owe the other delegates from my system. Or even to the To, who have chosen to get involved with humanity's next messy technological leap for inscrutable reasons of their own.

But perhaps it's not about who or what I owe. Perhaps it's more about who I am and what I believe in. And in spite of everything—or maybe because of it—I want to help. I want to make a difference, even if it's only a very small difference. I might be disheartened, but I don't want to leave my friends behind. Not because of what I owe them, but because of how much I love them.

I unmute my qualpad. "I'll come," I say. "I'll send you an estimated arrival time soon."

"Oh, thank you." Novelle sounds relieved. "We'll all be so happy to see you. And you should know Kuusta flatly refused to go meet the To unless you came too."

I feel a stir of affection for this latest demonstration of Kuusta's extreme stubbornness. "I'm looking forward to seeing you too," I say.

"Oh, Ereni wants to talk to you."

Novelle must know I don't really want to talk to Ereni because she passes her qualpad off quickly. "Hi, Sienna." Ereni's voice is unmistakable. I know she and Burke speak regularly, but she and I have only talked a few times since we left. Whenever we do, she brings up political topics and talks about what we might do together in the future. It hasn't been in keeping with my careful ignoring of said future, so I've been mostly avoiding her calls.

"I'm really glad you've been able to take this time off," Ereni is saying. "I hope it's given you something that you've been needing."

"I think it has," I reply carefully.

"I wanted to prepare you. The To have said they want to meet you personally, which I believe means they don't want to use their regular robot intermediary. They have extended an invitation for you and Kuusta to come up to their ship."

"Just me and Kuusta?" I ask. "Novelle just said all the delegates will be there."

"All the delegates will be at the meeting in Jundo," Ereni says. "But only you and Kuusta will be traveling into space. As long as you're willing."

A chance to see the first alien species humanity has ever met with my own eyes? How could I possibly refuse? An old, familiar excitement rises in my chest. "I'm willing," I say faintly.

"I also want you to know that I absolutely don't blame you for the results of the election." Ereni says the words with her usual force, and I feel like I've been punched in the stomach. "The odds were against me, and I think I would have lost regardless, but also I'm proud to be your friend, and I'm proud of the work we've done together. I just want you to know I've never apologized for any of that, and I never will."

My lungs squeeze. It's only hearing her words that I realize how much I've been feeling like I let her down. I haven't regretted befriending Kuusta when he most needed friendship or being supportive to Theckla while she was adjusting to a new school. But I've had the lingering feeling of being penalized for doing things I thought were kind. If I can't uproot that instinct within me, will there be a real place for me on Satori? One that doesn't involve me hiding away on a boat?

"I feel like when I care for people, it leads to bad consequences," I admit. Burke squeezes my hand tighter.

"Me losing my race is not a bad consequence," Ereni says briskly. "It's just politics. You have a big heart, and I would never want you to stop using it. *That* would be the bad consequence, in my opinion."

"But you always talk about how important it is to be strategic," I protest.

"Relatively important, yes. But I don't want us to lose our souls in the process. If you've taught me anything, Sienna, you've taught me that. Now come home and meet some aliens, okay?"

How could I refuse an offer like that?

CHAPTER 24

Kuusta and I don't meet with the other delegates when we arrive in Jundo. Instead, we're whisked away from Novelle and Allegra at the building entrance where the delegate meeting is taking place. Two grim-faced Satori take us directly to the spaceport where we'd initially arrived from Zamavat.

"If I didn't know better, I'd say we're being deported." Kuusta is joking, but I don't laugh.

We're escorted directly to the small spacecraft that will shuttle us to the To's ship, which is currently in orbit around Satori. I thought I might never travel into space again, but I'm surprised to find I don't hate the idea. In spite of the blank faces of the Satori who brought us here, I have to admit this meeting is more glamorous than anything I'd ever expected. I can't wait to meet the To. As far as I know, we are the first humans to meet the To face-to-face.

The spacecraft has no passengers but us, and as I strap myself in, my hands begin to shake. "I don't know why the To want to see *me*," Kuusta says. "I've never even visited your system, and I don't know anything about wormholes."

I don't know why they want to see me either. Surely they'd be better off negotiating with the delegates who traveled with them from my system, or else with seasoned Satori diplomats. Why are we, of all people, being dragged out into space for this meeting?

My nerves don't improve after we dock with the starship. A disembodied voice speaking in Truncish directs us to enter a decontamination chamber one at a time. "Is that the To?" Kuusta whispers to me. I shrug. Who can say?

The voice tells me to remove all my clothing before I am blasted on all sides by a hard spray. When I emerge from the chamber, naked and shivering, I put on the simple shirt and pants provided for me, wishing there is something I could do about my now very wet hair. The voice directs me into a stunningly white waiting area, hard benches against the walls on two sides. Floor-to-ceiling lockers, also white, take up one whole wall. The lights are so bright I have to blink several times before my eyes manage to adjust.

Kuusta emerges a few minutes later, also wet. He's wearing a larger version of my own clothes. "That isn't the most pleasant smell, is it?" he comments, taking a seat next to me on my chosen bench. I wrinkle my nose and nod. We both now smell like a combination of lye and an almost intolerably strong musk.

"This is the ship's computer," the voice says pleasantly enough. "We're sorry about the disinfectant process, which we understand is not ideal for humans. It is, however, important the To are protected from any foreign bodies you could have been carrying on your persons. You will be happy to learn our scans have shown you to be free from carrying any pathogens that are harmful to the To, so we may proceed."

I haven't considered the risks of two alien species coming into close proximity. I hope the To have been as thorough on my and Kuusta's behalf as they have been on their own. I can read the headline now: "First contact ends in tragic death of two young humans."

"We will ask you to open the lockers to your left. You will find breathing equipment for your use. I will confirm if you have donned the equipment correctly."

Kuusta and I stand and open the lockers, where we find oxygen canisters that we can strap to our backs, along with clear masks that easily mold to cover our mouths and noses. I check the gauge on my tank to ensure it's full. I don't want to catch an alien disease *or* asphyxiate to death.

"They sure are going to a lot of effort to meet us in person," I say. My voice sounds strangely muffled by the mask, but at least I'm able to talk normally.

"The To are very excited you have agreed to meet them," the ship's computer says in the same pleasant tone. "We understand you had to undergo personal sacrifice to do so, the one known as Sienna Tascioni."

My cheeks heat in embarrassment. "It was hardly a personal sacrifice," I murmur. I catch Kuusta grinning in my direction, and I glare at him. "I was happy to come," I say louder. After all, there are no guarantees the To aren't already listening to what we're saying.

"We are glad to hear that," the ship's computer says. "We would like to prepare you for the visit. You might find the temperature somewhat unpleasant, but it is within parameters acceptable for human lifeforms. In addition, the To have difficulty tolerating the light spectrums to which human lifeforms are accustomed. They fitted this ship with these custom light systems in order to accommodate human lifeforms comfortably should they require travel assistance, as has in fact occurred. However, for you to be in closer proximity to the To, these light systems will have to be deactivated. We apologize for any inconvenience this may cause you."

I draw closer to Kuusta. "Will we be in the dark?" I hope the ship's computer doesn't notice the small tremor in my voice.

"That is correct," they confirm. "It is our understanding that human lifeforms are very reliant on their systems of sight and that therefore existing in a space without your normal light wavelengths might be burdensome. The To have instructed me to apologize and assure you that they wish such measures were not necessary."

I take a deep breath. "We understand."

"In that case, might you be ready to join the To?"

Kuusta and I look at each other. He gives me a slight nod. "We're ready," I agree.

The door of our compartment slides open, leading to a hallway dimly lit by glowing panels inset in the floor and walls. The space is much wider and taller than similar hallways in Satori starships, making me wonder if the To might be very large. The panels light up in front of us as we walk, showing us the correct way. I practice breathing as normally as possible in spite of the oxygen mask I'm wearing. I can't smell anything.

Eventually the lights lead us to a large door. Once Kuusta and I are both standing in front of it, all the lights go out at once, leaving us in darkness. I hear a whooshing sound that I assume is the door sliding open.

"You may enter now," the ship's computer says. "I suggest you take approximately seven steps forward."

I decide not to worry about the "approximate" part of their instructions. Kuusta slips his hand into mine so we can stay together. We count our steps out loud. "One," he says. "Two. Three."

"Four. Five," I join him. The surface beneath our feet has become unexpectedly squishy, and the air around us has increased dramatically in temperature. "Six." We both pause, hoping the computer has calculated the size of our steps appropriately. It doesn't chime in to correct us. "Seven."

"Excellent," the ship's computer says. "The To will now try to initiate contact."

What do they mean, try? Are the To not in the room with us? A sudden panic grasps me, and I look around, straining my eyes in my efforts to see in the absolute darkness surrounding us. The great heat makes it hard to breathe, and I feel sweat collecting underneath my mask. I think I hear the swishing sound that means the door has just closed behind us, trapping us in this space. My breathing, loud in the oxygen mask, audibly increases in pace.

"We're fine," Kuusta says softly. He squeezes my hand as if to remind me he's still there. His palm is already slippery with sweat.

My breathing echoes loudly in my ears, until suddenly…we're not in the dark chamber at all.

No, we're back in the Forest of the Ancestors. I would know that smell of loam and evergreen anywhere. I spin around in confusion, taking in Kuusta standing beside me, a puzzled look on his face. Neither of us are wearing our special breathing gear any longer, and we're both wearing normal clothes, not our new sterile outfits.

Virve Tuomi, the Wise One who became my friend on Arbor, stands rooted before us, zher trunk and branches reaching up to the sky, the ferns planted by zher son looking as lush as ever at zher base.

"Virve," I breathe, and without thinking, I reach for zher in my mind.

Zhe doesn't respond. Instead, an older gentleman with a neatly trimmed white beard and twinkling blue eyes materializes out of thin air in front of us. He is wearing a formal black and brown outfit appropriate to Arbor. I blink and back up into Kuusta. "Who are you?" I realize I'm speaking Gallo, my native tongue.

"We are the To," the man says sagely. He is also speaking Gallo.

I turn to Kuusta in confusion. "He says he is the To," I tell him.

"Yes, I heard him," Kuusta says. He too is speaking Gallo, a language I'm certain he doesn't know. I swallow hard. "Surprises upon surprises, hmm?"

I turn back to the very human-looking man. "I don't wish to cause any offense, but would you mind explaining how you are the To? Or how we come to be in my friend Virve's clearing on Arbor, which is a planet located in another system?"

"Arbor," the man—no, the To—say thoughtfully, looking around with interest. "I was wondering where we were. What a beautiful spot."

"It's good to be home, however they managed it," Kuusta says under his breath. He seems much more interested in soaking in the atmosphere of the clearing than speaking to the strange old man in front of us.

"I regret to inform you that we are not truly on Arbor," the To say. "Not physically, in any case. We were searching for a place where both of you would feel comfortable and at peace, and this appears to be the compromise the two of you reached."

Kuusta looks as confused as I feel. "But Kuusta and I never discussed a meeting spot," I say.

"My apologies." The man—I'm having trouble thinking of them as the To—raises their palms upwards in a gesture of peace. "We are not used to conversing with humans in this fashion. This is how our species often communicates. We create a"—they say a garbled word I can't understand—"in order to have a shared consensus of reality in which to begin our communion."

"I'm sorry, I don't understand. What do you create?" I ask.

Kuusta wanders over to Virve and gently touches zher trunk. "It feels real enough," he remarks.

"A"—another garbled word comes out of the To's mouth. They try again. "A…dreamscape. We create something that isn't physically real but is equally real for all of us present." They grimace. "It is difficult to explain."

"I'm hearing Kuusta speak a language I know he doesn't know," I say. "Can you explain that?"

"Yes, it is easier to communicate here, isn't it?" the To say. "It is geared toward the comfort of each entity present. This way we can all say what we wish to say. We don't speak either of your most deep-rooted languages. We usually communicate with each other mind-to-mind, in a way more similar to the Wise Ones of Arbor of whom you are both so fond. That is why we asked to see both of you in particular. We surmised this mode of communication would be less alarming for humans with experience communicating in alternative fashions. Also, we don't have much experience with the devices that most of the humans present on this planet have imbedded in their brains, but our experience with the Luz while they were on board the starship indicate they might cause additional complications."

Given the To chose me for this meeting due to my experience with Virve Tuomi on Arbor, it seems fitting that the dreamscape Kuusta and I accidentally chose together is zher clearing. I feel a fresh pang knowing I'll never see zher, nor my good friend Pilvi, again, but this is confirmation they live on in my mind.

This is also confirmation there continue to be positive as well as negative consequences due to my refusal to have an N-CAT implanted.

"So we're not actually communicating out loud then, is that correct?" Kuusta asks.

"We are together in the compartment on our starship," the To say. "None of us is speaking aloud in that compartment at this time. But we can assure you that your physical bodies remain in good condition."

"Small favors," Kuusta says.

I try to think through what we've been told. "You said Kuusta and I compromised on choosing this location." The To nod. "But this form of communication doesn't feel like my experience speaking with a Wise One. When Virve and I spoke, it didn't feel out loud the way this does, and we could sense one another's feelings."

"Our method of communication is different from the one utilized by the Wise Ones," the To agree. "Especially the method zhey use to speak with those who are still human. Would you prefer to experience an emotional component? We thought that might be uncomfortable and confusing for you, but we are happy to adapt."

"That's okay," Kuusta says quickly. "Why don't you tell us why you wanted to speak with us?"

"We have received some intelligence," the To say. "We wish to share it with the humans and initiate a Reckoning. We chose you as our emissaries in this matter."

I look over at Kuusta, but he looks as in the dark as I feel. "I'm afraid the translation didn't come through clearly for us," I say politely. "What is a Reckoning?"

The To frown as though thinking. They are silent for a long minute before giving a brisk nod. "Perhaps there is no appropriate word in either of your root languages," they say. "What we mean by a Reckoning is a process of accountability, wherein the Satori come to an understanding of their actions and attempt to help those who were harmed become whole again. Is this an understandable concept to both of you?"

"Too familiar," Kuusta says. "I hate to say it, but I believe you chose correctly by having me here."

The To turn to me. "And you, Sienna?"

"Are you saying…the Satori have done something wrong?" I ask.

"The Satori must take accountability for their actions," the To say. "We hope they will want to do so, as well as contribute to creating the conditions necessary for both healing and harmonious relationships between humankind." They pause. "If it helps you to understand, the To's assistance in this matter is its own practice of accountability. We are honored to be able to be of service in this way."

Their reply only confuses me further, but the man who embodies the To is staring at me with such a pleased expression on their face. "Perhaps as you tell us more, I will understand better," I say. "You said you have information?"

"That is correct. Come, let us sit. That is appropriate in this setting, is it not?" The To fold themselves gracefully into a cross-legged position on the ground. Kuusta and I follow suit, and I'm surprised to find the ground damp against my backside, just as I remember it.

"We asked the Satori for the manifests and logs from a number of their starships," the To begin. "At first they were reluctant to provide this information, but we were adamant. We shared our belief that such a sharing of data was an act of good faith that would begin a strong foundation of trust and cooperation between the To and the Satori. The Satori recently acquiesced to our request, and we have performed an analysis."

"We were originally sent to investigate the wormhole in the Promise B system as part of our agreed-upon accountability plan," they continue. "Due to our monitoring systems, at the time of our departure we knew for a certainty that no other unusual wormholes had opened. The Promise B system wormhole was the first. Certainly, during the time of our voyage from the Promise B system to Satori, others could have been created, as we are not able to monitor the wormhole network unless we're in proximity to a wormhole ourselves. But we think the first wormhole is significant."

"Do you know why they chose our system?" I ask.

They hold up a hand. "I will tell you all," they say solemnly. "And then we can reflect and discuss until such a time as you may have certain biological needs that require your attention."

Out of the corner of my eye, I see Kuusta smirk. I shift uncom-fortably on the ground, not wanting to discuss a body I'm not even properly inhabiting at the moment. I hope it is behaving…appropriately while I'm gone.

"From our discussions with the Satori, we've been able to discern that the only planets we know for certain possess the wormhole technology are the Satori and the Doctrina from the Nova F system. While the Doctrina are typically very free with their research, it is our perception that most human cultures aren't equipped with the necessary knowledge base to understand the technology, let alone implement it. The Satori have clearly expressed their belief that the technology could have been independently discovered elsewhere, and we kept that in mind. They also led us to understand it was possible that one of the Satori mission ships might have shared the data with other planets. Due to the classification of this data, however, this was deemed by the Satori to be unlikely. Given the information we possessed, we thought it most likely that either the Doctrina or the Satori themselves had been involved in the creation of the wormhole in the Promise B system."

Kuusta makes a little humming noise, and I can tell he's as interested in what the To is telling us as I am.

"Unfortunately, we were unable to investigate the Doctrina with immediacy due to their distance from this system. We were, however, in an ideal location to investigate the Satori themselves. We set ourselves the task of discerning any possible Satori involvement. During the course of our inquiries, we learned about a pro-wormhole group who call themselves the Unity. We believe you are familiar with this group?"

I remember Aeson's political maneuvers and how we'd disappointed the Unity with Ereni's refusal to pledge them additional funding. "We've met."

The To nod. "We looked into the previous activities of the individuals associated with this group, and we discovered that several individuals who are integral to its operations recently returned from missions, just like yourself. They arrived on Satori about a year before you did, in fact. We asked for all documentation pertaining to that ship and mission. The Satori spent a long time debating whether they should provide such information to us, but eventually they agreed it was a reasonable request. Among the documentation, we discovered discrepancies in dates of departure and arrival that suggest the starship made an extra stop on its way home. The data confirms that a stop to the Promise B system would have been possible. We have just transmitted our findings to the Satori. We expect they will be able to locate either the wormhole creation devices themselves or their required components in the possession of the Unity down on the planet."

"Oh." I sit back on my hands in surprise. "So it was the Satori all along."

"A small group of Satori, who we believe acted without the knowledge of any of their peers," the To correct me.

Not completely unlike the decision Burke, Ereni, and I had made back on Arbor when we released private data about the Second Life process to the public. But not completely the same either: we had been making secret information available to everyone on Arbor, who could then decide on a course of action. The Satori involved in creating a new wormhole, on the other hand, had unilaterally decided to create a wormhole in a system with three human-inhabited planets without consulting any of them.

"It appears many of the Unity-affiliated members of the mission in question have already departed on two new missions," the To offer. I swallow and look up at Virve's branches. I wish zhe was actually here to offer zher counsel.

"Why are you telling us this?" Kuusta asks. "Neither of us are Satori. We won't have any influence over how they respond."

The man, I have come to realize, is sitting unnaturally still. Perhaps this is my subconscious's way of signaling they're not actually a human being but instead the speaking avatar of some unknown number of alien beings. "We would like you to be involved," they say. "Kuusta, you are neither Satori nor from a planet that is impacted by the new wormhole. As such, you possess a degree of perspective we believe will be valuable in the days to come." Kuusta nods slowly. "And Sienna, our hope is that you will act as a kind of bridge. You are from the system most impacted by the creation of the wormhole, and you have spent a longer time amongst the Satori than the delegates whom we brought to this place. You have studied Satori philosophy and participated on one of their missions. We believe you too provide a key perspective on the matters at hand."

The To stand and gesture to us both. Kuusta and I scramble to our feet. "We would like to invite the two of you to be part of the To delegation in the talks that are to come. We will deploy our robot, Milo, but we do not believe that will provide sufficient representation. Will you serve?"

Kuusta bows his head. "I will."

I try to ignore the churning in the pit of my stomach. I know it's an honor for the To to select me and Kuusta to represent them. But I've just spent the last many months deliberately disengaged and not wanting to be involved. There's a part of me that wants to continue to embrace that simplicity, not to mention the freedom from making mistakes.

But I know I can only contribute if I'm willing to make mistakes as I go, as messy and painful as that can be. And the To's discovery will impact both my old home and my new one, along with all the people I care about most in the universe.

I take a deep breath. "I will serve."

I only hope I don't regret it.

CHAPTER 25

I tell Burke everything when I get home to Seji.

It's not long before the Satori publicly confirm the involvement of the Unity and their previous mission in the creation of the new wormhole in the Promise B system. They call a summit to take place in a few weeks' time in Jundo. Representatives from the Greater Conclave and the Citizens' Assembly will be in attendance, as well as the delegates from the Promise B system, including Novelle and Allegra. And Kuusta and I will be there with the To's robot Milo.

It feels strange that for once, I'll be involved in something in which Burke and Ereni will not be participating. Ereni is busy with her work with the Seji Association, but Burke has spent the last several months with me on our little boat, which we're now giving up. He's been assigned a new room in a different building in Seji, and I'm staying there with him for the few days I have free before I have to return to Jundo to develop a proposal with the To and the delegates from my system that we can present to the Satori during the summit.

Burke and I decamp to Akari Park. It's been months since I've been there, but there's a familiarity to it that I find comforting in the wake of the larger events unfolding. Being in company with other people, even strangers, is surprisingly comforting in this moment. We walk in silence for a long while, finally settling on a bench in front of what Burke calls an infinity fountain, placed in the middle of concentric circles of blooming tropical plants.

Burke has been beaming with pride ever since I shared the To's request that I serve as a member of their delegation. "You are the perfect person to be involved," he tells me again now.

"And Kuusta," I can't help but add.

"And Kuusta." He shakes his head. "I can't believe we're the ones who have been responsible all along. These debates about the merits and dangers of the wormhole technology seem so insignificant now."

"I don't know." I shift, tucking my legs underneath me. "I think it's good those conversations have already started. I think that gives us something to build on, now that we need to reckon with the consequences."

"We met with those people," Burke says. "The Unity. I felt bad for Aeson when Ereni did her icy act with him. Before the meeting started, he told me I reminded him of himself when he was younger, did you know that? And now it turns out they opened a wormhole next to your planet without even talking to your people."

"To be fair, they wouldn't have received a warm welcome," I say. "I'm sure Sanctum would have strongly opposed the creation of the wormhole."

"That's exactly why they shouldn't have done it." Burke sounds indignant, making me want to kiss him. The fact that he cares so much, just as I do, is one of the reasons I love him the way I do.

"I'm sure they thought it would be easier to do what they wanted and apologize than ask for permission that would be denied." I raise a hand as Burke begins to splutter. "I'm not saying what they did was right. But we didn't ask for permission before giving Pilvi the Second Life data."

"That was entirely different," Burke objects. "You know it was."

"But like you said, it's not quite different enough to feel comfortable, is it? There's a reason we could relate to the Unity. That's all I'm saying."

"Yeah, I guess." The water tinkles musically in the fountain as he pauses to consider what I've said. "How do you feel about being back?"

I take a breath. "It feels kind of strange. It's wonderful to see everyone I care about, but we've been gone long enough I feel like I don't quite fit. Maybe I could fit if we stayed? But I'll need to be in Jundo for the duration of the talks. I got the impression it could be a lengthy process." I press my lips together, a wave of nerves increasing my heart rate. "I know you haven't been invited to play a role in the proceedings, but…would you consider coming to Jundo with me?"

I have no idea what he's going to say. I know we decided together to spend several months out on the boat, but after all this time away from his home city, will he really want to leave again? If he doesn't, I don't want him to have to give anything up for me. I've already thought about how often I can come back to visit in between sessions.

"I would love to." When he says the words, it feels as if my heart expands to fill my entire body. "And once the summit is over, we can figure out what we want to do next."

We. Burke and I are a we.

In my parents' relationship, my father always led and my mother always did as he wanted. She would have sacrificed anything for him, I truly believe that. But the relationship that Burke and I have is completely different, and the freedom of that…it makes me feel like I can fly.

I lean in to give him a kiss, and just as our lips touch, a gentle rain begins to fall. The water is warm, and we keep kissing, his hand slipping to caress my neck. I pull back long enough to see water beading on his hair, on the tip of his nose, at the ends of the hairs on his arms, and I know I must look similar. But appearances aren't everything here on Satori. I'm with someone who I love and who loves me. In this moment, everything about us seems like a miracle.

The rain begins to beat down harder, and Burke grabs my hand with a laugh and pulls me from the bench. We run through the collecting puddles, seeing who can splash the other person more, before coming to a breathless stop under a large gazebo in the garden. We aren't the only people seeking shelter here: there is another young couple, a trio of three older women, a man by himself with a peaceful expression on his face.

This place feels like home. But it's not because of the beauty of the garden or the mildness of the weather or the fact that I've visited this park so many times before. It's because Burke is here with me.

Sometimes the most important things sneak up on you when you're not paying the slightest bit of attention. I've been so busy focusing on the present moment in order to avoid thinking about the past. So much has happened since the Satori first came to Sanctum and I met Burke in another, very different, garden. I needed that time on the boat to come to terms with the choices I've made and grow comfortable with who it is I've become.

And somehow in the middle of everything, I began to think of Burke as my home. And looking into his warm brown eyes, knowing we'll be going to Jundo together, I know he thinks of me as his home too.

CHAPTER 26

*A*t the beginning of the summit, the Satori are very visibly sorry.

We all sit inside a gorgeous vaulted structure called the Akouo that reminds me of the cathedrals back home. Colorful murals decorate the walls and ceilings, and afternoon sun spills through large arched windows, providing plenty of light. The ceilings must stretch at least thirty meters high, and the setting lends gravitas to our meeting.

I sit with Kuusta and Milo, the To's rabbit robot, in one section of chairs. Novelle, Allegra, and the other delegates sit in a different section, the Lux in their glowing clothing and the Word in their silver robes. At least a hundred Satori sit in a third section. The chair molds to my body when I sit down.

For a while it seems as if each individual Satori will feel it necessary to deliver their own apology. Lyra takes place in the self-flagellation in her new role of Councilor, which I find particularly annoying given the part she played in the news show that damaged both Kuusta's and my reputations. I don't believe she's sincere, but that doesn't stop her from talking about her horror at learning the news of Satori culpability for the new wormhole in the Promise B system for a full five minutes.

I touch Milo's arm as Lyra is finally wrapping up, and they spring to their feet as if they've been waiting for my cue. A few delegates breathe visible sighs of relief at the interruption. We've been sitting here listening to the onslaught of apologies for close to three hours.

"These are all fine words of remorse," Milo says in their funny, tinny voice. "However, the To believe that actions are better suited for demonstrating accountability to those who have been harmed, as the three inhabited planets in the Promise B system most certainly have been. We suggest that we move on to having a productive dialogue with the delegates who have traveled so far to be here."

The Satori are clearly unused to being interrupted in their own space, but after some whispered discussion, one of the Councilors, a woman named Nyx who I know Ereni admires, agrees that the summit can proceed. There is a low grumbling from the Satori section, doubtless from people who had wanted to add their apologies to the words washing over the overwhelmed delegates.

Teofila, one of the Luz delegates, stands, her tail flicking behind her, which Novelle has told me is an indication of strong emotions. To my surprise, she doesn't give a formal bow. "We appreciate your professions of regret and responsibility," she says formally. "Before we begin our discussion about our accountability proposal, we would like to hear what further information you have discovered about the Satori who created our wormhole. Are any of them present?"

Nyx lowers her head for a moment before answering. "They are not here, no," she says. "We did not know if their presence would be welcome. However, Aeson has expressed his willingness to attend, should the delegates wish it. He could be here shortly to answer any questions you may have."

Teofila glances at the delegates beside her. "We do wish it," she says. "We want to hear directly from one of the individuals who made this decision."

Nyx nods at a woman behind her, and a few people leave the hall, presumably to fetch Aeson. "In the meantime," Nyx continues, "we can provide an update on our investigation. We have learned that the mission aboard the starship that originally traveled to your system to create the wormhole does in fact intend to open several more wormholes, although it will take them some time to do so. We have also discovered that several other missions that have left within the last year have done so with similar clandestine goals in mind. We have the lists of primary locations intended as wormhole sites, as well as a list of secondary locations should any of the primary locations not prove viable." Both her hands are balled into fists. "The list is sizable and contains many systems of note. All of them contain either human settlements or significant resources, which is unsurprising."

The Unity must have been feeling out Ereni's campaign, trying to decide if they could trust us. They'd clearly made the excellent call that they could not. While I agreed with Ereni that the wormhole technology needed to be actively dealt with rather than ignored, I would have never agreed to an operation like this one.

Then the import of Nyx's words sinks in. The starships have already left, and it's highly unlikely they can be stopped. Even if the Satori agree to opening their own wormhole here, there aren't yet enough access points in the network to allow us to travel faster than the original ships.

That means, whether we like it or not, the universe will fundamentally and permanently change. I feel a little queasy as I consider the significance of so many new wormholes created in a short period of time.

"Is the technology stable?" I ask Milo in a low voice. "Will creating many wormholes in relatively short order do any damage?" Damage to what, I wasn't sure. The network? Whatever space time consists of?

"We don't anticipate significant harm of that sort," Milo says. "The To will almost certainly need to deploy more ships to ensure the stability of the network, but we are able and willing to do so."

While Milo and I have been conferring, the delegates have begun a heated discussion amongst themselves. The Satori are strangely silent, given how many of them are present, but then, the information Nyx just shared is truly shocking, and I don't know how many of them had known the full extent of the situation until this moment.

After several minutes, Teofila steps forward, apparently the designated spokesperson of the group. Novelle is frowning, and Allegra has wrapped her arm around her, as if in comfort. "We remain strong in our conviction that there must be an accountability process between the Promise B system and the Satori," Teofila says. "But we are now realizing that there must also be a larger accountability process between the Satori and all the systems that will be impacted without their consent. Since those systems are not currently present, we are willing to act as representatives to initiate that process, with the understanding that individual acts of restoration will be necessary with all planets affected in the future."

The Satori begin talking amongst themselves, but they fall silent when a man, flanked by those who had been dispatched earlier, walks into the room. It's only when he draws closer I recognize Aeson. In spite of the trouble he's undoubtedly in, he sports the same mischievous smile and relaxed posture I remember from our previous meetings, his dark hair streaked with distinctive yellow stripes.

Nyx doesn't look happy to see him. "The delegates have asked to hear from you," she says stiffly. "I believe they are interested in your motivations, and they may have further questions."

Aeson's smile widens. "Of course. Like I said, I'm happy to engage in dialogue."

"Now that it's too late to stop them," Kuusta mutters in my ear.

"When the Satori learned of the wormhole technology, we were concerned about the implications," Aeson says in that confident way of his. "We tried to facilitate discussions on the matter, but it was clear a majority didn't want to seriously grapple with how a network of wormholes would fundamentally change humanity and our place in the universe. The economic possibilities alone are stunning, both for good and for ill. That being said, we are also students of ancient history, and given what we know about Earth, we were concerned, given how the wormholes quickly and drastically speed up travel between systems, about the military implications."

I can't keep my mouth shut. "So you secretly deployed the technology that makes military conflict more likely without having any plan?"

He turns the full wattage of his smile onto me, but it doesn't work. I'm too shocked by what he's just said. "We did have a plan. We acted to force the Satori to play a more active role in the deployment of the technology, given that its proliferation is inevitable."

Under the cover of the burst of conversation that follows this statement, I have time to collect myself. Same goal, different means. I hate that I'm forced to acknowledge that the Unity's strategy worked when mine and Ereni's did not. The whole affair makes me feel sick to my stomach.

Teofila indicates she would like to speak. "The delegates wish to know why your group selected the Promise B System for your first experiment with the wormhole technology."

"Of course." His cockiness is becoming unbearable to watch. "It was relatively close to the system we'd already been assigned, making it convenient. Then we heard about the failed Satori mission to Sanctum through a routine update beacon. That meant we could guarantee the absence of the Satori in the system, and it was clear from that mission's experience that we'd be able to create a wormhole undetected if we were careful. Which we in fact succeeded in doing." He shrugs. "It didn't hurt that it was obvious the people of Sanctum are incredibly primitive. There was certainly no risk of them being able to take inter-system military action any time soon. We had less information about Veritas and Buena Luz,"—he nods at the delegates, as if in deference, which is patently absurd—"but it seemed like a reasonable gamble, given our other options at that time."

I find myself leaning forward in my chair, wanting to yell at him again, but I restrain myself. After all, I'm helping to represent the To, not my own planet. One outburst was more than enough. Allegra looks as angry as I feel, but Novelle looks bored.

"That is quite a risk," Teofila says with what I think must be considerable irony. "Can you tell us why you chose not to communicate with us before coming to a final determination?"

"Oh, we did our due diligence." Aeson rubs his hands together. "I myself was dispatched to Sanctum's surface, but we sent small teams to each of the three planets, just to make sure we weren't missing anything."

"I take it you did this surreptitiously." Teofila says that last word with visible disgust. "But you didn't open official dialogue with any of us. Why weren't we granted that respect?"

"We didn't have to," Aeson said. "It wasn't part of the mission parameters. And we were going to open a wormhole one way or another, so it seemed kinder to simply do it. We didn't want to give you a false sense of agency. And because the process to create the wormhole does take some time, it seemed circumspect to avoid providing a warning."

"I see." Teofila's tail has begun twitching faster. She turns to Nyx. "May I ask what is going to be done with this man and his compatriots?"

Nyx clears her throat. "They will be required to undertake an accountability process," she says. "In addition, they will not be allowed to serve on any future missions nor in any position of trust. We can't prevent them from leaving the planet should they choose and should a foreign vessel agree to take them," she adds. "But they will not be provided with any resources to make their way easier."

"Where we come from, they would be put in prison," Allegra chimes in. "What about that?"

Nyx blinks, seemingly taken aback by the suggestion. Another Satori steps forward. "We do not have the prisons of which you speak," he says. "It has been our experience that punishment does not lead to further justice. Nothing we do now can grant us the power to go back in time and prevent the wormhole from being formed. What we can do going forward is limit the power of the involved individuals to cause any further harm through their actions."

The delegate from Veritas who I recognize from our conversation on the patio so many months ago, Abril Pacis, starts speaking urgently to Teofila and the other Buena Luz delegates, who appear to be translating for Novelle and Allegra. The conversation continues for quite some time while the Satori wait. I'm gratified to see Aeson start to shift his weight back and forth, the first sign he might not be quite as comfortable as he appears.

"We are willing to discuss this further," Teofila finally says to the wider group. "The delegates have some disagreement amongst ourselves on this point. For the time being, we have no further questions for this person."

The delegates wait until Aeson leaves the space before continuing. Novelle steps forward. "We would like to open dialogue on how the Satori mean to recompense our people for the creation of the wormhole in our system, as well as how they intend to ensure our safety and stability going forward."

Finally, our opportunity to present our plan. I take a slow, deep breath, preparing myself for the inevitable Satori resistance. We've worked so hard to reach agreement between all the delegates, but that is only the first step of many.

There is a long pause. The Satori look nonplussed, glancing in between themselves and communicating in inaudible whispers. Finally, Nyx speaks. "We've been here for several hours," she says. "I propose we adjourn until tomorrow."

None of the delegates want to make a fuss this early in the process, and Milo doesn't voice any objection, so the meeting unceremoniously ends. But when Novelle approaches me, she looks worried. "We'll present our proposal tomorrow," she says. "But I don't know if what happened today bodes well."

It is hard to tell with the Satori. "We will present it as planned," Milo says, twitching their nose. "We remain hopeful that our involvement might encourage cooperation on both sides."

Before I go to sleep that night, I make a call to Ereni. I tell her about our plan and ask her to come to the meeting tomorrow. She agrees without hesitation.

We need a secret weapon, and my hope is that Ereni will rise to the occasion.

CHAPTER 27

The To, in the form of Milo, are as good as their word, and they lay out our plan for the Satori the next morning. We transmit our detailed proposal to their N-CATs, and I know they're all furiously analyzing the material they've been given.

Ereni arrives in high form, wearing what I recognize as her favorite campaigning outfit: a high-necked dress in an eye-catching turquoise. She joins myself and Kuusta as a member of the To delegation. If anyone can convince the Satori of the merits of our plan and broker an agreement that all sides can agree to, Ereni can.

In essence, we're suggesting the Satori adapt their mission model to allow them to both communicate with the worlds that will already be impacted by new wormholes and speak to worlds that don't already have a wormhole but might like to consider one. If humanity is going to be closer to one another than we've been for generations, we are going to have to start with a lot of communication, and the Satori are well suited for the task.

The plan will mean, in essence, that the Satori will have to downgrade the collection of human knowledge to a second tier of priority. At any planet they visit, they can make any deals they wish with the locals, but the selection of destinations will need to depend on the information we have about the systems most likely to be impacted by wormhole technology.

On my mission to Arbor, the collection of data was paramount. For the wormhole-related missions, the Satori goal of helping humanity will have to rise to the top.

The other facet of the plan that I worry will become a sticking point is the requirement of creating a new wormhole right here in the Satori system. In order to be able to coordinate and communicate at the required scale, the wormhole will be necessary to facilitate the required travel speed. Once the Satori have their own wormhole, the To have agreed to teach them how to monitor the network themselves so they'll know when and where any new wormholes emerge.

The idea of the Satori *not* having their own wormhole also clearly sits poorly in the minds of the delegates, who have themselves been forced into all the problems and changes such a wormhole will inevitably necessitate. The least the Satori can do now is join them—us—in our troubles.

Meanwhile, if communication between all the worlds newly connected by wormholes is as important as everyone has been saying, we'll need a way to bring all the worlds together. There will be so many details that need to be worked out as humans are more easily able to travel between planets: issues of trade, of immigration, of social and religious mores, as well as agreements of nonaggression. Not every planet might choose to welcome the change of the wormhole in a peaceful way, but if planets are offered a structure and an easy way to choose peace, I'm hopeful it will lead to better outcomes than we'd otherwise see.

That's why I work hard to convince the delegates to include the idea of a Cooperative Council of Worlds in our proposal. If the Satori are willing to create their own wormhole, then the delegates will be able to travel in a reasonable amount of time back to the Promise B system. Satori, Sanctum, Buena Luz, and Veritas will be the first four worlds given the opportunity to join the Council. The To have agreed to serve in an advisory capacity as the Council is being formed, and to share the knowledge of how to monitor the wormhole network with any members who wish to learn.

I've also insisted on the importance of training a contingent of diplomats without N-CATs and with a strong grounding in languages and linguistics. It turns out there are the rare Satori that don't have N-CATs, usually due to health complications or injuries. The hope is that some of these people can be recruited so more mission teams sent out have at least one person without an N-CAT for those cases in which cross-cultural communication might benefit from its absence.

It's all a rather alarming amount of work, but if we can convince the Satori of the merit of our ideas, I think we have a chance to help humanity adapt to the new wormhole network in a more controlled way than the Unity have begun. It's not going to be perfect, but it's a promising start.

We have marathon negotiation sessions where Ereni and Milo cooperate to answer the many Satori objections. Some of them are logistical, some technical, but the most difficult ones are ideological. The Satori hold their mission program in such high regard, any changes to it are automatically met with skepticism and reluctance. But Ereni knows all the weak points upon which she can attack, and she slowly but surely converts a number of the Councilors and Citizens to her point of view.

It doesn't hurt to have the To present. Representing the first alien species to be in contact with humankind, they are largely unknown to the Satori. Their mystery exudes a quiet menace that both Ereni and I use to good effect in a few rare moments when pressure needs to be brought to bear. The Satori are invested in looking like good citizens of the universe, especially to a new alien race whose full technological capabilities remain murky. The To have also markedly refused to discuss the existence of other alien species, which leads to a further undercurrent of anxiety amongst the Councilors and Citizens.

Between all of us, we alternately browbeat, cajole, and reason the Satori into accepting the outlines of what needs to be done. As much as possible, we allow them to fill in the details themselves. "They need to feel a sense of ownership in what we're going to do," Ereni says more than once in the late-night meetings between ourselves, Milo, and the Promise B system delegates. No one disagrees.

In the end, the Satori almost act as if they've come up with this plan themselves, which they represent as a masterful performance of diplomacy and advancement. The day a new wormhole is created in the system, the entire planet celebrates the new epoch in human history.

The delegates are pleased. It's always hard to tell what the To think about anything, but Milo states they find this resolution to be acceptable. Kuusta tells me we've managed to pull off a miracle.

We learn there are eleven additional new wormholes in the network. More could appear at any time.

I might be the only one biting my tongue at what we've witnessed. But late at night when it's only me and Burke, I share my real feelings: how frustrated I am at how the Satori have behaved, even though they've been persuaded to respond responsibly. I know I should be happy, but to me the victory is bittersweet. I can't help but feel I will always be a visitor on Satori instead of someone who belongs.

Burke and I begin to talk about our future, and one idea that comes up with repeated frequency is finding an opportunity to leave the planet.

WHEN WE'RE BACK in Seji, Diantha invites us all—myself, Burke, Ereni, Kuusta, Novelle, and Allegra—to come over for dinner. Theckla is nearly overcome with excitement at having so many adults in the small home. She has made decorated place tags for each of us, set carefully around the table, and she chats happily about how much she loves to swim now that she's learned how.

At the appropriate time, we crowd around the table and share a simple meal made by Diantha, a hearty stew over rice. We talk about art and history, the latest land use decisions made by the Seji Association, various islands Burke and I had visited during our boating days. When I look around the table at my friends' happy faces, my heart feels nearly full to bursting. Back when I was trying to be a proper young lady on Sanctum, I could have never anticipated where I'd end up.

It is only when all of us have set down our spoons and Kuusta sits back with a loud sigh that Diantha gets down to business. She folds her hands on the table and leans forward, a focused expression on her face. "I asked you all here for a reason," she says. "Aside from the pleasure of your company, of course."

Ereni snorts. "I sensed some greater machinations at play," she says. I can't claim the same. I've simply been savoring quality time with some of my favorite people.

Diantha gives Ereni a quelling look. "I'm putting together a mission," she says. "Now that we have new priorities, I feel like I want to be part of the solution. And I'd like all of you to consider joining my Mission Council."

I don't even try to hide my surprise. Burke squeezes my hand under the table. "I don't mean to be rude, but have you thought this through?" I ask. "You know our various track records. We're not exactly…a conventional bunch."

"That's exactly why I want you," Diantha says. "This isn't going to be a conventional mission, after all. I've spoken to the Superior Mission Council, and they expect to have many assignments available to travel to new wormhole sites to provide information and start a dialogue about joining the Cooperative Council of Worlds. I think having a mission team with members from more than one planet will be a real asset for this type of work."

"I'm in," Kuusta says immediately. "Just tell me when, and I'll be there."

I'm not surprised at his answer. It's been clear to me since my return that he is making the best of his situation, but he's not at peace here.

Novelle and Allegra share a look, but Novelle is already shaking her head, and my heart sinks. "It's very generous of you to include us," Allegra says. "But we're both enjoying our lives here in Seji. We didn't leave Sanctum because we had grand ideas of becoming diplomats. We left so we could enjoy a freedom we would never be afforded at home. And now that we've found it, it feels hard to leave it behind again."

Novelle puts her arm around Allegra and leans her head on her shoulder. " My art is already becoming quite popular," she says. "We'd like to make Seji our permanent home."

Ereni chews on her lip, looking pensive. "What about Theckla?" she asks.

"I'm coming too," Theckla declares. "Wherever my mom goes, I go." She stares around the table fiercely, as if daring us to object.

Diantha sighs. "Theckla and I have discussed this at length," she says. "I thought things had improved since she made a few friends, but"—she shrugs—"it turns out there are still issues."

Theckla rolls her eyes. "No one understands me here," she says. "I'd rather go back in a starship and have more adventures. Everyone in my class will be jealous."

Diantha clears her throat. "You remember that we've talked about how that isn't a good reason to leave?"

But Theckla just sticks out her tongue and squirms more intensely in her chair.

"Last time we had a conversation like this, you didn't offer me a place on the Mission Council," Ereni says. "You told me I had a lot of growing up to do."

"And you chose to do that work on a different mission, which was a very reasonable decision to make," Diantha says. "I'd say you've learned a lot between now and then, wouldn't you?"

Ereni grins. "More than I could have ever realized."

"And now I think you're ready," Diantha says. "I didn't deny your request back then because I didn't believe in you. I think you know that."

"I do." Ereni shakes her hair, making it ripple down her back. "And yes, I accept. After spending so much time hammering out this deal, how could I refuse to be a part of it?"

That leaves me and Burke. He's still grasping my hand, and he has a little smile playing at the corners of his mouth. "Sienna and I come as a pair," he says. "What do you think, Sienna? I'm game if you are."

It's what we've been talking about, but being able to do valuable work with people I already care for is more than I've been hoping for. There's nothing more important I can think of doing than trying to help humanity come together in the face of this huge technological advance. And unlike Novelle, I don't feel any particular attachment to Seji. If anything, I feel the freest when I'm traveling to far-off stars.

I turn to Novelle, who still has her arm around Allegra. "I don't want to leave you behind," I say. "It's a miracle we found each other in the first place. After leaving Leo, I don't know...." My words die off, and I shake my head.

She reaches across the table then and puts her hand on my free one. "And I never dreamed I'd ever get to meet the famed Aunt Sienna. But we won't be going anywhere, and aren't the wormholes supposed to bring us closer together?" She leans forward. "We'll meet again, Sienna. Don't worry."

She has a point. With the wormholes speeding up travel times, it's not as if this will be goodbye. We don't even need the Satori lifespan extension technology to be assured of that.

I lean into Burke's reassuring bulk beside me. Joining this particular mission group is something that will give us purpose and allow us to work with colleagues who value our contributions. Ever since we left Arbor, I've been living through an open question, and finally I feel like I have an answer.

"Yes," I say. "Yes, let's try to do something good."

Diantha nods in approval, and Theckla is wiggling so much, I'm surprised she's managing to stay on her chair. Ereni raises one eyebrow at me, and I almost start to laugh thinking about the trouble we'll inevitably find. Kuusta gives me a little nod of understanding. He knows better than anyone how hard it can be to spend so long in uncertainty.

Burke doesn't loosen his grip on my hand. We've been through so much together, and now we'll be embarking on a new adventure, just as Theckla said.

The future shines brightly.

THE END

ACKNOWLEDGMENTS

I wrote the entirety of this novel in 2025, which has been a challenging year.

I started out the year in the middle of a mysterious and painful illness. While still recovering, I ramped up my journalism work, partly in response to the chaos that American federal policy was wrecking at a local level, about which I felt compelled to report. This included writing about a rapidly expanding surveillance state.

And then in the fall, after several months of declining health, my beloved little dog Nala died. She lived with me for more than sixteen years and almost made it to her eighteenth birthday.

So when I was writing this novel, it sometimes felt like an escape from a harsh and exhausting reality. How lovely that when our protagonists arrive on Satori, they are automatically given a place to live and food to eat. How wonderful that a main question of the novel is how to figure out what to do with your life when your basic needs are met and you have a wealth of options. How soothing to spend time with this cast of characters who have managed to come together into a kind of found family.

If this book can offer a respite for others as it has for me, I will be very well satisfied.

Books are not created in a vacuum, so I must thank my colleagues and friends who have taught me so much over the years, whether through collaboration, conversation, or their own work. Thanks also to the authors of more books than I could easily list here who helped me develop my thoughts.

Big thanks to my editor Kat Howard for her usual keen insight and sharp eye.

As always, thanks and appreciation to my friends and family for all your support, care, and encouragement. My found family means the world to me.

Thanks to my readers for accompanying me on this adventure. It's been wonderful having you along for the ride.

And finally, all my gratitude and much love to my little dog Nala. We were together through thick and thin and took very good care of one another. She sat beside me as I wrote 13 of the 14 novels I've completed, including this one that you're holding in your hands. She has been indelibly woven into my life, and I will always feel so lucky to have been her person.

ABOUT THE AUTHOR

Amy Sundberg is a novelist and journalist. Whether she is writing romping YA retellings of self discovery or psychological Gothic horror with trenchant social commentary, her novels feature intrepid heroines, high stakes, and questions of agency and power.

When she's not plotting how to someday have her very own library ladder or elaborate indoor reading tent, Amy is drooling over grand pianos and singing her heart out. She indulges her sweet tooth with some abandon (her favorite treat is pie, followed closely by ice cream). Driven by an insatiable curiosity, she has been lucky enough to travel to six continents. She can be easily coaxed into playing board games or going for a walk at a local park. She has a passion for theater, and she enjoys cooking a variety of delicious soups. She lives in the beautiful Pacific Northwest.

For more information visit her website amysundberg.com or follow her on Instagram at @sundbergamy or Bluesky at @amysundberg.bsky.social.

ALSO BY AMY SUNDBERG

<u>The Satori Chronicles:</u>

My Stars Shine Darkly: Book 1 of the Satori Chronicles

Stars, Hide Your Fires: Book 2 of the Satori Chronicles

<u>Other YA science fiction:</u>

To Travel the Stars: a Retelling of Pride and Prejudice

<u>Horror:</u>

Gold Diggers